BERLIN WALLS

A COLD WAR THRILLER

BY BILL RAPP

coffeetownpress

Kenmore, WA

A Coffeetown Press book published by Epicenter Press

Epicenter Press
6524 NE 181st St. Suite 2
Kenmore, WA 98028.
www.Epicenterpress.com
www.Coffeetownpress.com
www.Camelpress.com

For more information go to: www.camelpress.com
www.billrappsbooks.com

Berlin Walls
Copyright © 2021 by Bill Rapp

ISBN: 9781942078128 (trade paper)
ISBN: 9781942078135 (ebook)

Printed in the United States of America

DEDICATION

To my many colleagues at the CIA, past, present, and future, with whom I have shared a commitment to our country, its values, and its institutions. I know that commitment remains strong today and will continue well into the future.

ACKNOWLEDGMENTS

As one might imagine, there is a wealth of literature on the those heady days in the summer and fall of 1961, when the showdown over the Berlin Wall threatened to lurch from a unique urban and diplomatic dispute to a broader war between the United States and the Soviet Union. That was not the first time the world's attention had been drawn to Berlin, nor the first time that war seemed about to erupt. That, however, is not a story to be told here, at least not in its entirety. Rather I have tried to use that intense confrontation as the backdrop for an intelligence operation that hopefully captures and reflects some of that intensity, but on a deeper and more personal human scale. More complete histories can be found, among other books, in *Berlin 1961* (G.P. Putnam's Sons, New York, 2011) by Frederick Kempe and *The Berlin Wall* (Simon and Schuster, 1986) by Norman Gelb. *Escape from Berlin* (Boxtree Limited, 1987) by Anthony Kemp provides a number of fascinating accounts of escapes from East Berlin after the Wall went up. For those interested in the exploits of a real Soviet assassin *The Man With The Poison Gun* (Oneworld Publications, 2016) by Serhii Plotkhy is an interesting and informative read. And anyone who wants a more complete picture of American intelligence efforts in Berlin during the Cold War can find that in *Battleground Berlin* (Yale University Press, 1997) by David Murphy, Sergei Kondrashev, and George Bailey.

While those and other books provided the crucial background this story needed, *Berlin Walls* would never be the book it became without the great work of the people at Epicenter/Coffeetown Press, and especially that of Jennifer McCord, Executive Editor. She consistently insisted that I focus my revisions on telling a clearer and better scripted story for the reader. As always, my wife Didi, and on this occasion our older daughter Eleanor, performed the tough and critical chore of proofreading the manuscript not only for editorial and historical accuracy, but also for a cast of characters and a prose that speak to the world around them and, hopefully, those who will pick up this book. As so many writers know, it takes more than just an author to bring a book to life. I am fortunate to have such wonderful collaborators.

PROLOGUE

Christmas Eve, 1948

The invitation came as a real surprise to von Hoehn. Actually, it was more of a call or an order than an invitation. But then, perhaps he was in for some sort of Christmas treat. At any rate, the commandant's cabin would be warm and dry, much more so than the barracks where he had been living in the Donetsk region of Ukraine for the last year and a half. It might even give his feet a chance to dry out, and time to get some feeling back into his toes and fingers. *Mal sehen*, as his compatriots said with resignation every time something unexpected came from the Soviet guards. We shall see.

Another surprise awaited von Hoehn when he marched through the door. The air was definitely warm, if stuffy and foul smelling, thanks to the large stove in the corner burning the chunks of dark coal his fellow prisoners dug from the earth outside the camp. It was still a pleasant change from the drafty barracks that had a small stove in the center of the long wooden shack, which could never get warm enough. Most of the coal that was not shipped elsewhere in the Soviet Union and beyond went to stoves like this one where the commandant, his staff, and the guards could enjoy it. The snow piled against the walls outside seemed to provide most of the insulation for the other shacks from the freezing night air. Prisoners like himself slept more from exhaustion than relief at night. That is, if you slept at all.

The German had known the extra warmth would be there, and he had contemplated how he might be able to exploit whatever the purpose of this meeting was to extend his stay in the commandant's office. But von Hoehn had not expected to find the stranger seated at the commandant's desk. And he dressed as a civilian, not in the uniform of the Red Army. His suit looked to be tailored as well, the dark grey wool fitting his body like the two belonged together. Not only that, but he looked quite comfortable in the commandant's chair. Someone from Moscow no doubt. Von Hoehn glanced around the room. There was no sign of the commandant. Now he became very curious.

"Sit down, Comrade. Would you like a cigarette?" the Soviet civilian asked.

Now this was getting more and more interesting. Von Hoehn slid into one of the two chairs facing the commandant's desk and reached for the pack of cigarettes the stranger had pushed in his direction. After von Hoehn had selected one from the pack, the man leaned forward with a lit match at the end of his fingers. And this man had clean fingernails. Would wonders never cease? When von Hoehn inhaled, he felt dizzy and nearly fainted. It had been so long since his last smoke.

"Comrade?" von Hoehn replied. "Since when do I deserve that honorific?"

The man smiled and sat back. "Well it is hardly an honorific. Not in Soviet society anyway. And you are a member of the Free Germany grouping. That's a start."

"But with my background, I can hardly expect to be addressed that way."

"Ah, but you have been an exemplary prisoner. You have demonstrated none of the fascist leanings and preferences of so many others in these camps. We have noticed that."

"I am not a fool." Von Hoehn started to chuckle but then was suddenly struck by the Soviet's excellent German. It was almost as though the man was not a Russian at all. "You no doubt realize that I am doing what I must to survive. After all, you won the war."

Von Hoehn thought back to his capture after the fall of the East Prussian capital of Koenigsburg in April of 1945. He glanced at his empty wrist, where the watch from his father, a present for his twentieth birthday, had rested until a Soviet corporal snatched it away as von Hoehn waited to join the parade of his *Kameraden* beginning their march east into captivity. The corporal had given him a punch to the jaw with the edge of his rifle for good measure, only to have a Soviet captain seize the watch in turn. Von Hoehn had thought at first—naively—that the officer would return the watch. Instead, he had stuffed it into his own pocket and then winked at von Hoehn, as though to remind him who had won the war. Like there could be any doubt at this point.

The stranger in the commandant's office sat forward, resting his elbows on the desk. "Oh, I am aware of that. But it also suggests that you could be very useful to us when you return home."

"And when will that be?"

The Soviet reached for the cigarettes, shaking several out onto the desk. He selected one and pushed the rest—all four—in von Hoehn's direction. He struck a match and spoke between puffs as he attempted to breathe life into his tobacco. "Oh, soon enough. Probably next year. And since you have no family in the Western sectors, you will almost certainly return to the Soviet zone."

Von Hoehn slid the extra cigarettes into the pocket of his jacket. These would be very useful for bartering later on. "I guess that makes sense. But what would stop me from simply traveling to the American or British sectors?"

The stranger shrugged. "Nothing, I suppose. But we can make it very worth your while to remain in our zone."

"I can imagine."

The Soviet waved his cigarette in the air with his arms raised as he shook his head. It had gone out already. "No, no. It would not be like that. We would not force you into anything. You have demonstrated that that would be an unwise approach. It is clear to me that you are no fool." He smiled again and stood, relighting his cigarette. "In fact, you do not have to commit to anything now. We would like a more friendly and fruitful cooperation. One that would last over time. To both of our advantage."

"Then what do I have to do?"

The Soviet shrugged. He picked up the half-empty pack of cigarettes and tossed them toward von Hoehn. "Nothing for the moment. But someone will periodically reach out to you to see how you are getting along. There will be no pressure for you to do anything you do not wish."

"I see. That sounds almost too easy."

"Nothing will be easy for any of us from now on. It rarely ever is. Not if the goal has any value. Patience, that is, strategic patience is usually the best approach. I am sure you have learned that much over the last few years."

"Yes, I have learned to be patient. I am in no rush. Not anymore."

Again, von Hoehn's mind lapsed temporarily into the past. As the Red Army lurched toward his family estate in East Prussia, von Hoehn had been transferred to the 5th Panzer Division in February, 1945. That was supposed to be yet another display of the Fuehrer's alleged military genius: have German soldiers sent to fight near their homes, where their will would be stronger to resist the invading Bolshevik armies. Hitler had been right about that much, though. Those Asiatic hordes had indeed overrun the Fatherland, just as he and his henchmen predicted. Of course, it was all no small thanks to you, my Fuehrer. Von Hoehn had taken one last look at the red glow in the sky over the city that had once housed the great philosopher Immanuel Kant at the university of Koenigsburg, von Hoehn's own alma mater, the heart of the German Enlightenment. He pushed at the pockets of his winter coat to make sure the extra socks he had found in the ruined farmhouse down the road were still there. They would come in handy during his captivity. Of that much he was sure. To hell with the rest, especially the damn Nazis and everyone else like them on either side. Let's see if the Soviets do any better with their new burden, he surmised.

The Soviet civilian stood and stepped back from the commandant's desk. He leaned forward and extended his hand. "Well, good then. You will hear from us, not me, in all probability. At least not at first. But someone will call. Eventually, I hope we will be able to work together."

Von Hoehn stood and took the hand offered, then turned to the door.

"By the way, I have ordered that your barracks receive more coal," the Russian said. "It is far too cold in there. It seems to me that if they expect you to do worthwhile work, you men need to be better rested."

"And better fed, too."

"Yes, of course. And von Hoehn?"

"Yes?" The German looked back at his host.

"Your name. Is the 'von' really necessary anymore?"

"No, not anymore. Not for the world I inhabit now. I plan to change that. I just haven't had the chance in these camps."

"Good. We'll see what we can do."

"Thank you, Comrade."

The Soviet smiled as the German returned to his barracks. He looked down at the charred end of his cigarette, which had gone cold again. He had only taken a few drags on it. But it had served the purpose of creating a more congenial atmosphere. He tossed it aside as pieces of tobacco rolled out of the unlit end. As Kirillnikov watched the stub roll across the floor, he pulled a fresh pack from his jacket pocket.

Given his own background and experience in Germany and Berlin, he knew he would be spending a good deal of time there, especially with the Americans there now. Men like this von Hoehn could prove to be very useful indeed. They would need to be managed, of course. But it would still be worth the effort. He had learned that in this profession it was unwise to waste any opportunity. He would also have to acquire more American cigarettes once he got to Berlin. The Soviet ones simply did not measure up. At least not yet.

CHAPTER ONE

August 22, 1961

So it had come to this, Karl Baier told himself. And he wondered how. It was as though this operation was bringing his career full circle. Back in Berlin. And dealing with Chernov again, of all people. The man was Baier's KGB counterpart, his old nemesis and occasional colleague. Sometimes, they might even be called friends. Their relationship had begun here, in this very city, right after the war, when both men were stationed in the former German capital. And it had continued through their time together as their paths crossed in Austria and Budapest.

Sergei Chernov had always remained an enigma, his own man. And Baier never felt as though he really understood him. He even kept the moniker his wife had given Chernov those many years ago: 'the fucking Russian.' Still, his instinct told him the operation should move forward. But there were so many unanswered questions, so many things that could be wrong with it. And something probably would go wrong. After all, we are only human, Baier reflected. But wasn't it always like this? In the end, you had to go with your gut.

"Can you tell me why you're in such a hurry to flee the workers' paradise on your side of the Iron Curtain?" Baier asked. He glanced toward the window, the light from the lamp across the street casting a thin silver glow through the dirty panes of glass into the darkened vault, almost like it was a prison cell. This was probably the worst safe house in East Berlin, and Baier wondered who had been responsible for finding it. Even in August it made one feel damp and chilly. An empty socket dangled from a long black wire in the center of the room, as though reminding those inside of the absence of light. And the absence of any hope for light. The space was at least a little brighter—if you could use that term—than the stairwell he had climbed earlier, the walls and steps barely visible through a night so dark that the color black seemed too pale to describe it. It was a fitting setting for the eastern half of Berlin where Baier now sat in near silent conversation with a man who was supposed to be his enemy. History really does make for strange bedfellows.

"And what are you doing in Berlin in the first place?" Baier pressed. "The last time I saw of you, you were fat and happy in Budapest."

"A great deal has happened since then, Herr Baier. I now have unfinished business," Chernov replied. He leaned forward in his chair. His face was still, concrete-like and unmoving, his gaze glued to Baier as the American sat just a few feet away. The Russian held his own face away from the dim glow that had broken through the window to his right. "I need to get out, and as for Berlin, this seemed the easiest place to get through. At least, it has been in the past."

"Yes, well, you may a bit late for that. You've noticed the changes, I assume."

"Changes? Berlin has been divided among the victorious powers since the end of the war, Herr Baier." Chernov leaned back and tilted his head at an angle, a slow smile spreading across his face, as though he knew better. "And you still have your French and British allies here in the city with you. You still control the same territory as before. No one is going anywhere."

"No thanks to your people. Your side already tried to push out once, back in '48. But we were able to beat you then with the Airlift. And with the kind of noises Mister Khrushchev has been making, it sounds like you would like to try again. The result will be the same." Baier leaned forward in turn, his own head to match the angle of Chernov's. "Was it not Karl Marx himself who issued those silly words about those who do not study history are condemned to repeat it?"

Chernov nodded. "Always with your droll sense of humor, Karl." He paused to study the floor for a moment. "Of course, I should have known. It was actually too easy to foresee with this country bleeding to death. The attraction for what you have created in the western zones has simply been too great and the means of escape too easy. Something had to happen."

"Perhaps if the Germans under your system had been allowed to create something other than the Stalinist heap you all built in your own country."

Chernov shook his head and snorted. "Those sorts of reforms would have been a step too far. We would have lost our biggest prize from the war. So instead, people left on their own. I believe around 200,000 departed for the promises of the West last year." He waved toward the window and looked up at the American. "This thing they are building outside is the regime's answer."

"A new barrier to split the city and end free movement between the sectors. Basically, splitting the city in half and undermining Allied authority in Berlin in the process. Pretty drastic steps."

"You should have known, Karl, that it would come to this. Your country perhaps, but you for certain." The Russian laughed lightly and shook his head as he glanced from his companion to the window and back.

It was Baier's turn to nod. "Yeah, perhaps. 30,000 fled last month alone." He studied the buildings across the street, their facades still marked by gunshots from the battle for the city between the Nazis and the Red Army sixteen years ago, now covered in grime and neglect. "And the oppression has only gotten worse over on this side, especially with the hope for reform crushed back in '53. We suspected something would happen. But few of us suspected this."

The Russian laughed lightly and shook his head. "It didn't have to turn out like this, you know."

Baier turned back toward the Russian. "How do you figure? What are we supposed to do? Drop the big one on Moscow over this?"

Chernov shook his head some more. "No, no. Back in '45. If you had only kept on rolling east. There was nothing in your way then. The Germans were putting up what resistance they could against us in the hope that you Americans would get here first. You could have seized all of Germany up to the Polish border. Then the world would have been spared all this."

"Not really. There was no way you Soviets would have stood by and waited. We would have ended up fighting you. Besides, there was an agreement already in place. We had hammered all this out in Yalta and Potsdam. We were hoping to create a world of peace and cooperation. We trusted Stalin back then. Or at least Roosevelt did."

Chernov's laugh was harder and louder this time. "You were fools."

"We may have been naive then, but we're smarter now."

"Ah, but are you wiser?"

"I guess we'll see soon enough. This crisis is far from over. It's only been a little over a week since the barriers started going up." Nine days had flown by since the East German army and workers' militias had snuck out of their barracks and factories just past midnight on August 13 to throw their wire and concrete in the face of the West. Baier paused while he studied the Russian's face.

"But is this why you're leaving now, because of our mistakes 16 years ago, and the regime's inability to respond any other way to the differences between east and west?" Baier continued. "Why now? And why Paris?" Baier leaned forward in the thin wooden chair that he feared would collapse, like the state around them. "I mean, it is a beautiful city, but why select that one?"

Chernov sighed, sat back and threw a look of pity toward Baier. "Yes, that unpleasant surprise outside our window has created a new obstacle. I wish I had moved a month ago, but it was not possible then. In any case, this still seems like the best place for my escape. Especially with you here."

"Yes, well, thank you for bringing me back from my desk job in Washington. I am flattered that you insisted that I be the one to aid in your escape. I'm sure we'll work something out." Baier paused to study his companion. "But back to my question. The why?"

"You really expect me to explain everything, Herr Baier?"

Baier smiled. "If you expect me . . . us to help you, then yes, I would like some more information. As you are no doubt aware, we—both my organization and my country—are not a charitable foundation. We will expect something in return. Something valuable."

Chernov smiled in turn. "And after all these years of working together? You still do not trust me?"

"You are right, Sergei. We have worked together. And that does count for something. But we're still on opposite sides of this divide." Baier motioned with his head toward the world outside the window. "And your kind words and knowing smile do not provide the bridge I need. Not yet."

"I am prepared to pass along valuable information about my organization's work here in Europe that I am sure will more than compensate for any trouble you may have. And at a time such as this...." Chernov motioned toward the window once more. "I believe I can give you information on the Kremlin's plans for this city."

"And you know this how?"

"From my work in Moscow." He laughed lightly. "I am considered one of the German experts there."

"That would be very helpful, Sergei. Can you at least give me a hint now of what to expect? It would make my superiors in Washington that much more hospitable."

Chernov sat back and wagged his right index finger. "All in good time, Herr Baier. I have received nothing from you yet."

"Fair enough. But what really puzzles me, Sergei, is why now. You've had many chances in the past. Hell, you were even living in the West once but chose to go back."

"The 'now' is not significant. At least not as you understand it. I only learned of something recently, something that compels me to leave." Chernov's sigh was long and drifted far enough to fill the room. "I, too, regret that the need for me to leave has only come now that our German friends have begun to build that wall out there." He glanced toward the window. "I realize it will make things more difficult for me…and you. But given their German, even Prussian, nature, their wall will grow and only become more difficult to cross. They are very thorough. You, of all people, should know that much."

"Oh, I realize that well enough. But I must ask again as to why you need to leave at all. Are your people in Moscow suddenly aware of our relationship? Are you facing new suspicions and dangers?"

"Suddenly? There have been suspicions all along, Herr Baier. Certainly, you have known this, especially after Budapest."

"But then what has changed?"

"My brother…"

"The one that fled the Revolution and died in South America after the war?"

Chernov leaned forward, his face almost touching Baier's. When he spoke, it was barely more than a whisper. "He did not die back then. I was mistaken. He died more recently. Three weeks ago, to be exact. And he died in Paris."

"How did he die?"

"He was killed, Herr Baier. Assassinated."

"And you know this how? And if so, by whom?"

"The GRU killed him."

Baier's body shot back against the hard rails of the chair. He stood, then circled the room, avoiding the window. After a moment, he sat back down and leaned in close to the Russian. "Your own military intelligence organization? How can you be so sure?"

"I know, Herr Baier, I know. I still have friends and comrades in our organization. And as you know, there is little love lost between my organization and the GRU."

"And your sister? Is she still alive?"

Chernov sat back and shrugged. "I thought she had died over there as well, possibly in South America. But now I cannot be sure. The only traces I have found disappear in Paris as well." He shook his head. "She is probably dead also. It is what usually happens. Those people believe it is best to leave no one behind."

"Those people?"

Chernov's smile returned. "Yes, those people. The GRU and even some in the KGB. Not all are like that, but enough are."

Baier's brow wrinkled in confusion. "But why? For God's sake, Sergei, why would your people kill your brother? What was he doing in Paris?"

"That's what I need to find out, Herr Baier."

"Will there be anything else that you plan to do? I mean, before you come to us?"

Chernov smiled through tight lips, but the sense of certainty and experience behind it was clear to read. "If necessary, I will take my revenge. That should be enough. Baring complications, of course."

CHAPTER TWO

August 24, 1961

The sparks bounced off the car's sides and roof like small firecrackers. Baier thought briefly of a small town's Fourth of July celebration, one in which the biggest things the local kids could get their hands on were a couple of cherry bombs. Or a roll of caps. The driver swung the vehicle wildly from side to side, as much out of desperation as design. He must have thought this would make him a more elusive target. Most of the shots seemed to be finding the car, though, shattering the windows and ripping through the small body that looked as though it was made of aluminum or thin strips of plastic. It was a wonder he was still alive, much less able to steer the damn thing.

Baier hung back in the shadow of the doorway to an apartment building directly across from the Bernauerstrasse crossing between the Soviet and American sectors of Berlin. Probably not as busy as the one at Friedrichstrasse, or Checkpoint Charlie in local parlance. But that made more sense to try to escape here, since it just might attract less attention. Theoretically at least. But these bullets were not following the theory.

Until just a few weeks ago, movement between the two halves of the divided city was an easy thing, perfunctory actually. Eighty-one crossing points in all. But the Stalinist rulers in the eastern half of the city had begun to build a barrier between the East and West that ran like a scar through the heart of the city. Now, there were no more than 13 left open. All of it designed to staunch the flow of East Germans pouring into the land of political freedom and consumer comforts that they were sure awaited them on the other side. Probably more for the latter, Baier guessed, since the Germans had not exactly enjoyed great success at building democracy during their troubled history. Still, though, this new venture in the west, the Federal Republic with its capital in Bonn, looked like it had gotten off to a good start. And the appeal of it all was bleeding East Germany dry of its people, especially its younger and more talented ones.

The barbed wire and concrete blocks going up through the middle of the city were obviously an attempt to cut that flow off. It was August 24, just 11 days since the first barbed wire had been strung along the sector boundary, and the East Germans were well into it. Only time would tell if this wall would succeed in transforming West Berlin into an island cut off from the citizens of the Communist state in the east. But for now it was proving to be a real hell for the driver of the little black sedan that was hurtling its way through that barrier. The car was one of the new model Trabants that had only been out for a year or so. Unfortunately, the car's dark color did not help it hide in the blackness of the late summer Berlin night. Nor did the sides that were rumored to be made of little more than pressboard, which were splintering like cheap plywood.

Good Lord, Baier thought, how was the man inside able to breathe and see, much less steer, as bullets continued to rip through the siding and glass with explosive force. Two East German border guards, almost certainly members of the vaunted Felix Dzerzhinsky Brigade, named for the first chief of Soviet intelligence, fired away with machine pistols levelled at the sides of their hips. They could only have been at it for about a minute, but standing there helplessly Baier felt as though it had been going on for hours. The lights that had been erected to assist the construction work helped the soldiers keep track of their target while also casting a glow of mock heroism on their own positions. Baier could have sworn he saw thin smiles creasing lips tightened by the effort to aim and fire in rapid succession as they observed their handiwork.

Two West Berlin policemen stood at the front of the ambulance they had brought with them little more than a block away from Baier's post. They shifted their weight from foot to foot, clearly uncomfortable with the fireworks display. One cast an appealing glance at Baier, who shrugged and held his palm out. Baier shuffled his own feet every few seconds or so, desperately trying to think of something to do, something to end the slaughter. But he was stuck. There was no sense in starting a firefight between East and West. He could not step in while the car was still in the east. They would simply have to wait for the car to cross the sector boundary. If it ever did.

In the end, the car did make it through. If Baier had been a religious man, he would have regarded it as another miracle. Maybe this guy would become the patron saint of escapees. Then again, he was Sergei Chernov, so he would have to be a saint in the Orthodox Church, not the Roman Catholic one of Baier's birth. The Russian had hardly led a blameless or exemplary life, however. Especially now, given the mission he had set for himself. Well, we'll see, Baier thought, as he moved from the doorway and trotted to the car that had rolled to a stop not more than twenty or thirty yards from the crossing. But it was in the western half of the city now. The CIA's Chief of Base in Berlin, Tom Hendricks, hustled along beside Baier, hanging a few feet back, as though to give Baier the first look. And the first reaction.

"Come on, Tom. We're not in Durango anymore." Baier turned to his companion, who had grown up on a cattle ranch in southwestern Colorado, and waved him forward. "Then again, this does look kind of like the Wild West." Baier slowed, an instinctive caution taking over. "Son of a bitch," he muttered. His hands started to shake a little, and his stomach got that queasy feeling when your body and brain knew that something wasn't right. He could feel the perspiration beading along his forehead.

Hendricks caught up to Baier and took his sleeve. "All things considered, Karl, you seem pretty calm about the whole thing. You've been through this before?"

"Not exactly." Baier took a deep breath and ran his forearm over his brow. "And nothing inside me is telling me to stay calm."

Baier paused in mid-stride and shook his head before continuing. "Goddammit." He tried to catch his breath and suck in some air. "You never do get used to this kind of stuff. It's always a shock. You probably know as much already from Korea, eh, Tom?"

"Not really. I never saw that much action. Spent most of my time in Seoul. You know, military intelligence, like you in the previous war." He motioned toward the car with his head. "Let's see if there's anything left of your Russian friend."

They resumed their hurried pace. Perhaps the man was still alive and in need of first aid. When they were about 10 yards from the car, though, reality struck. The two Americans halted, then sneaked closer, their eyes occasionally glancing in the direction of the East German border guards. Those men remained stationed just to the East German side of the crossing, their weapons still levelled and aimed in the direction of the car. And the Americans.

"What do those assholes think is going to happen? That this poor sap might try to return fire or something?" Hendricks asked. "Or us?"

"Their probably just following orders, Tom. I'm sure that's something they've learned well."

"Yeah, the Prussian pricks."

Baier stepped to the driver's window. Remarkably, it was the only piece of glass that had not been shattered by the hail of automatic fire during the escape attempt. Light from a street lamp about fifteen yards away allowed Baier to see the figure slumped inside. His head was resting on the front seat, pointed toward the passenger-side door. His suit jacket had been shredded by the automatic weapons fire, small holes and ripped fabric scattered over the upper body like he had been wearing a target. A big one.

"Dead?" Hendricks asked.

"I'd certainly guess so. There's enough blood for several passengers, or so it would seem." It took several attempts to free the door from the ripped and crooked remains of the car's body, but Baier eventually yanked it open and poked his head inside. "Give me a hand getting this guy out so we can check for certain."

He reached back outside the car and motioned for the West Berlin police van to pull up alongside the car. "We'll have to get him to a hospital as quickly as possible."

Hendricks shrugged and cursed until he was able to pull back the dented door on the passenger side and felt along the neck for a pulse. "Make that a morgue, Karl. Your Russian friend is gone."

Baier pulled himself from the car and slid down along its side. He sat in the street and looked up at the darkened, four-story apartment buildings on the eastern side, now empty but still wearing the scars of the battle for Berlin sixteen ago. Vacant windows and broken panes of glass stared back at him. He wondered how many new pockmarks would scar these same buildings in the weeks ahead. The East German regime had begun to empty the buildings along the sector boundary of their occupants to make way for the new wall and to prevent any more escape attempts before the construction was complete. So many of the buildings straddled the line between the Western Allied and Soviet sectors that some even opened on one side and closed on the other. Many residents in the eastern half—even old grandmothers—had taken to leaping from the windows down into waiting arms and even bed mattresses assembled in the western part of Berlin to beat the regime's construction schedule.

"Motherfucker," he whispered. He pivoted to catch the two East German border guards in his view. So, this was the world these assholes wanted to create. "You fucking pricks!" he yelled.

He sat for a while on the pavement, taking deep breaths to regain his composure. Despite the summer heat, the blacktop felt cool through the seat of his tan cotton slacks, and Baier rolled onto his side. Two days had been all the time he had to help bring his Russian nemesis and sometime friend through to the West. And two days had clearly not been enough. But it had also been too long. The shoot to kill order had gone into effect that very day.

Baier blew out a breath of anger and frustration that had been building since the shooting began. His heart felt like it might explode if he jumped up too quickly. After about a minute, he brushed the dust and grime from his hands and pants, then stood up slowly and moved back to the car. He leaned inside and studied the face of the dead man. He paused for a moment longer, then began searching through the pockets of the ripped and bloodied jacket.

"What are you looking for, Karl? Some kind of message?"

Baier shook his head. "Nope. Identification."

"What the hell for? I thought you knew this guy, your Russian friend and accomplice."

Baier retreated from the inside of the vehicle, shaking his head further. "This isn't my Russian defector."

"Then who is it?"

Baier shrugged. "Beats me. Some poor clown who was trying to escape to the West before everything got sealed shut, if you ask me."

"Then where the hell is your guy?"

Baier turned and looked into the eastern half of the city, focusing on nothing in particular, just the blend of brown and grey and black that marked the East Berlin skyline. And its present and future, as far as Baier was concerned. It was as though his thinking had swept into broad geographical and historical terms, not of any time or moment, like tonight. But his mind did focus on this particular city and country. He thought back to the sweep of history that had overwhelmed this town, well back before this wall, before the Allied occupation and division, back before the war and the Nazis. You didn't have to work very hard to imagine the waves of journalists and statesmen and politicians and military people that would flood this city once more with all the attention that would come from around the world. Hell, the American Vice-President had already come and gone, hoping to reaffirm the American commitment to this city and its freedom, to restore the locals' faith in the United States and its allied friends as their guardians and protectors. He wondered if history would ever give Berlin a break.

"I guess I'll have to go find out."

At just that moment, a tall East German in civilian clothes walked up to the two border guards and appeared to dismiss them.

They lowered their weapons and marched off in the direction of a hut that had been set up behind the piles of construction materials in the street that ran behind the crossing. Then he turned to the west and looked straight into Baier's eyes. Shadows and streaks of light played behind him, almost as though he was performing a part in one of those German Expressionist films from the Weimar period, acts of surrealism that nonetheless captivated their audience with their own eerie reality. The man's face was immovable and finely chiseled, as though it had been set in the same concrete the East Germans and their Soviet masters were using to build their new border. It also shared the dark lines and shadows of the surrounding night. And his deep hazel eyes held a look of contempt and hatred, the latter colder and harder than the first.

In that moment Baier knew he had been challenged. I do hope we meet again, you son of a bitch, Baier thought. It looks like we have some scores to settle. And I'll be happy to oblige.

CHAPTER THREE

August 24, 1961

"This cable back to Headquarters is going to be a bitch to write," Hendricks said. "I know it's late, but are you going to be able to give me any help?" He steered his dark blue Opel through the deserted streets of West Berlin, back in the direction of his office on Clayallee. "We should knock this thing out so that it's waiting for them when they get into work tomorrow."

"Like what kind of help," Baier asked.

"Oh, maybe an insight or two. And some answers for the questions we know they're going to have. Like why we didn't set up the escape ourselves. We do have the means and ways available, you know. I've got a feeling they're going to be all over us on that one."

Baier looked out the window on his side of the car and sighed. His right arm rested against the side of the door as he leaned toward the open window. "Chernov didn't say why, but he wanted to handle that part of it himself. He said he only needed our help once he crossed the line and then getting out of Berlin and over to Paris."

"And you went along with that?"

Baier shot a look of anger and frustration at his companion. A lamp from an apartment window threw a flash of white across the car's windshield. "Of course, I did. Obviously. It's not like the guy was an asset of ours, taking orders. Besides, he probably knows more about getting around in the new environment over there than we do. Our networks in the east have come under a lot of pressure since that thing started going up. Or at least that's what you've been telling Washington. And anything we're constructing now to move people back and forth has got to be pretty preliminary, Tom. Preliminary enough not to expose it so early in the game."

Hendricks slammed the steering wheel and shook his head. "I know, I know, Karl. That's all true." He paused as though considering some weighty rebuttal. "It just seems odd that we let the lead on this operation slip away before we even got him out of the Soviet sector." He smiled. "Besides, who better to test a new escape mechanism than some fucking KGB guy? It's not like it would be a great loss if it all goes belly up."

"I'll let that one go, Tom. But that's the operative phrase you used earlier. Soviet sector. Who better to know how to move about and leave it than someone who's a part of it?"

"Ah shit, Karl, but how's Washington going to take this? They weren't real enthused about letting this character call any of the shots in the first place, certainly not for this part, even if it does make sense out here. You know what kind of control freaks they can be." He paused to study the street ahead. "And what does this tell us about the rest of this operation? I know you've got a history with this guy, but I've always had the feeling that the people back in D.C. were never really comfortable with him and his story. It was like you were a one-man band singing his song. And this whole thing this evening is sure to bring all those doubters and naysayers back into full chorus."

"Maybe so, but they'll have to admit we've had some pretty good results."

"You don't need to sell me on him, Karl. I know what it's like out here in the field, and I've handled my share of questionable characters."

"I know that, Tom. We all do at some point."

"As you once told me, we work with a lot of broken toys, so nothing's ever going to be perfect or easy." Hendricks's stare roamed between his passenger and the dark blacktop broken by shafts of yellow light from the occasional window or streetlamp. "But you could have one really busted toy on your hands now."

Baier sighed and refused to bring his own gaze back inside the car. It was as though he was trying to divine some future episode that would sort all the confusion from this night, sort it enough to make sense to himself, to the local chief of base, and the minions back in Washington as they strolled along the reflecting pool in the Mall during their work day.

"You guys must have known something was up, Tom. Thinking back, can't you identify anything that might have warned us of what was about to happen here?"

"You mean this botched escape attempt? How the hell would I have guessed that?"

"No, no. I mean this fucking wall in the heart of our occupied city."

Hendricks shook his head. "Not really, Karl. We all thought that the regime would have to do something to restrict movement in the city or try to isolate us. We were even beginning to transition away from the meetings in the East to a form of two-way radio communication. You were aware of that, since you all back home had to approve the funding for the gear."

"And how has that been going?"

Hendricks smiled for the first time that evening. "I guess an optimist would say that progress has been uneven. It's been a tough adjustment for many of the crew over there. Most of them are getting on in years, you know. And it was just so easy to arrange our meetings in what had been an open city with freedom of movement through any sector."

"In any case, I can always argue that it's better we didn't expose any of those people or the new exfiltration routes or methods you've begun working on," Baier said. "Especially seeing how this one turned out. Besides, we're assuming right off that this shooting was connected in some way with Chernov's plan. It could have been coincidental."

Hendricks looked over at his passenger, who continued to stare ahead. "Really, Karl? I mean, the poor sap showed up at the exact spot and the exact time we were expecting Chernov to come through." Hendricks almost laughed. "And on the exact day, or night, when the guards are allowed to shoot to kill."

Baier thought back to the look on the East German's face at the border crossing. "Yeah, probably not. They sure didn't waste any time putting that piece of cruelty to work."

"And what's with Paris, anyway? Are we paying for some kind of vacation for this guy?"

"Trust me, Tom, it's an important part of the operation."

"So where do you propose we go from here?" Hendricks asked. "I'll have to put something about that in the cable."

"Shit, Tom, I have to go in and try to find Chernov and figure out what happened." He finally looked over at his driver. "I don't see any other way. I'm not going to simply walk away and forget the whole thing." He thought back to the look on the East German's face. "There are other issues, too."

Hendricks glanced over. "Like what?"

Baier shrugged, his lips set tight and eyes focused back on the road. "Nothing. Never mind."

"Well, Karl, you're the deputy chief back there for the European Division. You should be plugged in well enough to know how to sell this thing."

Baier half-turned toward Hendricks. "They're not going to pass up the chance to bring a senior Soviet spook over, Tom. Believe me, they've been drooling in their coffees over this one, regardless of what anyone might say. And I'll bet they still are. Especially with everything going on around us. We really don't know what the Soviets and their henchmen are up to right now. There are people back in Washington worried about World War III erupting from this city. Chernov could prove to be a real gold mine of information."

"You think your Russian pal is that well plugged in?"

"He claimed to have access to some valuable information along those lines."

"Well, that would be sweet. That is, if he isn't bullshitting you." Hendricks paused. "So what can you tell me? Are we going to war over this?"

"I don't think it will happen over this wall, or whatever the hell it is they're constructing right now. Washington is focused on keeping the corridors into the city open. If the Soviets try to shut those off like they did in '48, then we could see some real shooting."

"That's not exactly reassuring, Karl. I mean, the Soviets have got several divisions ringing the city already. We wouldn't last long. Are you sure the people in Washington are certain of their response and where the red lines are? Don't you sit on the Berlin Task Force over at State?"

"I go to some of the meetings, but I'm not what you'd call a regular member. I'm not sure anyone knows who they are, if there are even any permanent members. One of the Agency's analysts is there more often than I am, actually."

"So, what's the word? Are we getting any insights into how the White House views all this?"

"Not really. I get the sense that once again we're fighting the last war, as it were." Baier noticed the puzzled look on Hendricks's face. "No, not World War II. The Berlin crisis of '48. The one where Stalin tried to force us out of the city by cutting off the road and rail access. It's why we're so focused on protecting the access routes. We definitely do not want to give up our place and role in the city. The mantra you hear in Washington is that whoever controls Berlin, controls Germany; and whoever controls Germany controls Europe." He smiled. "I think Lenin was the first to say that, and we've adopted it as well."

"Are people ignoring the implications of what this all means for our right to be here as members of the Allied occupation force that has rights throughout the entire city? I've also heard talk about 'salami tactics' on the part of the Soviets. You know, whittling away at our position and rights here. You noticed how those guards were East Germans, not Soviets tonight?"

Baier nodded. "Of course. Those fuckers aren't even supposed to be here. That regime doesn't have any authority in Berlin."

"Well, I think that issue has been decided—and not by us or the other Western Allies. It looks like Washington—not to mention London and Paris—is prepared to let those guys do whatever they like on their side of the city."

Hendricks drove the car over the cobblestone driveway that led to the U.S. compound on Clayallee and pulled his car into a parking slot to the left of the entrance. "I guess then getting approval from Headquarters is the least of your worries. Especially if they want to know just what the Soviets are up to."

He cut the engine and stepped from the car. Baier emerged on the other side, and both men leaned on the roof of the Opel. Hendricks looked out over the long perpendicular driveway that ran from the front entrance of the compound to the gate separating it from the world outside. Baier followed Hendrick's gaze with his own.

"I think you're probably right, Tom. The real challenge will be connecting with Chernov and figuring a better way out. Somebody already seems to suspect that something is up, and he does not look like an amateur. That whole show tonight was orchestrated for a purpose." Once again, the image of the East German's face floated back into Baier's memory.

"Yeah, finding another way out will be tough. If your Russian friend is still alive, that is."

"Good point, Tom. Good point."

• • •

He drove slowly through the darkened streets of West Berlin, heading for the temporary quarters the Base had set up for Baier and his wife Sabine down the street from their old house on Im Dol, about a quarter of a mile from the U.S. Mission compound. Berlin had a well-deserved reputation as the town that never slept, but here in the well-to-do residential sections of the city, the streets were almost deserted this late at night. Baier drove through shadows and silent streets as he turned down his own just off Clayallee. He glanced over at the new Mobile gas station on the corner of Im Dol and Koenigin-Luise-Strasse. In many ways it symbolized the changes to the city that had come since he was here last in the late 1940s. Back then, Berlin was little more than piles of rubbish and wreckage left from the Allied bombing and final battle to seize the capital of the Third Reich. Housing had been scarce and tough to find for most Germans, especially when the Allied forces seized a good number of the homes in the nicer neighborhoods, like Dahlem and Gruenewald, for themselves. Baier's house on Im Dol had been one. That it had still been available made him wonder back then just where the original owner had ended up. If he even made it back to the Fatherland, that is. He eventually found out, and he found a wife in the bargain. She was the woman who had been married to the original owner, but he came back from the Eastern front a changed man, physically and psychologically. He was not alone, of course, among the thousands of his countrymen who made it back to the Fatherland after years of fighting and harsh and punishing captivity.

Now the western part of the city was changing its landscape as rectangular apartment blocks of cement and steel blossomed throughout the city. The most color one could find came from the painted sheets of steel and tin that sprouted from the rows of steel pillars and concrete slabs. At least the locals were no longer sharing space in the few livable square feet they could find, often in the basements or few rooms in the upper floors that still offered a modicum of shelter.

Baier pulled the Mercedes sedan the Base had provided into the carport that stood to the left of the house he had been assigned for his brief stay in Berlin. When he drove past the house Baier saw his wife Sabine seated in front of a blank television screen, staring into some dark future like a seer frightened to guess at what it might hold. Although it was unusual for a wife to accompany a CIA officer on a trip such as this, their mutual history in the city in which they had met, fallen in love and gotten married allowed Baier to argue for an exception this one time. Besides, the black market smuggling networks she had built to survive in the months immediately after the war had proved to be invaluable for Baier in running agents between the city's Allied sectors. And he never tired of pointing that out to his colleagues and superiors back home whenever they saw fit to question her reliability and clearances for a trip such as this. Baier knew she would keep her distance from this operation, about which he had given her only a vague outline. And even that was pushing it. But she had been the first to know Chernov and work with him to bring hundreds out of the Soviet-occupied East, and it gave her a right to know something about Chernov's efforts to leave himself, possibly for good. At least, that's how Baier saw it.

She came running down the hallway toward Baier when he pushed through the front door and into the living room to his right. She had wrapped a light grey and dark green shawl around her shoulders and over her nightdress, and her face wore a look of deep anxiety that left her lips trembling.

"Karl, what happened? You've taken so long. Is everything all right?"

Baier leaned against the arm of a sofa, then slid into the cushion on the end. "No, Sabine, everything is not all right." He explained the shooting and the man they found in the front seat of the shattered East German mini-sedan. "I waited back at the Base while Tom drafted his cable back to Washington explaining what had happened. We both thought it best if I read through it to make sure it reflected both our views on what had taken place. Or gone wrong, is more like it."

"But what about Chernov? Don't tell me that fucking Russian is finally dead."

"Well, I can't tell you that, Sabine, because I don't know. It's something I need to find out. He wasn't there. It was some other poor sucker."

Sabine dropped onto the cushion on the sofa next to his. Her left hand reached out and stroked his forearm. "How do you plan to do that, Karl? Can't you just leave well enough alone?"

Baier sat up straight. "No, Sabine, you know I can't do that. I'm not going to just walk away from a botched operation, especially when I agreed to help bring the man out."

"Why did our fucking Russian want to come west in the first place?"

"Sabine, please, he no longer deserves that."

"Ha." She sat up straight and pulled her hand back to her lap. "He has never changed and never will. He's playing you, Karl. You trust that man far too much."

"He recently discovered that his brother had survived but was killed in Paris. He wants to find out why."

"And exact his revenge, right?"

Baier nodded. "Probably, depending on what he finds. And I am prepared to help in that. We've been through a lot together, Sabine, and he's helped me a great deal over the years."

"So you think. Your feelings toward this man have changed, Karl. Changed a lot. You no longer see him for what he is. Sometimes I find that so hard to understand." She frowned and looked away from her husband. "No matter what he has done, I will never trust that man. Or any Russian, for that matter."

"Yes, I know. You're right, Sabine, for all your own reasons. And I respect that. But you don't go through what we have together and not develop some respect for the man. I suppose my feelings have changed the more I've gotten to know the man. Besides, why shouldn't I help him eliminate a Soviet assassin if I can?"

"Eliminate? That sounds so much more genteel and refined than the reality of murder."

"That will depend on the circumstances, Sabine. First, though, I need to find him and bring him out. If he's still alive and free, that is."

Sabine stood and took both of Baier's hands in her own. "Let's leave that for now. There's something else, Karl. My dearest husband."

"What is it, Sabine, my dearest wife?" He smiled at the thought of her sudden tenderness. It was something to which he would always be vulnerable. And she knew that.

"My parents are in East Berlin. They've finally decided to leave East Germany and come to the west."

Baier shot up and gripped his wife's hands tight enough to make her wince. "Good God, Sabine, now? But why now, and why so suddenly? All these years they could have simply driven to Berlin and walked over the line. What made them change their minds?"

Sabine rested her head on her husband's shoulder. "I think the wall going up finally brought home the reality of the Germany we live in now. Divided and not likely to be reunited in our lifetimes."

"But I thought they were content to stay behind in their old home in Erfurt, that they had survived the Nazis and could certainly survive the Communists."

She leaned back and looked into Baier's face. Her own eyes waded in the tears of a bitter realization. "They said they also realized that the wall meant there would be no more easy movement between the sectors and no chance of escape in the future. They know now that they would never be happy in the eastern zone. That no one would." She squeezed Baier's hands. "And that they would probably never see us again if they stayed. They need our help, Karl."

"But why have they come now? What do they expect us to do?"

"They said they just wanted to see if there was some chance of a crossing now. But, Karl, things have tightened so much already."

Baier let her hands fall and shoved his own deep into his pants pockets. He paced the room like a German staff officer contemplating his next tactical move, hoping it would not undermine his grand strategy. "Of course, I'll do what I can Sabine. Just let me think a bit." He marched some more, his face studying the rug. Then he stopped and glanced at his wife.

"Do you think you can contact some of your old friends in the east, the ones who used to help you back in '45?"

She approached him. "But, Karl, so many of them are dead. Or long since retired and fled here to the west. Besides, this is an entirely new situation. It would be so hard to trust them with my parents' lives."

"Yes, you're probably right. But we need to think this through and come up with some kind of plan."

As Baier spoke these words, he knew that he would have to find more than just one plan. There was no way he could bring Sabine's parents and Chernov out together. That would require more than luck. A miracle would be more like it. He had been robbed of a miracle at the crossing tonight, so maybe he had one coming to him. But he doubted there was a patron saint waiting to intervene for him. No, his task had just gone from difficult to impossible.

CHAPTER FOUR

August 28, 1961

He followed the same route he had been running for the past three days. This particular path took Baier through a dense warren of streets in the section of Berlin known as *Mitte*, or 'middle,' the old heart of the city now sitting in the Soviet sector just beyond the line that separated the East German capital from the American zone. Here lay the heart of the East German government and Soviet occupation authority in Berlin, as well as many of the historical sites from Germany's imperial and Prussian past. The border between the American and Soviet sectors was also the most active part of the new wall as its barrier of concrete blocks and barbed wire fencing rose to replace the invisible but official border that had sprung up back in 1945 when the Allies had divided what was left of the Reich capital. The new barrier even crossed right in the front of the famous Brandenburg Gate, giving the world perhaps the most iconic picture of the new barrier breaking the city in half. Ironically, this was close to where the Soviets and East Germans had left the one of the few workable crossing points between the east and west: Checkpoint Charlie. Since its history and monuments made *Mitte* that part of Berlin most likely to receive western visitors, this also made it the most obvious place for a westerner to be seen driving into and out of the eastern half of the city, which gave Baier the best cover for his trips to Berlin's eastern half. Or so he figured.

On each of the last three days, Baier had followed the same route. And he always had company, of course, in the form of local surveillance. Both Soviet and East German. He just hoped that three day's worth of countersurveillance had allowed him to pick out who was who on his tail and the methods they were using. Each trip took at least two hours, sometimes three, plenty, he believed, to give him the time he needed to single out just who his tails were and what routes they followed, and where the trade-offs took place. He could never be sure, of course, but it was a chance he would have to take. More time would have been nice, but any longer would have probably brought even more surveillance if they thought he had gone operational or was simply running a surveillance detection route, 'SDR' in professional parlance. And that he definitely wanted to avoid—even though that's precisely what he was doing. So, he had to mix in some social errands and sightseeing to build a plausible cover.

By the third day, Baier was pretty sure he had found a gap in the coverage, that period when the team following him turned off and their replacement took over. When he drove down Unter den Linden, Berlin's main drag, and turned off on Friedrichstrasse, the Ladas on his tail drove straight on if he turned once more down Werderstrasse and headed for the Gendarmenmarkt, the plaza with the French Cathedral and Opera House. Maybe they didn't want to be too obvious, sticking that close after two quick turns. Or perhaps they really did think he was planning to do some sightseeing or pick a few things up in the shops surrounding the square. Not that there was much to choose from.

But there had been a gap of a few minutes before the next sedan picked him up again. And fortunately, there was a café on the corner across from the Cathedral, where he had an excuse to get out of the car and stroll over for a coffee. During that walk, as luck would have it, he could leave his chalk mark on the side of the trash bin in the square on his way into the cafe, as he had arranged previously with Chernov.

Finally, on the fourth straight day of his excursions through the lingering ruins in what was in many places still the bombed-out capital of the self-anointed German Democratic Republic, Baier finally felt confident enough to leave the signal. The surveillance had been the same as before, and Baier was relatively certain that he had not been seen. After a long, leisurely coffee and pastry, Baier left and decided to do some shopping. Thanks to the Soviet requisitions and economic mismanagement there wasn't much worth purchasing in the eastern half of the city. But having gotten a handful of East German Marks before crossing over, anything he did find was certain to be a bargain. Rather than exchange his West German currency at the East German official rate of one-for-one, most westerners purchased their *Ostmark* at the more favorable western rate of about eight or nine to one before heading east. Besides, he needed more time to see if Chernov had found the signal and responded.

Three boring hours later, Baier returned. He had actually found some linens for Sabine, as well as four bottles of Radesburger Pils, a solid German beer from Dresden. Most of the time, however, had been spent browsing. But it paid off. The mark Baier had left had a diagonal cross through it, running from left to right. So, he had to hurry to the locale he and Chernov had selected as the site for Plan A, an abandoned—because it had been bombed to crap—warehouse just off Prenzlauer Allee and behind Alexanderplatz.

'Shit,' Baier swore. He had less than hour. And he would definitely have to go operational, as they say, because of the need to shake his surveillance. He would almost certainly have hell to pay when he crossed back over. That is, if he did succeed in getting rid of his tail long enough to meet Chernov and plan the Russian's escape to the west. If the tail stuck, he would have to abort and find a way to make contact again. Fortunately, they had a Plan B as backup to reestablish contact, if necessary.

Baier tossed the copy of *Neues Deutschland*, the official East German rag, into the same trash bin and trotted to his car. He began his drive by tooling at a leisurely pace toward the west and the crossing that was still open at Friedrichstrasse near the shell of Anhalter Bahnhof, once one of the busiest rail terminals in Europe. Now, only the facade of the old station still stood. Then, before he reached Checkpoint Charlie, Baier took a sudden swing to the east down Leipzigerstrasse, over onto Werderstrasse and across the River Spree, gradually building his speed along the way. When he got to Alexanderplatz, where the pedestrian and automobile traffic was heaviest, he accelerated through the throng and ran two red lights to create some distance between himself and his companions. The good Germans yelled curses and instructions about careful driving as he sped past, and one policeman waved his steel traffic sign, blowing on his whistle hard enough to bring the Red Army running.

'Fuck 'em,' Baier thought. His temporary assignment to Berlin for this trip gave him not only diplomatic immunity, but Allied Occupation status. They couldn't do shit to him. At least not officially.

He pulled off Prenzlauer Allee as soon as possible, just three blocks in, and ditched his car in front of one of the apartment blocks. The functional and ugly style sprouting everywhere in the west to provide housing as quickly as possible was missing here in the east, from what he could tell in *Mitte*. But there was nothing yet to replace the gaps and ruins that spotted the landscape. You'd think the regime would have been quicker to create more housing and a more hospitable image, but the vaunted German efficiency was not in evidence. Not under the Soviet administration anyway. He guessed that blocks of new housing were not in the Five-Year Plan. At least not yet. The meeting site was just three blocks down and one over. He could always cut through a courtyard, if necessary. But he did not want to pick up any foot surveillance, or alarm some vigilant neighbors, so Baier walked as briskly as possible along the sidewalk and toward the old warehouse. Time was really important now, and he quickened his pace. But he did not want to bring too much attention to himself by running. Some conscientious citizen might call the '*Vopos*,' as the East German police—or *Volkspolizei*—were known.

Once inside, Baier darted through the barren room and tumbled down a set of stairs into the basement. The stairs were slick with moisture, and he almost fell, grabbing onto a handrail for balance. When he reached the bottom step in one piece, Baier looked up across the stretch of dark empty space bordered in crumbling concrete and dirt. Dust danced in the drafts of air that circulated with the bits of wind penetrating the spaces with windows that housed little more than shattered glass. After a moment, his eyes adjusted to the shades of grey and black, and he saw Chernov. The Russian was standing in a back corner on the ground floor, hidden in shadows except for the glow of a cigarette that periodically moved up and down from his mouth to his side.

"Pretty questionable tradecraft," Baier said, as he walked slowly toward the Russian. Baier motioned toward the glowing ash. "Don't they teach you about that kind of thing in KGB school?"

"Of course, they do, Herr Baier. But I was able to follow you all the way as you approached. That, too, was pretty questionable tradecraft, as you call it. Rather hurried and ad hoc. Fortunately for you, you were alone. In spite of yourself."

"I did not have much choice, Sergei. You put some real pressure on by opting for our meeting plan here and right away. What's wrong?"

"What's wrong, you ask?" Chernov crushed the cigarette under the toe of his shoe and stepped from the shadow to confront Baier. "You ask that after the shooting a few days ago? Do you have any idea of the sort of pressure I have been under? The effort to avoid any possible surveillance alone is exhausting. And sleep you can forget, for the most part."

"So, what happened with your planned crossing? I thought we had lost you. I was all set to give my wife the good news."

"Your wife?" Chernov arched his eyebrows. "She is here? In Berlin?"

"Yes. She couldn't pass up the opportunity to return home. I don't think Washington is quite Germanic or orderly enough for her."

"Joking aside, Herr Baier, that may actually be a good sign for me. I know she still harbors some resentments, for reasons that are beyond me. But if she still has any of her networks operating, we may have to rely on her."

Baier shook his head and stuffed his hands in his jacket pockets. "She's out of it now. Has been for years. And the same goes for her old contacts. I'm afraid we're on our own. And the other night?"

Chernov threw his hands in the air. "I never even got started. There was a crowd of East German Stasi officers near the crossing I had chosen. I realize now that was understandable, since they are funneling all travelers through selected points. I have heard that there are only thirteen now."

"Check that," Baier said. "I think Checkpoint Charlie may be the only one available at the moment. There may still be a few others, but the regime is really clamping down. Which, of course, will not help us."

"Yes, well, in any case they were led by this real son a bitch, Johann Gracchus. They call him *Der Jaeger*, 'The Hunter.' He was one of those German Communists that lived in the Hotel Lux in Moscow during the Nazi years."

"I take it you don't like him."

"I hate the bastard. If he survived Stalin's purges, he must have informed on his comrades at the Lux. God knows enough disappeared into hands of the Cheka. That is how those other self-serving pricks, Markus Wolf and Erich Mielke, survived. They brought Gracchus back to Berlin with them when they returned."

"So, what were all these border guards and Stasi creeps up to?"

"They pulled some poor sap from one of their cars and threw him into a little black Trabant." Chernov snorted. "That alone was like a death sentence. They handed him a set of documents and told him to drive to the other side, that it was his last chance to leave his socialist homeland for the Americanized West." Chernov shrugged. "I guess he thought they were actually letting him go."

"Do you have any idea where they got him?"

Chernov shrugged and fumbled in his pockets for another cigarette. "Who knows? Perhaps we was a political prisoner of some sort. In any case, they were able to kill two birds with one stone, as you say."

Baier looked off to the side, then back at Chernov. "Well, he did escape this place at least. Presumably for someplace better, depending, of course, on the kind of life he lived." Baier smiled. "But if he wanted out of here, he must have been a decent sort."

Chernov's face showed no emotion whatsoever. He stared hard at Baier, his eyes like gray stone against a pale sheet. He held the cigarette he had found in his right hand. "Yes, apparently. But they appeared to be aware of my plan and that you were waiting on the other side. You know what that means, don't you?"

"Why not tell me yourself? I'm sure you're dying to do so."

"It means, of course, that they have penetrated your office here. Or at least the U.S. Mission."

"Then why not stay behind? You could help us find the culprit."

"There are probably more than one, Herr Baier. And probably more than a few. I will leave your people to do their own work. As you now know, I have my own things to settle."

Baier frowned. "In any case, you should have been able to travel on your Soviet documents."

Chernov shook his head. "No, I did not have time to get the proper documentation. You have to be stationed here as part of the occupation forces. You might say I am now 'AWOL,' as you Americans say. And I think someone has also betrayed my presence here. It would explain the indications of surveillance I mentioned earlier."

"Jesus, so you're incognito? They must be dying to grab you, Sergei. So, what was your plan?"

"My plan was not so brilliant, I'm afraid. I was going to get close enough with the papers I do have, then burst through. That will clearly not work now. So, I must ask, what do we do now, Herr Baier?"

Baier stepped in closer. "Did you say you are under surveillance, Sergei?"

"Yes, I am pretty sure. But it is not constant. It is actually very limited." Chernov smiled and shrugged. "I have been able to shake it, as best I can tell. I am not an amateur, you know."

"So, your side knows you are here. Why haven't they arrested you?"

"They have to catch me first."

Baier sighed. "I see." Baier paused, as though weighing a new thought. "You are going to have to trust us on this one now. I guess I'll have to bring you out myself."

"Oh, really? And how do you propose to do that?"

"You see, I have diplomatic and Allied status in Berlin." Baier raised his hand when Chernov looked as though he was about to resist. "I got the designation from our U.S. Army Commandant for my temporary assignment here. That means that I have free access throughout the city and that the locals may not search my car. You're not claustrophobic, I hope."

"Bullets can still penetrate a car. Even the trunk."

"They wouldn't dare. The key will be to get you into the car and hidden without their knowledge. I'll think of a way." Baier smiled. "Like I said, you'll just have to trust me, Sergei. I'll pass along the new plan as soon as we've worked out the particulars."

Chernov smiled in return as he lit his cigarette. "I would feel safer if your wife were in charge. But I guess you will have to do."

• • •

When Baier returned to his car, he had a welcoming committee waiting for him. Three East German civilians, presumably from East German intelligence, the Ministry for State Security or Stasi, leaned against the passenger side of his car. Their dark suits and impassive faces gave them away. Two of them even flexed their hands and forearms when they saw Baier coming. The other one separated himself from his colleagues and approached Baier.

"Nice move, smart guy. What do you think you're doing?"

"I never cease to be amazed by the lack of progress in rebuilding your half of the city," Baier replied. "I just wanted to get a closer look at some of the handiwork. Or lack thereof. I thought there might be a reason for all the inactivity here."

"Whatever." The East German motioned with his head for his companions to join them. The other two took Baier by his arms and led him to their own car, parked about ten yards behind his own.

"What the hell do you think you're doing?"

"Someone wants to talk to you before you go home tonight," the first one said. "Or tomorrow. Or the day after. Whichever." He snorted. "But don't worry. I will drive your West German car." He pointed at the sedan. "A Mercedes? Your organization must spoil you."

"Don't get carried away with the moment. Once you experience Western technology, you may want to defect. And you'd better hurry before your side finishes that monstrosity through the middle of town." Baier laughed at the man who appeared to be the group's leader. "But if you decide to leave tonight, please wait so you can take me with you."

All he received in return was a cold stare from blue eyes that had gone vacant.

• • •

Fortunately, as far as Baier was concerned, they drove westwards. And definitely not toward the Stasi headquarters in Hohenschoenhausen on Normannenstrasse. Instead, they ended up at another one of the small temporary-looking huts that were springing up along the new barrier dividing the Soviet sector from the other Allied sections of Berlin. This one sat behind the crossing at Friedrichstrasse. Baier recognized it as depressingly similar to the one from several nights ago. This one, though, had two rooms, and the three-man team escorted Baier into the back portion. The walls were painted a dull grey that appeared to be intended to rob its occupants of any sense of humanity. In fact, coupled with the barren urban landscape in the rest of this part of the city, Baier felt as though he had been transported to some alien planet, dispirited and all but abandoned, far, far away from his home in the West. The only relief from the drab and dull surroundings came from the wave of lighting that burst through the one window at the back, streaming from the rare appearance of the sun in this north German city. If that failed because of the usual cloud cover or the arrival of night, there were huge temporary lamps that had been placed along the new wall to assist in the construction underway. And to illuminate any would-be escapees, of course.

He was not really surprised to see the familiar face of the East German civilian from that night four days ago sitting behind the lone desk in the back room. This was the man who had delivered his challenge to Baier across the sector boundary in a stare of cold hatred. The long black raincoat was missing tonight, though, replaced by a light gray, two-piece woolen suit and a thin black tie that spoke of casual, bureaucratic violence. Without asking or being invited, Baier sat in the chair facing the desk that separated him from this new nemesis.

"You must be Gracchus," Baier said, by way of greeting.

The Stasi officer smiled. "So, you have heard of me."

"Nothing complimentary, I'm afraid. But I would like to know just what the hell you think you're doing, hauling an American diplomat in here."

Gracchus sat back and smiled again. "Oh, come now. An American diplomat? If that is what you are, then you are an American diplomat who has been engaged in espionage in the heart of the German Democratic Republic."

"Bullshit. I was doing nothing of the sort. And if you have an issue with my presence here, you will have to take that up with your Soviet masters and the Allied Kommandatura. You know, the group that coordinates Allied policy in Berlin. It might actually behoove your allies, the Soviets, to resume their participation there." Baier settled back in his chair, despite the discomfort of the hard, wooden slats digging into his back. "As you well know, your government has no authority in Berlin, which remains an Allied occupied city." Baier leaned forward. "Now, it's time for me to go home."

Gracchus leaned forward in turn. "Oh, you will go home, Herr Baier. Eventually."

"What the hell is that supposed to mean?"

"It means, my American friend…"

"I am definitely not your friend."

"…That you will leave when I am satisfied that we have an understanding."

"I don't intend to come to anything of the sort with you.

Unless, of course, it has to do with your illegal and inappropriate activity here. Hell, this whole fucking wall is illegal."

Gracchus's face went hard suddenly, and the look from the other night returned. Baier was unprepared for the sheer hatred emanating from the man's eyes as his lips curled in disgust.

"This wall is necessary to protect the first socialist state on German soil. You capitalists and imperialist are doing everything in your power to destroy a true socialist experiment that will eventually benefit all Germany. Indeed, all Europe. Justice demands that you not succeed."

"Justice demands, you asshole, that the people who live here have the chance to choose a life free of oppression and poverty, which is not what you'll ever give them."

"That remains to be seen, you American asshole." A smile broke through the steely countenance. "You see, I can shower insults as easily as you. But, more important, this wall will give us a chance to build our state and our society without you people luring our citizens to the West. Or kidnapping them."

"I guess this will come as a surprise to you, dickface, but we don't need to kidnap them. They come of their own free will."

Gracchus paused to catch his breath. His face had grown red, and his chest heaved with anger. "But rather than allow this discussion to degenerate into an exchange of insults, I will leave you with a warning."

"A warning? About what?"

Gracchus stood and leaned over the desk. "A warning that I know what you are up to. I know that you plan to bring someone, possibly a Soviet officer, over to your side. Why he should want to leave for your crowd is beyond me…"

"There's a great deal that is beyond you."

"But I know something of your plans, I will stop them in any way I can. Today, you were lucky, Mister Baier."

"Excuse me? Lucky? In what way?"

"Lucky in that we did not catch you in your act of espionage assisting the Soviet officer's betrayal. Lucky in that you are going home tonight. Alive, that is."

Baier jumped up. "Are you threatening me?

Gracchus leaned back, the smile once more spreading across his face. But it was a smile that contained no warmth. Rather it reminded Baier of the face of a skeleton, cold and uninviting. "No, Mister Baier, I am extending to you a warning, a courtesy even. From one professional to another. The next time you will not be so lucky."

"How so?"

The smile evaporated, replaced by the same look from the other night, only harder and more serious, if that was even possible. "The next time I catch you in our city engaged in this or any other illegal operation, I will make you sorry you ever came to Berlin. If necessary, I will kill you."

CHAPTER FIVE

August 30-31, 1961

"It is hard to believe that it has been 13 years since I was last in Berlin," Sabine said. "Maybe even a little bit longer on this side of the city."

"Do you recognize anything?" Baier asked.

Sabine stared for a minute or so, gazing through the windshield and the window on the passenger side of the Mercedes. "Oh, some, of course. My memories of this city are a mixture from before and after the war. And, of course, during it as well. So, it is all a bit confusing."

Baier nodded. "I would guess that the eastern part here looks much the same as the last time you saw it."

Sabine smiled. "Don't be so condescending, Karl. Of course, there hasn't been the recovery we have in the western zones, but they have done some work here." She pointed out her window. "I mean, look at that gigantic apartment building. Or buildings. I'm sure it looks like the ones Stalin had built in Moscow." She studied the massive complex that stretched the length of several city blocks. "Not that I've ever been or hope to go. But I have seen pictures."

Their car breezed through the light traffic along the renamed Stalinallee. "You mean that 'wedding cake' monstrosity?" Baier asked. It actually did remind him of something akin to a blend of medieval castle and a pastry concoction.

"Karl, it may not be to our tastes, especially since it inherited the name of the style Stalin preferred back in Moscow. But at least it has a little more character than those plain, soulless apartment blocks thrown up in the West."

Baier frowned as he glanced over at his wife. "Function over form, dear. I'm sure some local architect claimed that those western buildings were a kind of Bauhaus artistic revival, but I suspect the real reason was the need for lots of housing, and fast." His head tilted towards the apartment complex. "And I doubt any of those units," he motioned toward the huge apartment complex, "are available to the average citizen over here. Only the best for the party bosses. You know, the *Bonzen*. Just like the Nazis."

"And how is that any different from the other side of Berlin?"

"Oh, come on now, Sabine. You know darn well there is much more available to the average Kraut in the West than here."

"Well, then I guess you can say our side has succeeded. Perhaps we should give the Easterners more time."

"Why?"

"Karl, whenever you speak of the East Germans you have this embittered tone. Why are you so passionate in your distaste for them? What have they ever done to you?"

Baier shrugged and sighed, his hands gripping the steering wheel tight enough to sweat. "It's not so much about what they've done to me, which is relatively little." He paused while the car switched lanes. "Maybe it's my family history."

"What does that have to do with this situation? What have these people ever done to your family? You left years ago."

"I know that, Sabine, but one of the pervading sentiments in our house when I was growing up was resentment."

"Resentment about what? The Nazis?"

"No, not just that. Resentment about the unfairness of German history, I guess. It's a nation that has rarely gotten good or even fair leadership. At least not over the last hundred years or so. Things were supposed to be different after the last war." Baier swung his arm in a large arc over the steering wheel and out toward the windshield. "And now look at all this shit. They're doing it again."

Sabine threw a look of mild disdain at her husband, who stared straight ahead. "Yes, well, remember, Karl, we Germans did bring much of that on ourselves. And after all, this bunch is dealing with those fucking Russians." She hesitated, chewing her lower lip. "Speaking of which…"

Baier waved his hand in the air. "Never mind, Sabine, I've got a plan."

"Is our little tour of East Berlin part of that?"

"As a matter of fact, yes. It is."

"Does that mean we have to keep driving around this godforsaken zone much longer?"

"I thought you liked it here."

"Don't get carried away by a few simple comments to get you to tone down your own sense of superiority. I still prefer it in the western zones." An East Berlin police car roared past, its siren blasting the quiet air of a sleepy East European capital. "Just what are we supposed to be doing?"

Baier smiled. "I want to make sure we're seen cruising the area."

"You mean you actually want to draw their attention to yourself?"

Baier smiled again and nodded. "Precisely."

"But won't that throw us off if I want to try to reestablish contact with some of my old friends. You know, we still have to figure something out for my parents, Karl."

"Yes, it would make that more difficult. Possibly, anyway. But I thought you didn't see much point in that."

"It may still be worth a try. And it may still be necessary."

"Well, we'll have to handle that separately, Sabine. In a few days, I'm hoping they'll be tired of me. Although I suspect they'll hate me even more."

"Just so long as they don't hate you so much that they crawl all over you when we try to get my parents across."

Baier smiled once more, his grin wider than before. "That, too, Sabine, could be to our advantage."

• • •

That had been on a Tuesday night. Now it was Wednesday, just over two weeks since the new barrier had gone up. Baier toured the same parts of East Berlin, driving nearly the same route and looking at the same dilapidated buildings that lined the shadowed streets. And he had a tail, just as he suspected he would. Baier had not seen Gracchus himself in any of the cars following him so far. There had been three that he picked out, shifting their coverage every five or six blocks to avoid having one car too obvious in its pursuit. The problem in that strategy was that his Stasi friends needed more vehicles. Three automobiles were easy to see and remember in the less-than-crowded streets of the Soviet zone. Four and five made it more difficult to remember them all, but, fortunately, they all looked alike. As did their passengers.

Baier figured that that situation represented the two sides of the absence of the prosperity growing in West Berlin. Fewer vehicles meant you could track strangers like himself more easily; fewer vehicles also meant it was more difficult to hide yourself in a crowd. Then again, maybe the Stasi and their Soviet masters meant for Baier to find the first two or three cars, the better to hide others that periodically appeared and then disappeared. It was all part of a game, in some ways. Except when it was a matter of life or death. Either way, it never failed to start that flow of adrenaline that would fuel him for hours.

But tonight, that was of less importance. There were other elements at play. Baier drove down Prenzlauer Allee for the second time that evening and parked in front of the same apartment block he had found the night he met Chernov. Cutting through three courtyards, Baier ran to the same abandoned building and jumped down a set of stairs to the basement. He trotted through a quick 360-degree survey of the basement itself, then ran back to his car. He knew his little exercise would probably end the utility of the building as a safe house or meeting place, but that was okay. It had outlived its usefulness for that the other night. The Stasi had gotten too close, and he knew it wouldn't take them long to discover the spot. But now it functioned as a convenient decoy.

Surprisingly, there was no welcoming committee this evening waiting to give Baier a warm Stasi greeting when he got back to his car. He hopped in the Mercedes, then drove straight for the Western side of the city. He raced through Alexanderplatz, then swung down Werderstrasse and Franzoessiche Strasse. Just before he reached Friedrichstrasse, they struck. An unmarked GAZ Volga rammed into the passenger side of Baier's Mercedes. Or maybe it was a Moskvitch, perhaps the 402. Baier could never be sure with these Russian cars. In any case, the lighter Russian car did little damage to the West German panzer, but Baier was still forced to pull over. Although he was just shy of the crossing that led back into Berlin's western half, he did not want to give some trigger-happy Vopo an excuse to fire on an American. Baier was quickly surrounded by a phalanx of East German border guards. This time Gracchus was among them. He had changed his light gray suit for something more somber, a black number that looked as though he planned to attend a funeral. Baier did not like the symbolism.

"Just what the hell do you think you're doing? And where the hell did you clowns learn to drive?"

"Open the trunk, Herr Baier," Gracchus demanded.

"Go to hell. I don't have to open anything for you bastards."

Gracchus did not hesitate. He drove his fist straight into Baier's midsection, doubling the American over in pain and gasping for breath. "You will open that trunk, or we will force it open."

"Why should I?' the words escaped in the middle of gasps as Baier searched for breath. "I am an American diplomat with Occupation status in this city. Your writ doesn't cover me, asshole."

Gracchus stared at the sky, his fists clenching and unclenching as he struggled to contain his anger. "Listen to me, you American jackass. I know you are trying to smuggle a renegade out of here. I know you have been operational in our city this evening. I will not allow you to proceed unhindered. Nor will I allow you to evade responsibility for your actions, once we have the proof we need."

The sound of Baier's trunk popping open forced him to turn his head toward the Mercedes. He couldn't keep from letting a smile of triumph spread wide across his face. A dark empty cavern stared up at the East German border guards, members of the elite

Felix Dzerzhinsky brigade. Their puzzled looks told a story of confusion and frustration.

Gracchus marched over to the trunk, bent low, and ran his arms inside the empty space.

"You might as well search the rest of the car, now that you've broken it. Asshole."

All heads turned to the rear as a black Zil pulled up alongside the small crowd. A tall Russian, who Baier assumed was Vladimir Kirillnikov, the local KGB resident, stepped from the back seat and walked over to Baier. Despite the warm August weather, he wore a long black raincoat that gave him an air of mystery and authority. Perhaps it was just Baier's imagination. The Russian stood in front of the American and stared into his eyes for what seemed like a full minute. The dirty blond hair was swept straight back and his cloudy blue eyes almost made him look like a native of the city. This was reportedly the Russian's third tour in Berlin, so maybe he had adopted the look of his unhappy hosts. Whether he had taken on the outlook and perspective they had developed after years of occupation remained to be seen.

"Have they harmed you?" he asked.

"Not really," Baier sputtered, as he struggled to regain his breath. The pain had subsided enough for him to make a passable attempt at appearing to be tough enough to handle Gracchus's assault. "I am glad that you've arrived, though."

The Russian nodded and looked over the East Germans before turning back to the American. "I am sure you are." He glanced at the Mercedes. "But if you don't mind, my people would like to have a look at your car."

Baier swept his arm in the direction of the impressive but damaged West German sedan. "Be my guest."

The two men who had emerged from the front seat of the Zil and planted themselves behind Kirillnikov turned and strolled to the Mercedes with little more than a glance at their chief. They were quick and efficient. After a few minutes, one of them looked at Kirellnikov and shook his head.

"I guess you can go now," the KGB chief said. "That is, if your automobile is still drivable."

"Of course, it is. It's a Mercedes," Baier said.

Kirillnikov smiled. "I noticed. Good luck getting home tonight."

The Russian turned and began to walk to his car. Then he stopped and turned again toward the American. "You may have won this round, Mister Baier, but as you well know, this is not over." He nodded in Gracchus's direction. "My German colleague here will not let it go. And neither will I."

"I know that," Baier answered. "I would expect nothing less."

• • •

The construction at the Checkpoint Charlie crossing was still relatively incomplete, at least well behind the schedule that the Agency's Berlin Operations Base—or BOB, as it was known—had picked up in reporting from some of the few assets with whom BOB had been able to maintain contact. Perhaps that was because the East Germans were being more thorough than efficient, given the importance of their assignment and the focus of the world's attention. The Volkswagen and its two passengers passed through the checkpoint in an uneventful crossing, then swung right and headed for the American compound on Clayallee. It was almost ten o'clock, but the streets of West Berlin were still full of traffic, despite it being a weeknight. It was almost as though Berlin was beginning to recapture the glamour and allure it had won during the Weimar Republic, when it had served as a mecca of sorts for the *avant garde* and the exotic.

"Please pull over so I can take off this ridiculous disguise," Chernov asked.

The young American intelligence officer, Robert Mikulski, could barely keep the Volkswagen on target to slide next to the curb. He had been understandably nervous, pulling his first exfiltration assignment just two months after arriving in Berlin. Not only that, but it was his first overseas tour after a life that had taken him not more than a few miles from his home by the steel mills of East Chicago to DePaul University on the Windy City's northern side. His shirt clung to his underarms in a pool of sweat and cotton, and his breath came short and heavy in the humid night air.

"Sure, sure. I know that kind of thing gets heavy and hot, but it was necessary to make sure you matched the picture in the passport. You were lucky we were able to find a photograph of someone who looked so much like you."

"Yes, yes, I understand," Chernov replied. "But it also itches. Quite a bit, actually."

"Okay, I get it. You don't need it any longer, anyway."

"And, please, do not think I do not appreciate the effort your people have made to bring me out. I understand it was a difficult operation. Even if it did go smoothly. I hope Herr Baier is okay."

Mikulski nodded as he pulled away from the curb. "Oh, I'm sure he's fine. He's done this kind of thing before. He's pretty experienced."

Chernov smiled at the memories. "Yes, I am aware of that. I have known him for some time now."

Both men were silent for the rest of the ride. When they reached the American headquarters at Clayallee, Mikulski drove the car past the Post Exchange, or PX, shopping center across the street and turned right at the next intersection. Chernov touched the American's arm. "You can let me out here."

A worried look spread across Mikulski's face, as his brow wrinkled with concern and some confusion. "But we're not at the place I was told to drop you off, the place you're spending the night. It's really pretty nice and spacious." Mikulski smiled. "Your biggest problem may be finding the bedroom. Or choosing which one to use."

"I realize we are not there yet. And I am sure it is quite pleasant. But there has been a good bit of excitement and anxiety this evening. I would like to walk for a bit to calm down. Tell Herr Baier that I will see him tomorrow, as we have arranged."

"Well, okay, I guess so."

When the car stopped, Chernov slid out the passenger side door and stepped to the sidewalk. He watched as the young American drove the Volkswagen in the direction of Zehlendorf, the suburb between Berlin and Potsdam on the city's southwestern corner. When it rode out of sight, he turned and crossed the street to the subway station at Onkel Tom's Huette, then disappeared down the stairs to the tracks.

CHAPTER SIX

September 1, 1961

"**M**an, but this house is huge. How come nobody is living here permanently?" Baier asked. He stood in awe of the three-story overgrown mansion built in a mock Bavarian chalet style that even had the painted wooden porches on the upper floors, complete with flower boxes hanging from the railings. It may have seemed out of place in Berlin, Germany's Prussian capital, but then it was situated along the curve of Mexicoplatz, not the most Teutonic of names. He glanced up toward the beamed ceiling in the living room. "It must cost a fortune to keep this place up."

"Not really," Hendricks answered. "Or maybe it does, but that's not my problem. The Germans pick up the cost as part of the occupation budget."

"Which they fund. How convenient." Baier peeked through the opening into the kitchen, a short and narrow passage flanked by the stove and oven on one side and refrigerator on the other. Keeping with the Continental style, neither appliance was very large. "You could use some more cooking and counter space, though."

Hendricks shrugged. "Whatever. Also not my problem."

"So how come no one's living here now?"

"It's between occupants. The last family here returned stateside in July as part of the normal rotation. But not for long, poor sap. He's currently suffering withdrawal pains from all this in Jakarta."

"Well, that interlude is convenient. Or at least it seemed so yesterday when my Russian friend was supposed to show up."

The two Americans climbed the stairs to the second floor and began wandering the hallway, poking their heads in the bedrooms and baths for a final cursory glance, hoping in vain that somehow Sergei Chernov would magically reappear. To inspect each one took longer than Baier originally thought would be necessary. But there were more than he realized—six in all— so it took a little while. Still, all was in vain. Not a clue of anyone's presence, much less of a Soviet.

"What do you suppose happened?" Hendricks asked.

Baier blew out a breath that left a hint of his breakfast of scrambled eggs, bacon, and orange juice. His first coffee of the morning was still resting in a porcelain mug on the floor of his car, half empty by now. "If I had to guess, I'd say he's half-way to Paris. If he isn't there already." He halted and marched through the master bedroom. "Do all of these bedrooms have their own bath in this place?"

"No, only four do. But about your buddy…"

"He's not my buddy. He's my sometime asset, not recruited and certainly not controlled. What did your boy Mikulski say again?"

"He claimed that Chernov wanted to unwind after all the excitement of the crossing. Of which there was apparently not all that much. Certainly not as much as you encountered. They sailed through like some kind of summer breeze off the Pomeranian plains. So, Rob let him out a couple blocks from here to walk the rest of the way. Then Mikulski drove home."

"Very poetic, Tom. Well, chalk it up to a lesson learned. Never give up control of an asset so easily and without establishing exactly when you will meet him next and how. Especially when you're dealing with a sly fox like my fucking Russian."

"Well, that's true enough, Karl. But you just said he's only a sometime asset and not controlled. And you did have the next meeting scheduled and arranged. It was supposed to be today, and here. Remember? He could just as easily have turned around and walked away once Mikulski dropped him off here anyway. I mean, he did not have instructions to tuck the bastard in for the night."

Baier sighed and headed toward the staircase. "I suppose you're right." At the head of the stairs, Baier glanced around, then turned to the chief of base. "I guess we're done here. The fox has definitely flown the coop with whatever hen he wanted. And since he was never here, he didn't exactly leave any clues. Not that I really need them."

"You really think he's gone to Paris, like he said?"

Baier nodded. "Yes, I do. In fact, I'm positive. It's what he said he would do, eventually. And it looks like I'm going to have to follow him there to wrangle him back." He rested his hand on Hendricks's shoulder. "But don't worry, Tom. I will find the son of a bitch, one way or the other?"

"'Other?' Be that as it may, I do like your choice of verb, Karl. Wrangling may well be what it takes. But you know Headquarters is going to have a humongous shitfit over this."

Baier smiled and nodded. "Of course, they will. But I've dealt with that before."

"You mean Budapest?"

Baier nodded. "For starters, yeah. Let's head back to your office and let Washington know of my change in plans. Do you still have a copy of his photograph we used to prepare the fake documentation that brought him across last night?"

It was Hendricks's turn to nod. "Of course. You want me to send a copy to Paris for identification purposes? I'm sure they'll be happy to join the hunt."

"Thanks, Tom. I can make my travel arrangements while we work on the cable for Washington. Do you think Paris will have any problems with me showing up there?"

Hendricks actually laughed out loud as he started down the stairs. "Will they say no to their deputy division chief hunting for a KGB defector?" He laughed again and shook his head. "I hardly think so." His shoulders rolled as he chuckled further on the way to the ground floor. "You've been back at Headquarters for too long, Karl. You sound like you're losing your edge."

Baier followed, then reached for his colleague's arm when they made it to the front door. "Tom, I have one other question for you. And this one won't be so funny. It's a personal one, actually."

Hendricks turned, a look of concern wrinkling his brow and narrowing his eyes. "What is it, Karl?"

Baier paused to rehearse the words in his head before speaking. "It's about Sabine."

"Sabine? What's wrong?"

"Well, Sabine and her parents."

"What about them?"

"You may not know this, but they remained behind in the East after the war. They didn't want to leave their home during what they thought would be a temporary division until a peace treaty sorted things out here in Germany."

"And now they want to leave," Hendricks guessed. "Now that that fucking wall is going up."

"That's right, Tom. Do you think there's anything you can do to help?"

Hendricks was silent for what seemed like a full minute, maybe longer. "I don't know, Karl. That's a tough one. After all, it is a personal matter. And you know that the rules are pretty strict about that sort of thing."

Baier reached out to touch his colleague's shoulder. "Tom, it's more than that. Sure, there's a personal angle, but you know the kind of help we got from Sabine back in the days after the war running our asset stable in the east. A big chunk of that grew out of the black market network she had established and then turned over to us. We got all kinds of contacts and traveling routes from her, and they lasted for years."

"You do make a pretty good point, Karl. But that was over fifteen years ago."

"But still not to be forgotten. And then there's the work she put in helping me run that debriefing center in our property on the Austro-Hungarian border back in '55 and '56, before the Soviets sealed that border completely."

"Okay, Karl, you make a strong case. Strong enough for me, anyway. I'm sure we can look into it." Hendricks rested his hand on Baier's shoulder. "As you just pointed out, it's the least we can do."

Baier paused to think for a moment, his teeth working his lower lip. "What about that new asset you recruited in East Berlin? The Syrian diplomat."

"He's pretty green, Karl. We've only used him once for a border crossing. Are you sure you want to trust him with your in-laws? Would Sabine?"

"What kind of choice do we have, Tom? Things are only going to get tighter."

"Yeah, but I doubt we can pull together some more false documentation on such short notice. Are they already in Berlin?"

Baier shook his head. "No, not at the moment. They were here earlier but returned to their home in Erfurt. They were afraid that hanging around too long would make the authorities suspicious. But Sabine could bring them up here pretty quickly."

"Do you think they'd be willing to cram themselves into a trunk, or ride in a hidden compartment?

Again, Baier shook his head. "I seriously doubt that, Tom. They're pretty old and not in the best of health."

"Well, that certainly complicates matters even more, Karl. Let me think on it. Together we can probably come up with a plausible reason to cooperate on this for Headquarters when the bureaucrats start to howl. But it's the method that will be the real challenge."

"Thanks, Tom. I won't forget this."

The two men walked towards the base chief's car. "In the meantime, let's get those cables to Washington and Paris going. Your Russian buddy already has a big head start on you."

"Like I said before, he's not my buddy. And there is no way I'm going to let him get away."

• • •

At his Normannenstrasse office, Johann Gracchus sat rigid behind his metal desk, his swivel chair turned at a right angle to the wall. He stared through the window at the back of his office as though he wanted to melt the glass. His solid blue tie was already loose at his collar, the top button of which was undone. His white shirt felt like a sackcloth lined with the taste of last night's failure. The entrance of his three colleagues brought him around to face his visitors standing to the front of his desk.

"Comrades, that must never happen again."

"What exactly do you mean?" the tallest and oldest of the three asked. He could not have been much more than forty, perhaps a year or two more. His frame was little more than bone and muscle, as though he had yet to recover the body fat lost during years of deprivation during and after the war. "I thought we were relatively successful last night. After all, we confronted the American, as you had wished."

Gracchus nearly spat his response in disgust. "Successful? Are you a fool, Hoehn? How do you define success?"

The man shifted uneasily on the balls of his feet. "We gave the American a clear warning. Or at least *you* did, Comrade. And we disrupted whatever plans he may have had."

"And the Soviets? How do you explain their presence? Was that part of our success?"

Another officer spoke up in defense of his colleague. "They arrived at the right time to assist us. We are, after all, on the same team. Are we not?"

"Are you really so naïve, Barenbrugge? Are all Saxons so simple?" Gracchus shot back.

"What would you have preferred, Comrade Gracchus?" Hoehn asked.

"I would have preferred more time to work the American over to discover his plot. I have no doubt now that he was a merely a decoy last night. Unfortunately, we do not have enough information from our sources at this stage to find out what is really going on."

"And the Soviets, Comrade?" Barenbrugge continued. "Are they in the dark as much as we are?"

Gracchus laughed. "I doubt it. It's not like they share everything with us." He thought for a moment. "Perhaps they are, after all." Then he shook his head and stood behind his desk. "No, no, it's too difficult to tell. I would not be surprised if they have their own agenda at work here in hopes of working something out to reduce tensions in the city."

Hoehn stepped forward. "But they are our closest allies,

Comrade. Surely, they gave their approval to our plans for the wall here in the city and were well aware of the tensions that would result. We are working together on this, are we not?"

Gracchus shrugged and turned to the window again. "Do not spread a word of this conversation beyond this room, or you will live—briefly—to regret it. But we did not share the details of our plans for the new division of the city with our allies. Yes, yes, of course Comrade Khrushchev knew of them. He got the general plans and timing from Ulbricht, who had to say as much to gain the Kremlin's approval. But we kept everything as closely held as possible. And I doubt Khrushchev shared it much further within his own circles. And certainly not with anyone else in the Warsaw Pact."

"But why?" Barenbrugge protested. "Are you saying the Soviets are no longer to be trusted?"

Gracchus threw a look of disdain at his underling, as though he was looking down from some Olympian political heights. "We can no longer assume that our interests and those of our socialist brothers in the Kremlin are always one and the same. Look at how First Secretary Ulbricht had to badger and pressure that fat prick Khrushchev to take a stand here to remove this cancer of West Berlin from our heart. He thinks of his relationship with the Americans first."

"And what does that mean exactly, Comrade?" Hoehn pressed.

"It means we have to be very careful when dealing with our Soviet allies and the Americans. And we can assume nothing." Gracchus turned toward his colleagues and the front again. "Hoehn, the American is going to Paris in pursuit of something or someone. I want you to take these two and follow. Find out what he is up to."

"Of course, Comrade Gracchus. We will prepare our departure immediately. What should we do once we have discovered his purpose?"

"I will leave that up to you and your judgment, Hoehn." Gracchus paused and looked hard at his subordinate. "Do not let me down, Hoehn." He glanced at the others. "You other two are dismissed. But Hoehn, I'd like you to stay for a moment longer."

When the others had left, Gracchus sat back down and motioned toward the single chair at the front of his desk. Hoehn sat in the narrow piece that appeared to have little padding or stuffing, stiffly at first but then relaxed and fell back against the chair and crossed his legs. His charcoal gray pants leg climbed his shin, exposing the dark blue sock and about an inch of calf. Hoehn glanced down, then smoothed his deep red tie over a pressed white shirt. He started to undo the top button, but then thought better of it. Before Gracchus could speak Hoehn jumped in with a question of his own.

"How can you be so sure that the American is traveling to Paris?"

"Because I have an asset in the travel office at the U.S. Mission over there." Gracchus threw his head in the direction of the west.

"Excellent, Comrade. Are there more?"

"Perhaps. But I wanted to speak of something else, Comrade. I want to find out more about you and what drives you." Gracchus leaned forward, his elbows resting on files scattered across the top of his desk. "Your evaluation reports are all excellent," Gracchus picked up a sheaf of papers to show them to his officer, "but you still remain an enigma to me…and others here. For example, you served the Fatherland well under the fascists, even winning decorations for bravery during the assault on the Soviet Union. And then there is your family's background. Hardly proletarian, I am sure you would agree. I mean, a Prussian Junker? We do not find many of those here."

"That is all part of the past. Which I have left behind. I have explained this before."

"And your faithful and rather effective service for the Third Reich?" Gracchus let the last two words slip out in a breath of condescension and disgust.

"That was a matter of survival, Comrade, not pleasure."

"I see. Then why did it take you so long to join the Free Germany movement in the prisoner camps?"

"You are aware, Comrade, that there were still many unreconstructed fascists in those camps who exacted revenge against any who turned against the Reich, are you not?" Hoehn shrugged. "In any case, I always say better late than never."

Gracchus smiled as he leaned back. "Yes, of course, I understand completely. But I still wonder just how deep your loyalty to the new state is, Comrade Hoehn."

"Have I given you any cause to doubt me, Comrade?"

"No. Not yet, anyway."

"Will this Paris trip be a test? Of sorts? And if so, how many more will you expect me to undergo?"

Gracchus leaned back. "We are all undergoing tests all the time, Comrade. Deviations can come along at any time, especially when one lives and works so close to the enemy and his schemes."

Hoehn leaned forward in his seat. "May I ask you another question, Comrade Gracchus?"

"Yes, of course."

"Just how did you spend the war years in Moscow? Was there ever a time you had doubts about the inevitability of our victory. The triumph of Socialism, I mean, not that of the Third Reich. Naturally."

Gracchus's smile evaporated as he paused to look out the window. When he turned back to Hoehn, his face had grown tired, as though weary of the memories of his personal history and of the struggle his family had engaged in for decades now.

"No, of course, not."

Hoehn rose to go. "Alright then, Comrade. I think I understand you better. I will try to live up to your expectations."

"But it was not always easy."

"Excuse me?"

"It was the nights that were most difficult. But it wasn't the silence that comes with the darkness. Rather it was the eerie, frightening and isolated sounds of the footsteps that would echo through the hallways. It was the time they came to make their arrests. You held your breath as they passed, as though by not giving forth a sound you might convince the NKVD that there was no one left behind your door. Only when they had passed, did you allow yourself to let that breath out, a breath that had become foul with fear."

"And that never gave rise to any doubts?"

"Of course, it did." Gracchus looked up from the floor with its distant memories. "But you overcame them. Just as you must overcome them now. You remembered your cause and the ultimate victory that History has forecast. Have you ever read Marx's, *Das Kapital*?"

"No, not yet."

"There is a certainty there. It can be very reassuring in those dark moments. And you leaned to trust the Leader in his program to protect the Motherland of Socialism, because it was necessary."

"I see."

Gracchus stood. "But enough of that." He paused. "Do not let me down, Hoehn. I am depending on you here. We must learn to depend on each other."

"Of course, Comrade. I will do my best."

•••

"Paris? Well, that's certainly nice. For you."

"Sabine, I have to go. Our friend has disappeared, and I'm pretty damn sure that's where he's gone."

Sabine let loose with what sounded like a full-blown harrumph. "I told you not to trust that fucking Russian. Maybe now you'll learn."

Baier smiled and shook his head. "And after all these years, and all that we've been through together. I think I know the man better than that."

It was all he dared to say. Sure, she knew Chernov well, perhaps as well as he did. His wife had been there at every turn in his career that involved the Soviet KGB officer, from Berlin to Vienna to Budapest, and now back to Berlin. It was as though their careers had come full circle, returning to the town of their origin. Of course, each man had followed different paths and objectives, but those paths had crossed often enough to give Baier, at least, a sense of what made his counterpart tick, what drove him along his own roads of searching and desperation, of longing, fulfillment, and identity. And for the moment, that road almost certainly had driven him to Paris, where Baier now had to follow. He would never try to explain it all to his wife, certainly not in all the details of their shared past. Sabine had probably—and understandably—never gotten over the horrors of those first months of Soviet conquest and occupation in Berlin. Sergei Chernov would never be more than a reminder of that time, regardless of his own behavior and actions, however innocent. How could a woman ever overcome that? No matter what he went through with Chernov, he would never press that point very far with Sabine. She and all that she had endured clearly came first.

"Besides," Baier continued, "there's enough for you to do here."

"Like what?"

"Like help prepare for your parents escape."

Sabine's eyes brightened and grew wider with anticipation. "Oh, Karl, can you really pull it off?"

He held up his hands, as though to ward off any sudden and unrealistic hopes. "Sabine, we're looking into it. There is one possibility, but it's all very preliminary. And even if this doesn't work out on the first try, we'll keep at it. I promise."

"So, tell me. What is the plan?"

Baier grimaced, afraid that he had already raised her expectations too far. "There is no plan yet. We're looking into some possibilities. I think the less you know at this point, the better it will be. Believe me, you'll know in due time."

"So, what do you want me to do?"

"Can you reach your parents? Are they still back in Erfurt?"

Sabine nodded eagerly. "Yes, yes. Should I tell them to come to Berlin?"

Baier thought for a moment, his eyes studying his wife's face. "Not just yet. But tell them they should be prepared to leave on very short notice. When the time comes," Baier raised a finger here, "if it does, it will probably all happen very fast." He stared deep into his wife's eyes again. "And for God's sake, please ask them to act naturally, not to raise any suspicions. I'm sure the local authorities there are aware of their familial connections to the West."

"But so many people have those, Karl. They can't watch everyone."

"But they can be selective. And we have to reckon with those bureaucratic pricks focusing on people like your parents who have official connections with anyone with authority and influence in the West."

Sabine turned and paced the living room as though she was measuring it. "Yes, yes, of course. I'll tell them to be very careful. They are aware of the dangers, Karl." She stopped to take in her husband with a look of love that would have melted the most committed intelligence officer, even the most committed Communist or Capitalist. Baier was no exception. "Please don't let me down, *Liebchen*."

"Of course not, my dear. Of course not."

But try as he might to imagine it, Baier was not at all certain he could pull this off. Especially when he was running across Europe to corral a troublesome and puzzling Soviet officer intent on pursuing his own agenda.

• • •

He decided to leave his car parked along Breitestrasse, where he could look back toward the city center and see the ruins of the Hohenzollern palace. The regime had blown what was already a pile of ruins into even smaller bits a few years back, probably to make the total removal of such a powerful reminder of Berlin's— and Germany's—imperial past that much easier. The parking spot was far enough away from Berlin's city hall, the *Rote Rathaus,* to allow Hoehn to make sure there was no surveillance. It also not too far away, which allowed him to reach his destination in a reasonable amount of time. The city hall had been so named for the red bricks that made up the building's façade, but he was pretty certain the regime would find some way to tie the popular label into a convenient political narrative as well. And to be sure, there was a bit of revolutionary heritage there. King Friedrich William had been forced to attend a parade honoring the victims of the initial attempt to suppress the revolution of 1848 from its front balcony. This regime would probably forget to note that he eventually got his revenge, though.

In any case, Hoehn had a purpose that was more immediate. He walked briskly with stops at street corners and shop windows to check for a possible tail but was reasonably confident that he was free. One still could never be entirely certain of whom to trust.

Once at the *Rathaus*, Hoehn strolled down a back street and popped into a bar kitty corner from the old Saint Nicolaus Church, one of the oldest churches in one of the oldest neighborhoods in the city. It was still largely a collection of rubble, having been heavily bombed by the British and Americans, but some day the regime might find it to its advantage to reconstruct the area with a taste for the neighborhood's historical atmosphere. In the meantime, it provided another point for resentment against the Anglo-Saxon *Luftpiraten*, or air pirates, as they had been so aptly labelled by the Nazis.

Hoehn headed straight for the telephone hanging on the back wall, ordering a beer as he sped by the bar. The call's connection was immediate and actually clear, a minor victory on a phone system that had yet to be updated since its installment in 1939.

"So, do your colleagues know the whereabouts of the Russian?"

"I do not think so," Hoehn replied. "They are as confused as anyone about the man's location. And about his intentions. In fact, I am not even sure they are certain as to his identity."

"That does not surprise me. It may explain your superiors' obsession with their interference in the operation."

"They really have no way of finding out either. That is why, I am certain, Gracchus is so obsessed with the American." Hoehn laughed. "Aside from the fact that he really seems to hate the bastard."

"He probably hates all Americans. The man is an ideologue, pure and simple."

"Not exactly, Comrade. The man is more complicated than that. Although I have to admit that I am still trying to figure him out myself."

"Whatever. Try to make sure that he does not find Chernov first. I would like the opportunity to interrogate my Russian colleague here, perhaps even try to turn him once more."

"Do you think that is wise?"

"I think it provides a wonderful opportunity. Speaking of complicated men, this one has layers none of us have seen yet." The voice on the other end of the line paused for a moment, and Hoehn could hear papers rustling in the background. "In fact, I have his file in front of me now. It makes for some very interesting reading."

"How so?" Hoehn asked.

"For one thing it does raise some questions about what his intentions are and what he may know of things in Moscow."

"Are you concerned about what he could betray to the Americans?"

"Yes, there is always that. It is not clear, however, just how much he knows or whom he knows. And that could be a problem."

There was a pause, and Hoehn started to wonder if the connection had been broken. But then the Russian Kirillnikov spoke again. "For another, though, it confirms what we suspected after the American's escape from Budapest. And there have been other times of collaboration."

"That sounds very much like treason, Comrade."

"Yes, but it can also lead to the opportunities I mentioned."

"Again, Comrade, how so?"

"It means he has gained the confidence of the Americans. Or, at least one of them for sure. And that can be exploited, if we play it properly."

Hoehn smiled, nodding as though the person on the other end of the line could see him. "I am beginning to think you are right, Comrade. Is there anything you would like me to do?"

A short laugh traveled across the wires. "Just continue as planned for now. We shall see how the situation develops."

"Agreed, Comrade. I will do my best."

CHAPTER SEVEN

September 3, 1961

The City of Light. Okay, it was cloudy, and Paris was almost empty of locals and swimming in tourists. It was just past August, after all. Yes, it was September already but technically still summer. Not that it mattered that much to Baier. The history and beauty of this city was inescapable, regardless of the time of year. It always would be, as far as Baier was concerned. He had taken up his post at a small café across the Seine from Notre Dame Cathedral, content just to sip his coffee—*au lait*, of course; he was an American—and pick at his croissant and strawberry jam while he pondered the medieval majesty of that famous church. Admiring it from a distance also allowed him to pass on the temptation to climb all those steps in the bell tower, like some reincarnation of Hugo's Quasimodo. Besides, there were enough crazy tourists to watch doing just that.

"I knew I'd find you here. Nice spot you selected, by the way."

Ralph Pittman was the local chief of station and a classmate of Baier's from their early days together, having joined the Agency and taken their oath on the same day. They had also spent countless hours together during their initial training, and Baier had come to respect his colleague as a 'natural,' if there was such a thing in this business. Since then, their paths had crossed rarely. Only once, in fact, and that during Baier's tenure in London almost a decade ago when Pittman had been temporarily deployed to the British capital for a six-month stint. Knowing that his old classmate was here in Paris had made the request for assistance in tracking down the wandering Chernov that much easier for Baier.

In his experience, the informal networks of colleagues and friends often counted for more than the flow of paperwork through the bureaucratic in- and out-trays that populated the desks back in Washington.

"Glad to see you've kept your edge in a soft assignment like this one," Baier responded. He studied his colleague, dressed in a pair of tan trousers and a light blue dress shirt with the sleeves rolled halfway to his elbows. The tie and jacket were notable for their absence. All in all, his appearance was a surprising break from the upper Midwestern working-class background he had carried from Minnesota to Washington. "Even if your casual attire suggests otherwise. No tie today?"

Pittman pulled out the chair opposite Baier and took a seat, his back to the river and the cathedral. "Hey, it's August in Paris. Close enough, anyway. And whatever the season and whatever the dress code you still need your edge. Have you ever tried working with the French? Besides, I knew you'd pick a spot like this one, although all your message said was to meet you at Notre Dame." Pittman smiled and seemed to fold into his chair and the scenery around them. "The scenery and history here really are hard to beat. So I decided I would relax a bit. Unless you want to attend Mass. But even then…" Pitman threw a suspicious and curious glance at Baier.

Baier put his coffee cup back on its saucer. "Not much chance of that. I have yet to rediscover my childhood piety, I'm afraid."

"It's just as well. We're a bit late for the morning Mass schedule. There's always Vespers, of course…"

Baier motioned with a nod of his head toward the book and art stalls lining the upper level of the sidewalk along the Seine. "This is also a great spot to look for a tail. Lord knows, there's plenty of opportunities to stop to browse and check your company."

"Good point. Did you find anything?"

"Thankfully, no. No unwanted company."

"Were you expecting any?"

"I'm finding a surprising number of people interested in this case. And there are always the locals."

"I don't think you need to worry about our French hosts on this one. How about some books?"

Baier smiled and shook his head. "No. I didn't feel like carrying anything around all day."

"Too bad. It would be good cover." Pittman swiveled in his chair to study the stalls. "There's some interesting stuff over there."

"True, but I don't read French. If anyone asked I wouldn't be able to tell them about the books I was carrying." He gazed at the remnants of coffee in his cup and fingered the last third of his croissant. "So, have the French been helpful on this one?"

"Actually, they have." Pittman signaled for the waitress and ordered a small canister of coffee. "You'll be having some more, I hope. At least another cup. They're small here."

"Yeah, I've noticed. But about the French."

"Well, it's a good thing I'm so diplomatic and resourceful. They've been quite cooperative for us. Or, I should say for you."

"Don't think I don't appreciate it." He pointed to his cup and nodded when the waitress brought the order to their table. "How have they helped?"

"For one thing, they were able to find Chernov among the recent arrivals. Just yesterday, in fact, thanks to the picture you sent."

"I take it he's traveling under a different identity."

"Of course. Which has naturally gotten our friends here all excited and interested. I mean, any time a KGB officer visits their capital under a false identity, you can imagine what that will do to their daily routine."

"Is he at least traveling as a Soviet?"

Pittman shook his head. "Apparently not. He has a Czechoslovak passport under the name of Milos Havilek."

"Do they have an address? He would have been required to give one, right?"

Pittman nodded again, this time more vigorously. "Oh, yeah. He's got himself a room in a small hotel not far from the Hotel des Invalides and the Army Museum."

"The what? You mean, where Napoleon is entombed?'

"That's right. It's on the Avenue de Breteil. You get the irony, don't you?"

Baier looked up after finishing his croissant and washing the final remnants down with some fresh coffee. "No, why?"

"That's the street where De Gaulle lived as a child."

"I doubt whether my Russian knows or even gives a damn."

Pittman shrugged. "Whatever. I thought it was interesting." He studied Baier over the rim of his coffee cup as he sipped at a speed that made it look as though he was trying to catch up to the caffeine level his guest had already attained. "So, what can you tell me about Berlin? Just how great is the danger? The French are in quite a huff."

"How so? It's not like they're out front in trying to stop the Soviets and their East German buddies from splitting the city."

"Ah, but you have to see how important it is for them to be a part of the game there. It's reminder that they were actually one of the victors in the last war…"

"Despite having been overrun in a matter of weeks and then occupied for a little over four years."

Pittman nodded as he reset his cup on its saucer. "True, true. But they will always look for opportunities to remind everyone of how they see themselves. Which means in this case that you can expect them to focus on the principles, as opposed to the practicalities. And for them that means, of course, that Berlin must remain a four-power city under Allied occupation. Period. And Khrushchev's threat to sign a separate peace treaty with the East Germans means nothing and should be ignored. De Gaulle even said as much publicly. They're holding to a very hard line right now and probably will for the foreseeable future. Whether they will do anything about it is another matter."

"Well, I'd say Washington is a lot more confused. Half the people involved say it doesn't matter, while the other half believe we're on the brink of World War III."

Pittman tipped his coffee cup back as he drained the last drops before setting it back on the table. "So, it's like the Berlin theologians are still working to convince everyone that city is the center of the universe. And I suppose you are right in the middle of that, singing the same tune." He smiled as Baier shrugged. "But hurry up, we need to take a walk."

"What the hell, Ralph, there's still half a container of coffee here. And I'm paying." He drank some more of his coffee, frowning at the bitterness. "Besides, Berlin is the center of the universe. And not just for me. It has been since the end of the war and will continue to be so. At least for this week. And probably for several months more."

Pittman stood and nodded toward the coffee canister. "Leave it. There are some other things I want to pass along but not while we sit here in comfort. You never know where there are extra ears in this city." He opened the lid of the coffee pot, then set it back down. "Besides, someone of your rank can afford the coffee. Congratulations, by the way, on getting your GS-15. You certainly deserved it after your work in Lebanon."

"Thanks. Mark my words, Ralph, we are not done with that place yet."

"No kidding. There are still problems aplenty with the ethnic and religious divisions that the French and British cobbled together into a collection of nations without any pasts or heritage after World War I. That whole region remains a tinderbox." He shook his head. "The imperial delusions our two big allies suffer under have really gotten anachronistic. You see that every day here with the Algerian war."

Baier stood, tossed several francs on the table, and hurried to catch up with the local station chief, who was already strolling along the sidewalk. When he caught up with him, Baier reached for his colleague's sleeve.

"It seems we agree with each other on that, Ralph. I guess it's part of our OSS heritage. But what's so important that we have to walk and talk at the same time? I was hoping to go stake out my Russian friend's place."

They swung left when they reached Boulevard Saint Michel. "All in good time, my friend. I want to show you the pleasant wonders of the Luxembourg Gardens." Pittman glanced at the sky.

"Although it would be nice if the sun came out. But tell me, is your hotel satisfactory?"

"I guess it's okay. Kind of small, though, and I'm not crazy about having to share a bathroom on the second floor. Then again, the location is pretty nice. I can even see the corner of the National Opera if I strain my neck at a certain angle."

"We wanted to give you some place that is out of the way and discreet. But also a place that isn't too far out of the way, where we could easily reach you and give you a good access point in your hunt."

"What's my story with the staff there?"

"We told them that you were a moderately successful Hollywood producer who wants his privacy while he researches locations for his next film."

"Moderately successful?"

Pitman shrugged and smiled. "We didn't want to excite too much interest or attention. Besides, the local owner is an asset of ours. He's proved to be very useful in the past in keeping people isolated whom we needed to have isolated. And the staff has been instructed to look for anyone showing an unhealthy interest in your presence."

"What kind of film am I working on?"

"That's up to you. But you know, they still love *The Maltese Falcon* here."

"That's right. Wasn't it the French critics that gave it and its many successors the *noir* label?"

"Good for you. Apparently, you haven't been spending all your time in the office. And if anyone asks, be sure to work in your admiration for the French New Wave stuff. That will score a lot of points."

"You mean Truffaut and Godard and that crowd?"

"Yep. Here, take a look at this place." They were ambling along a path through the middle of the Luxembourg Garden, sharing the walk with about a dozen Parisians, half of them with their families in tow. The Garden was blessedly free of tourists. "Now we can talk shop again. It's not that crowded here at this time of day."

"So, what's up, and why do we need to be so secretive about it?"

"We will cover that. Don't worry, Karl. But first, look over there." Pittman pointed toward a path that ran along a busy street one could barely find through the foliage. "That's where the Closerie des Lilas is located. You can barely see the building from here. But it's the restaurant where Hemingway wrote his first novel, *The Sun Also Rises*. At least, he reputedly wrote it there. There's a plaque at the bar where he's supposed to have sat as he wrote it, anyway."

"What's with all the tourist stuff? Am I supposed to give you a tip at the end?"

"I just want to be sure you enjoy the fullness of Paris while you're here. It is your first time, right?"

"Sadly, yes. But I'll be happy to call on your background here when I return with Sabine. In the meantime, however, I'm hunting for a Russian."

"Apparently more than one."

Baier stopped in his tracks, a slight breeze ruffling the leaves overhead. "Say what? How many more?"

The local chief walked over to Baier and planted his feet several inches from those of his colleague. He spoke just above a whisper. "Just one more." Pittman surveyed the path, the trees, the people, even the blades of grass. Or so it seemed. "You recall that I noted how excited the French got when they discovered your Russian friend's presence here and the circumstances of his travel?" Baier nodded. "Well, they did some more digging on their own, and they discovered that another Soviet intelligence officer—this one from the GRU—arrived three days before your friend got here. And this one is reportedly an assassin."

Baier nodded in appreciation. "That fits. It's why my guy came to Paris. At least, I'm pretty sure it is. He told me that was his reason for coming here, and I believe him. There's quite a family history there. What's this one's name?"

The Americans resumed their walk. "Oleg Marchenko. And I notice that this part of your story was missing from the cable traffic."

"I'm sorry, Ralph. But I did not want any of that in the official record, which, of course, would have happened if I put it in the cables."

This time Pittman pulled up short. "Just what sort of game are you playing here, Karl? I don't need to tell you what something like this can do to your career, do I? That is, if what I suspect is true."

"Just what do you suspect, Ralph?"

Pittman's gaze drifted over the treetops, almost as though he was avoiding Baier's eyes. He blew out his breath before returning his focus to his colleague. "I'm not really sure, Karl. But I hope you're not assisting this Russian in any way if he is on a quest that involves an assassin. If you are, then you've started down a dark and devious path. I would have expected a professional like yourself to realize that."

Baier closed in on his colleague. "I am truly sorry, Ralph. You can deny all this, of course, and claim I never told you any of it. I wanted you, of all people, to know. But only after I had the chance to tell you in person. The real reason my Russian defector came over from the East is that he has a score to settle. He believes that this Marchenko assassinated his brother after he fled the Revolution back home."

"Why would he do that?"

"I'm not sure. But my Russian is pretty damned certain of it. And he plans to settle the account."

"Is this part of the family history you just mentioned?"

Baier nodded. "As best I can tell. My guy's siblings fled the Revolution back home around 1918 or 1919 and came first to Paris. From there they kept going to South America, where they disappeared. Or so the Soviet officer claimed in the past."

"So, what's with an assassin in Paris?"

"The Russian now believes that the brother, at least, survived and returned here, where he was assassinated. He asked for my help in getting him out of East Berlin so he could hunt the killer down."

"And what do you—or we—get in return?"

"He's promised to reveal what he knows of Soviet operations not only in Berlin, but the rest of West Germany as well. Possibly beyond that."

"Will we gain anything on Soviet planning for Berlin? Khrushchev has been up and down on the Western Allies' place in that city ever since he gave Eisenhower that ultimatum in '58 about a separate peace treaty with the East Germans."

Baier nodded. "I know, I know. And, yes, he claims to have some special information or insight into the Kremlin's plans. But even if we can't get anything directly from this defector, then hopefully we be able to pull some hints or indications from learning what their plans and requirements are operationally. Besides, he might help us focus our efforts to get the information Washington has been screaming for. You know, the real decisionmakers in Moscow and their interests. He could tell us who is directing their efforts here in Europe and at what targets."

"When were you planning to let me know about this guy's history and his true intentions?"

"Before I left Paris. I wasn't sure myself, and I didn't want to give you only part of the story. Although I still don't have much more at this point."

"And has Headquarters approved all this?"

Baier hesitated before answering. He wanted to choose his words carefully. "They've approved what they know of it."

"Which, I take it, is not everything."

"Well, not every last detail. Let's leave it at that."

The two Americans were silent as they made their way out of the Gardens. Baier wondered if he had lost the cooperation— friendship, even—of the local station chief. And where that might lead. Pittman grabbed his attention with a slight punch to the shoulder.

"Off to the right, along Monsieur le Prince, is a local dive called Polidor. It was another of Hemingway's hangouts because it's relatively cheap for Paris. It's one of the spots where Balzac used to hang out as well. You can still get a pretty good meal there. Try the beef Bourgogne and get a carafe of the table wine. It will be a real Parisian meal, the kind the locals have. In fact, the place will probably be full of them. The students from the Sorbonne like to go to the Polidor, too. Maybe you can take all your Soviet friends there, and you guys can hash things out."

"Okay, enough with the tourist stuff, Ralph. I feel bad enough already. Maybe I won't come back at all."

"Oh, you'll be back, Karl. Everyone comes back to Paris."

• • •

It had been two days now, and Baier had only had intermittent sightings of Chernov. During the first day, Baier had stationed himself close to the Army Museum and Hotel des Invalides, thinking that this offered the best combination of intercepting Chernov, while also blending in with the crowds visiting Napoleon's tomb.

It had worked the first morning. Around 9:30—Chernov must have just finished his breakfast—the Russian strolled past the entrance to the tomb, circled around to the front, then marched straight through the park at the museum's front and headed for the Seine. Once there, he had turned right along the Quai d'Orsay (did he have an appointment at the Foreign Ministry? Baier doubted it.), only to veer left again and cross the river at the Place de la Concorde. He then spent the rest of the morning wandering in the Tuileries Garden by the Louvre, where he alternated between strolling, sitting on benches to smoke a cigarette and sipping coffee at the park café. After a small lunch with a salad and sandwich, Chernov had taken a long, slow walk back to his hotel. Baier had not seen him again that afternoon.

Chernov had met no one, nor had he followed anyone that Baier could see. Perhaps he was running his counter-surveillance routes, but then he had probably been doing that for several days already. Or a meeting could have been aborted—but not, Baier believed, because Chernov had sighted Baier's tail. How much longer was this likely to go on, he wondered. It was understandable, though, in that Chernov had a host of people to worry about. Not only was there this assassin the French had spotted and who was most likely Chernov's target, but there were the Americans, the French, his Soviet colleagues, and, of course, Baier himself.

He sighed as he looked out across the park's expanse that ran from the front of the Hotel des Invalides to the Seine and hoped his stay in Paris would not be too long. It wasn't like he was getting to enjoy the touristy things Pittman had pointed out. No, this was definitely boring and at the moment seemingly pointless. He would have gladly returned to Berlin and Sabine, but he needed to know what Chernov was up to. All those years working together one way or another and the personal bond of sorts that had grown between the two men had generated some, but not all that much, trust. If Baier was going to lay his career on the line for the defection of this 'fucking Russian,' as his wife liked to call him, then he would have to have some kind of certainty as to what the Russian's plans were.

Baier's luck turned a bit that first night when Chernov selected a table in one of the restaurants on the Ile Saint Louis down river from Notre Dame. He chose a small bistro along the Rue Saint Louis just a few blocks from the church that had supposedly once held the remains of Jesus's crown of thorns. At least, Baier recalled having read something along those lines. He wondered momentarily what had happened to them. He was also hoping Chernov would eat a little more quickly, since he was getting pretty damn hungry himself, lurking in the shadows of an alley across the street and two buildings down. But he soon lost his appetite when a bulky visitor climbed into the empty chair at Chernov's table. The man kept his hat low over his face, so Baier could not compare it to the photo of the assassin Pittman has passed along from the French. But the warm greeting Chernov gave the stranger suggested it was not the same man. Certainly not the assassin. Instead, Chernov's new companion ordered a carafe of red table wine but no food. At least this would not prolong the evening, Baier hoped. Their conversation proceeded non-stop for the next hour—Baier's hunger returned—and the two men parted, as near as Baier could tell, as the closest of friends. It was the warm embrace and cheek kissing that gave it away. Chernov paid his bill, stepped from the front door of the bistro, glanced both ways along the avenue, then walked back to his hotel, stopping occasionally to window shop, or, more likely, use the glass window panes to check on a tail. Baier was too tired to eat when he got back to his place near the Opera and fell into bed without any supper.

He made up for it the next morning at breakfast, foregoing the croissants for a full plate of ham, sausage, cheese, and rolls to accompany his juice and his first café au lait of the day. Over his second cup of coffee, Baier thought about the stranger from last night. Was he another Russian, someone from the local *Residenz* perhaps? That would suggest that Chernov had the support of the Soviet base in Paris, or least that of some friends there. Baier thought about bringing his own colleagues in, but there was so little he could say about the man or give Pittman as a description. And he doubted the American chief of station had the resources to give Baier to allow him to check on what could well be nothing more than a friendly encounter. No, Baier would have to spend at least another day trying to sort out Chernov's intentions and agenda in the City of Light, little of which was being thrown on Baier's problem at the moment.

Only then did it strike Baier how unprofessional he had been all day yesterday, neglecting to check on any surveillance against himself. He had been so focused on Chernov and worked on the assumption that he had little to worry about regarding his own mission and safety because he was on friendly territory, such as it was. True, the French are our allies, he thought, but they are not our lackeys. They had demonstrated their own interest and competence by running down the presence of a GRU officer linked to several deaths, and Pittman had already stated explicitly how unhappy they were to find out that this sort of game was afoot on their patch. And Baier doubted they faced the same kind of resource constraints on their home turf.

And then there were the Soviets. Chernov had implied that he was on the run, and who else would be in pursuit? And not only them. The East Germans had already threatened Baier, claiming they knew he was up to something with an operation on their ground. And they were right. In fact, they had nearly disrupted Chernov's escape from East Berlin, and they may well have guessed about his—or someone's—successful trip west by now. And if they knew, the Soviets certainly did as well. That is, if they weren't aware of it already through their own means. But what did that say about Chernov's position and game? Jesus, but the field was getting crowded.

Baier gulped the last of his coffee and was determined to restore some of the expertise and experience one would expect from a seasoned professional like himself. He may not have been the sort of super spy one encountered in espionage novels and the occasional Hollywood film, but he did know his business. And he was determined to execute his tasks the way he knew he should.

This time, Baier dispensed with the luxury of waiting with the other tourists at Napoleon's tomb and set up his post in a café down the street from Chernov's hotel. He was there by 8:30, and alternated between coffee at his table and trips to the small grocer next door. Chernov showed precisely at 9:30 once more, and Baier wondered at the man's predictability. It seemed that Baier was not the only one letting his professionalism lapse in Paris. Baier paid his tab and slipped into the street behind Chernov. This time Baier periodically checked on any tail he might have as well, while working to avoid being spotted by Chernov. He even took off his sport coat at one point and draped it over his arm to give himself a slightly different appearance. It was a bit of a grab, but it beat giving his target the look of consistency that would expose his surveillance too easily.

Chernov ended up once again at the Tuileries, but there was no coffee this time. Instead, he immediately took a seat on a bench next to a tall stranger, this one much thinner than the man from the previous night. The two shook hands, and Baier was certain that he caught sight of a quick brush pass, the stranger slipping an envelope into Chernov's hand, which went immediately to the inside pocket of his suit jacket. Now we're getting somewhere, Baier thought. Perhaps this note included an address or contact instructions for Chernov in his own quest.

Assuming of course, that this was the real reason for his trip to Paris. But there was only one way to find out. Tonight, Baier would brace the 'fucking Russian'—Sabine's phrase seemed truly appropriate right now—about his agenda and the game he appeared to be playing by keeping Baier in the dark on his travels and search.

After about half an hour of this and some seemingly friendly chit-chat along with a cigarette, Chernov rose from the bench. He saluted his colleague or whomever, and then made his way back to his hotel. Baier was determined not to lose him, since things appeared to be coming to a head. Maybe Chernov had been waiting for the same man yesterday, and possibly other days as well. It could have been that this was a pre-arranged plan, to wait for him at the same spot every day until the stranger could find the information Chernov needed and break away to deliver it. This meant the new figure was almost certainly a Soviet officer. Or did it? Maybe Chernov had turned to another service, maybe even the French, or possibly a criminal organization. Lord knows, there were enough of those operating in Paris. And who was the fat guy from the night before? An ally perhaps of the thin man, another player entirely, or maybe just an acquaintance. People tended to forget that intelligence officers had friends and acquaintances like everyone else.

The journey had brought the two men almost to Chernov's hotel. They had just entered the Avenue de Breteuil with Baier still deep in thought pondering the possibilities. That may have been why he was so easily surprised. The car, a dark Renault sedan, pulled alongside the curb, and two men leaped from the car. One came from the front, and the other from the back seat, effectively sandwiching Baier between them. They grabbed Baier by each arm. When he resisted, one of the men must have clubbed him with a sap of some kind behind his left ear. He never saw it coming. Hell, he never even saw the son of a bitch move. Darkness swept toward him, and Baier glanced up to catch a glimpse of the Hotel des Invalides. As he was spun around, he caught sight of the military academy down the street that Napoleon had attended. What a shame, he thought, that Generals De Gaulle and Napoleon would allow this sort of thing to occur at a place so close to their childhood homes.

But then the night swallowed him before he could give it anymore time and consideration.

CHAPTER EIGHT

September 6, 1961

"Who the hell are you?" Baier asked.

When he tried to move, his head felt as though it would explode. Oddly, he awoke to find himself laying on his side, facing a stranger who did not look very French. Maybe that was because he looked vaguely familiar. He had two companions that Baier could see from where he lay. Both men stood behind the first and wore short black leather jackets that came to the waists of their loose brown slacks. It was like they were the working guys, ready for some heavy lifting. That brought up some worrisome possibilities when he tried to figure the whole damn situation out. He didn't try for long, though, because it hurt too much. So Baier rolled slowly onto his back and contemplated the off-white plaster ceiling that looked to be about eight feet over his head. He groped with his hands along the side and found a canvas cot underneath him. Baier decided he'd go back to sleep, so he closed his eyes as gently as possible.

It was not to be, however. A heavily accented voice asked him in French if he felt all right, or if he wanted to throw up again.

"I'm afraid my French is not very good. In fact, it's almost non-existent. Can we try something else?" Baier asked in English.

The voice returned in what sounded like native German. It asked the same question.

This brought Baier fully awake. He shifted his weight in the direction of the stranger, who occupied a solitary wooden chair facing the cot and Baier. He leaned forward, his hands hanging between his legs. The gray suit did not have a tie to go with it, or with the white shirt underneath, but Baier felt he could forgive this lapse in etiquette. Not that he had much of a choice. And the idea of vomiting didn't sound all that bad. But again? That would explain the smell.

"Are you German?" Baier asked, displaying his own comfort with the language.

The stranger nodded. And as he did so, Baier got a good look at the man, his dirty blonde hair that had begun to recede from his forehead above the right eye, the chiseled chin and long, aquiline nose. But most of all, Baier was impressed by the deep blue eyes that did not shine as much as penetrate. The face was also coming into focus with the memory from one of his confrontations in Berlin. That was also not very encouraging, even though this particular face had remained in the background that time, speaking very little.

"Why are you here?" Baier asked. "And while we're at it, why am I here? More to the point, where are we?"

The German looked out the window, as though he was searching for a street sign. "We are in the 16th Arrondissement, if that helps. We are close to where the *Abwehr* had their wartime headquarters in Paris, interestingly. "

'It's also where France's most notorious serial killer lived and was active during that same war. So, which is more appropriate for the situation I'm in now?"

The stranger smiled and leaned back against the wooden slats at his back. "You needn't worry about your safety, much less the ghost of a serial killer. Marcel Petiot, I believe his name was. His crimes have nothing to do with our business today."

"Well, that's good news at least."

He switched to English. "No, I became curious as to what your business here in Paris was and why you seemed so interested in the Russian. Just who are you and whom do you work for?"

Catching the clue that his interrogator wanted to keep his companions out of the conversation, Baier followed suit and continued in English. "I am a State Department officer on temporary duty here in Paris." Baier fumbled in his inside jacket pocket for his diplomatic passport to demonstrate his credentials. Of course, it was missing.

The German held the passport in his right hand, so that Baier could see where it had gone.

"Naturally, we checked your pockets. That should not surprise you. But what did surprise us was how clandestine your activities have been in Paris. It's not like anyone is likely to find you at a diplomatic reception, or in the reception books at the Quai d'Orsay. Or, I mean, the Foreign Ministry.

"I know what the damned address refers to." Baier was surprised at how easily he was taking the bait and rising to anger. Then again, he had been beaten over the head. "If you need to establish my position, you can contact the American Embassy. And who the hell are you, by the way?"

"Let's just say I am an interested party."

"Do you have a name?"

"Joachim will do for now."

"And why are you in Paris. For whom do you work?"

"You get two guesses. No wait, make that one guess. It should be obvious."

"East or West?"

"East, I'm afraid. If I worked for Bonn then we would hardly have had to assault and kidnap you."

"Naturally not. But then why did you feel you had to do that in the first place?"

"Our superior is very demanding. He wanted us to maintain a tight surveillance on the American visitor from Berlin and find out who else was interested and why. Imagine our surprise when a Russian appeared and fell into our net."

"But he's not in your net. I am. Unfortunately."

"Yes, well, I think you Americans have a phrase, 'so to speak,' or something like that."

"Very good. But this superior wouldn't be an asshole by the name of Gracchus, would he?"

"Ah, so you know Johann Gracchus?"

"We've had a few encounters in Berlin recently. I hate the son of a bitch, and I believe the feeling is mutual."

"You may be surprised to learn that you are not alone in that. On our side of the border as well."

"How about you?" Baier had lapsed back into German.

The German shrugged. "I think it would most definitely be in both our interests if we continued our conversation in English at this point." He nodded at his companions. "He is not my favorite. For a number of reasons. But he remains my superior. He has Mielke's ear. They knew each other back in Moscow during the war and before. They lived on the same floor of the Hotel Lux."

"Ah, yes, the refuge for German and European Communists during the Third Reich. Did you live there as well?"

The German let slip a look of disgust barely hidden behind the scowl he wore, even if for only a moment. He stood and walked to the window before returning to the chair by Baier's cot.

"I did not enjoy that luxury, such as it was. No, I remained behind to serve the Fatherland."

"*Wehrmacht* or SS?"

"The former. If I had been in the latter I probably would have risen much higher and more quickly in our service."

"That is, if you survived your capture. But how did you come to work for the Ministry for State Security, or should I say the MfS, in the first place?"

"You do not refer to them as the Stasi?"

Baier shrugged, as though the label made little difference.

The German sat back and stretched his legs before responding. Baier guessed he stood at over six feet. Easily.

"Ah, well, that is an interesting story. You see, I was originally approached by someone from your side. Or rather, he was an intermediary for your side. The CIA, I believe. We were in the early stages of building an army for the German Democratic Republic…"

"Oh, please," Baier groaned.

"…and he probably thought I would make a good source for you because of my military background and service for what was an extremely anti-Communist regime. I had been providing some assistance to the new regime, mostly in the way of consultations and recommendations. So, I had access to some information that would have been of interest."

"Well, what happened?"

"I decided that it was not worth the risk. I turned him in."

"What happened to the poor sap?"

The German shrugged once more and leaned forward. "I never heard. Nothing pleasant, I would imagine. In any event, a call from the Ministry for State Security, or MfS as you called them, followed shortly thereafter."

"Interesting, if sad. But tell me something. Why is Gracchus such a prick? Is that common among your superiors?"

The German waved his hands and glanced over at his companions before looking at Baier again. "Ach, that. I believe it stems from his personal history, his family history."

"And that would be?"

"You see, his father was killed in a street brawl with the Nazis before 1933 when they seized power. It left a quite a scar on the young man's psyche, as you can no doubt imagine."

"I see. So how is it you continue to work for those bastards in the East? You do not sound all that dedicated."

The stranger stood again and moved back toward the window. 'You do not bother to hide your sentiments, do you, Herr Baier?" He smiled. "I, however, must be more careful."

"So why haven't you defected? Lord knows, it was not that difficult before your side started building that barrier through the city."

"After the collapse of our front outside Leningrad I was part of a unit that moved west and tried to re-establish a defensive line in Poland. That collapsed as well, of course, and I was taken prisoner and shipped to a camp east of the Urals. It was horrendous. I joined the Free Germany association led by that worm General Paulus, whose leadership had been so disastrous at Stalingrad. But it was a way to get more food and get out of the cold more often. Besides, I convinced myself that we could build a strong new Germany under a Soviet umbrella, instead of an American one."

"How did you come to that brilliant conclusion?"

The German smiled again. "I will assume that you are being sarcastic, Herr Baier. But how appealing do you really believe the prospect of a self-indulgent consumer society in my homeland appeared to be in 1945? You Americans can be very naive and self-centered at times. Not everyone wants to live on Coca-Cola."

"Well, things seem to have turned out pretty well on our side of the border. I mean, you finally have a prosperous, free, and democratic German nation."

"That may be. But how free is it really? Do not try to convince me that in the end you Americans do not call the shots, as you say."

"Don't worry. Once there's a real peace treaty—not that bullshit Khrushchev has been pushing for the last year or so about the one he wants to sign with East Germany and Ulbricht's lapdogs—then we'll be gone. Right now, though, that appears to be a long way off, especially since your Soviet masters are not about give up the jewel in their crown, this nice chunk of Germany they seized at the end of the war."

Baier slid his feet to the floor and attempted to stand. His anger was rising again and he felt compelled to score debating points with this German who appeared to be confused by Communist propaganda and blind to the realities of Central Europe. "I mean, are you really trying to argue that you enjoy as much freedom in the East as your compatriots do on our side of the divide? That's ridiculous."

The German approached slowly and held out his hands. "I am simply trying to give you the benefit of a perspective beyond your own. It explains much of the thinking of your opponents in the Warsaw Pact and East Germany, in particular." He paused. "And how can you speak so forcefully of freedom when there have been persecutions underway for the past decade or so in your own country? I am speaking of the McCarthy group and all the Red-baiting in America. Yours is hardly a model society, you know. In fact, one could argue that you are little better than the Nazis in that regard."

Baier stepped forward, but the pain in his head drove him back to the cot. "That's all over now, damn it. Besides, if you weren't blinded by your propaganda, you'd see the better side of that."

The German smiled. He almost laughed. "Oh really? And what is that?"

Baier held his head in both hands. "That we were able to react and rein all that in. The witch hunts are over now. And I think we're stronger for getting through it.' The German did not laugh this time. "At least I hope so."

"Perhaps," the German said. "Only time will tell. But since we are alone, I can tell you that I no longer believe that. About the Coca-Cola society in western Germany, I mean. But there is little I can do about it now." He paused and bent down to look Baier in the face. "I'll leave your own American politics to you. I really do not care."

"So why are you telling me this?" Baier fell back again onto the cot.

"Because it explains why I am letting you go. And why I do not plan to report our meeting to Gracchus when I return to Berlin." He glanced over at his compatriots. "Although I will have to be careful and find out what they report. Whatever does go forward, though, will not contain any of this conversation. I might also add some other pieces of my own."

"Are you suggesting that we might even work together?"

"On this particular case?"

"For starters."

The stranger smiled again. "That is an interesting proposition, Herr Baier. I will have to think about it. Your interests, whatever they may be, are not the only ones at work here. But if we do begin a liaison of our own, it must be kept secret from your West German friends."

"Why is that?"

"Because we are beginning a program that is designed to penetrate the West German government. Thoroughly. And it may well go beyond that. But in any case, even if that effort does not succeed it would not be long before my role would be discovered." He held up a finger. "That is, if I agree to work with you."

"You'll be well taken care of. And we would get you out, if needed."

"Be that as it may, Herr Baier, we will have to leave that for a later discussion. Right now, I am off to Rome."

"Rome? Why there? Are you that badly in need of some decent food? After Paris?"

"Sadly, Paris has been all work and no play, as you Americans say. Hopefully, Rome will prove to be different."

"But why Rome then?"

"Because that is where your Russian target Chernov has gone. Part of his own quest, apparently."

This time Baier succeeded in standing. "Rome. How did you find out? What have you learned?"

The German raised his finger again, but this time he waved it back and forth. "No, no, Herr Baier. I am afraid you will have to learn that on your own. We are not working together yet. At least not closely." Then, he seemed to reconsider. "It is where the Ukrainian has gone."

"The assassin?"

The German nodded. "Yes. I am not sure why, but Marchenko is probably on the trail of another victim. So, of course, the Russian is following."

Baier's German host strode to the door of the room where Baier noticed for the first time an overcoat hanging on a peg on the inside of the door. The stranger pulled the coat from the rack, then turned and gave Baier a final smile, this one broader than any that had preceded it.

"I shall leave you to it, Herr Baier. I am sure you can find your way out of here. And perhaps we shall meet again in Rome, if not Berlin." He opened the door and began to move out into the hallway. Then, just as quickly he stopped and turned to Baier.

"By the way, my name is Hoehn. Joachim Hoehn. *Bis spaeter*, Herr Baier. Or as the French say, *a bientot*."

• • •

"Rome! That fucking Russian is really starting to piss me off," Baier shouted.

"So, I guess you're going after him?" Pittman asked.

Baier jumped up from his chair and paced the office of the Paris station chief, then marched to the window behind his desk. "Hell, I have to. I can't let go of the thread now."

"Well, before you go tell me some more about those guys our Russian friend met here."

Baier moved from the window and took a position at the desk next to the local chief. He reached down and rifled through the photographs on Pittman's desk for the third time. "Nope, they weren't any of this crowd."

"In other words, you're telling me that they do not appear to be part of the official Soviet residence in Paris. These photos are the whole lot of officers they have assigned to their post here that we are confident are KGB or GRU, both declared and non-declared." Baier nodded as Pittman continued. "And, as a result, you're also telling me that we have other problems in our town with the Soviet contingent here."

"Maybe they came here on a visit, or temporary assignment. Like me."

"Yeah, maybe. But we can usually keep track of those guys as well."

"How well plugged in are you to the Soviet or Russian diaspora here in Paris?"

Pittman sighed. It was almost as deep as the frown along his forehead. "Not very much, unfortunately. You know what sort of resource constraints we have here. We're busy enough as it is keeping on top of the real Soviet spies, as well as all the other targets we pursue. All of which you are well acquainted with, seeing as how you're the European Deputy Division Chief."

Baier stepped back and smiled. "Believe me, Ralph, I would love to give you some extra officers. That is, if we could get the State Department and White House to give us some additional slots to place those guys in. There are plenty of people who would be more than happy to take a posting in this town. Hell, I'm sure Sabine would love it for us to come here."

"Be that as it may, Karl, these meetings in Paris suggest you may have some real trouble on your hands with this Russian friend of yours."

"How so?"

"Well, on the upside you can see that he is not in any official contact with the Soviet community here. Like I said, these do not appear to be members of their regular team in our town."

"But?"

"Yeah, 'but' is right. He seems to have his own network for support, and they happen to be people we—and you in particular—know nothing about."

"So?"

"So, you have no idea just what sort of game he's playing here—and wherever else he may go. These guys could be fellow exiles, disenchanted with the recent course of Russian history. Or they could be a new network of illegals."

"You mean the long-term plants the Soviets have been sending west for future use?"

Pittman nodded vigorously. "That's right. The people who burrow into a local society, hidden like parasites to emerge when they're needed. If that's the case, then you could be in for some heavy disappointments. What did you once tell me Sabine called this guy?"

"That 'fucking Russian.'"

"If so, he may have fucked you over good. And now you have some East Germans involved in the chase? What was the guy's name?"

"Hoehn. Joachim Hoehn. There were two others, but I never got their names. However, I'm pretty sure they were among those who braced me a couple times in East Berlin."

"Great. I'll send the name off to Hendricks. But how the hell did they catch up to you in Paris? How did they find out what you've been up to?"

"Excellent questions, Ralph. I hate to think what this could imply..."

"A leak. Or worse."

Baier nodded. "Yeah. 'Or worse' is right." He paused to study the floor before looking up. "What I really find interesting is that the German said they were originally here to follow me, and that the Russian's presence came as a surprise."

"Do you believe him?"

"Ralph, I'm not sure what I believe at this point."

"And why would they want to follow you?"

"Christ, I wish I knew. It's obviously something I'll have to follow up on back in Berlin."

Baier walked to the door and glanced back at his colleague. "If I have been fucked over—now in more ways than one—then I guess there's only one way to find out. Let Frank Carberry know that I'm coming to Rome, will you? That's the first stop."

Pittman rose from the desk with a wave of his hand. "Sure thing, Boss. And good luck. I think you're going to need it."

• • •

"Are you sure it was wise to let the American go, Comrade?" Barenbrugge asked.

Hoehn smiled and moved to the window to study the street below from their hotel room across the river from the Eiffel Tower. Groups of tourists—Americans almost certainly—strolled toward the landmark with a determination and pace that suggested some kind of El Dorado awaited at the end of their brief journey. And to think that the piece of world-famous architecture had been reviled by the critics when it was first built. Perhaps the same would be said of his new country in the truncated Fatherland. That is, if the rebuilding ever got properly underway.

"What purpose would it have served to have held him? And do you realize how much it would have burdened us?"

His colleague who posed the question moved forward, standing just behind Hoehn at the window. He appeared to be uninterested in the scene below. "Still, it would have been nice to take a few more shots at the bastard. I really hate Americans."

"And why is that?"

"They act so superior. And they're really only richer. Disgustingly so. Not really smarter or better."

Hoehn smiled and turned to his colleague. "Don't be so quick to dismiss such luxuries. There are those among our leadership who live quite well, you know."

"But it's for a good cause, isn't it? It's not just personal enrichment, is it?"

Hoehn moved to the edge of the bed, where his suitcase rested. It was open. He threw the two sides together and buckled the case shut. "Let's hope so. But more to the point of this operation, do you not see the advantage of having the American lead us to where we need to go and providing the information we need?"

His colleague persisted, while the other man remained by the door, as though waiting for the conversation to end so they could catch their train. "But do we really need the American? What more do we need to learn? Why not just dispose of him? We can always blame it on the Russian."

"You are too easy with the lives of others, Comrade. One can always use some bait, or a lure. Besides, I am quite sure our superiors back in Berlin would not be happy if we left dead bodies in our wake here in the West. That's not what one would call discretion." Hoehn smiled as he lifted the suitcase from the bed. "That sort of thing has a way of raising uncomfortable questions." He strode to the door. "And creating unexpected repercussions. Now, let's get that train to Rome."

CHAPTER NINE

September 7-9, 1961

Rome. The Eternal city. There were signs of the city's long and rich and turbulent history everywhere you looked. And for someone who had studied and reveled in history as much as Baier did, this was perhaps as close to paradise as one could come. The food wasn't bad either. And there was the wine, of course.

If Pittman was right, though, then it was appropriate to be in Rome now, more than ever. Necessary, too. Absolutely. Chernov may have gotten me eternally screwed, he thought.

Baier watched Frank Carberry, the Agency's local chief of station, stroll across the Palazzo del Quirinale to the café—or what the Italians referred to as a 'bar'—on Via della Dataria, just down the street from the Presidential Palace. As Baier remembered it, the palace used to be the home of the popes until the revolution of 1849 forced them to move to the Vatican and Saint Peter's, where they became ensconced and practically barricaded once the newly united Italian Kingdom seized Rome as its capital in 1870. And Carberry looked every bit the part of a casual European—Italian even—dressed in his khaki slacks, white shirt open at the collar despite the thin, red tie loosened ever so slightly, and pale gray silk jacket. *Bella figura*, after all. Just like his days at that prep school in New Hampshire, up the road from his parents' home in western Massachusetts, or so Baier imagined. So, when in Rome… especially when it fit so easily. Even the shoes looked Italian: light brown leather that gave off a scent of expensive. Dapper, Baier thought. Everyone assigned to these famous and stylish European capitals seemed to turn dapper.

"You know, you're only supposed to drink cappuccino in the mornings, before noon." Carberry pointed at Baier's cup and shook his head in an affectation of disappointment and disapproval. "A café macchiato would be more appropriate now. And for God's sake do not order a wine to go with your pizza, should you have one. Beer only. It will mark you not only as a foreigner, but an American for sure."

"So, you're telling me I have to drink an Italian beer?"

Carberry shrugged. "Well they may not be up to the standards you're used to in Berlin, but they're not so bad. You get used to them."

"I'll keep all that in mind. I'd hate to stand out. But I'm not really sure how long I'll be here." Baier's arm swept the horizon. "I do appreciate the setting, though. How come you asked to meet me here and not at your office?"

Carberry took a seat across from Baier and motioned for the waiter. He ordered a mineral water and an espresso. "I thought you might want to stay away from the Embassy or any official American presence for the moment, given as how you not exactly here on official business. At least, not entirely or not formally approved."

Baier nodded and stared at the crowds rolling past. "Agreed, although I am hardly here as a tourist. But why this spot?"

Carberry added sugar to his espresso, stirred, then sipped. He grimaced, presumably at the unexpected sweetness of having emptied a full packet into his drink. "Ah, well, I had to attend a meeting with the Prime Minister and several of his advisers this morning, including the Foreign Minister and the head of their intelligence service." Baier's eye rose in admiration. "Yeah, they had all had been called in by the President," Carberry explained. "They wanted to get the latest from us on the situation in Berlin."

"Ah, I see. And you attended alone from our side?"

Carberry sipped some more and shook his head. "No, of course not. The Ambassador and DCM were there as well."

"The Deputy Chief of Mission? Not the political counselor or defense attaché?"

"No, they're both traveling. Anyway, as you can probably imagine, the Italians are pissing nickels like everyone else in Europe over what's going on up in your home away from home. I gather you've been up there for much of the fun."

"'Fun' is not the word I would use, of course. But there has been plenty of excitement."

"And? Are we going to war? That's what the Italians want to know."

Baier sat back and studied the crowds again. He wondered where they were all heading on this hot but sunny early September afternoon. The Pantheon was just down the street, and the ruins of the Roman Forum were not all that far away. Even the Coliseum was within walking distance. "It's really hard to say. I doubt it will come to that unless the Soviets and East Germans try to cut off our access again, like they did in '48. But I don't get the sense that Washington—or London and Paris, for that matter—are ready to go to war over a sector boundary in the middle of Berlin. It looks like we've been outmaneuvered. That is, if the other side is content to stop there, which is pretty hard to forecast. Khrushchev is so unpredictable and mercurial even." Baier sipped his coffee, as though to gather his thoughts. "Even if nothing else changes, they will have undermined our policy to respect and preserve the four-power arrangement and standing of Berlin."

Baier finished what was left of his lukewarm cappuccino and contemplated an espresso to satisfy local custom. "Why are the Italians so worried? I doubt the Soviets will try anything like that to threaten Rome. The Trieste dispute has been settled, and both sides seem to be satisfied. The Italians kept the city and sone surrounding territory, but the biggest chunk of land went to the Yugoslavs. So Belgrade is probably happy enough."

Carberry frowned. "No, you're right there. Ironically, the only outstanding territorial issue is with the Austrians up north. You know, over South Tyrol. But as members of NATO and with a sizeable American military presence in their country, they would inevitably be drawn into any fighting that breaks out between us and the Soviets. And there are still a lot of memories from the war here. There was plenty of heavy fighting in this country, you know."

"Oh, for sure. But their own record in that war and the years leading up to it are not all that admirable. They do seem to be pretty good at the blustering and less so at the actual combat. The Germans still joke about Italian tanks having one gear for forward and four for reverse."

Carberry nodded and polished off his tiny cup of coffee. "Granted. And let's not forget, they were led by the master bluffer himself, the big bad Mussolini. But given as to how easily they switched sides, you can understand why the government would be worried about popular attitudes and support should it come to that."

Baier nodded. "Yeah, tell me about it. The West Berliners and West Germans have been directing a lot of their frustration and anxiety at us for not doing more to stop the building going on and the hard division of Berlin that looks to come of it. They seem to have forgotten how we saved the city from Soviet domination back in '48. Just think what a miserable life they'd be having now if Stalin had gotten his way back then."

Carberry poured his mineral water into the glass beside the green bottle, which all looked so refreshing to Baier. He motioned to the waiter to order one for himself. "People are fickle, Karl. The Romans began to turn against the Allies during the German occupation when our forces got stalled at Anzio for several months. They couldn't understand why we didn't just roll right in and why they had to go on suffering the deprivations that came with the German occupation."

"Well, I can understand why Kennedy sent General Clay back to Berlin as his personal representative when LBJ paid his visit last month. Not only that, but the fact that Clay is sticking around should hearten the Berliners. I just hope Clay doesn't do anything that precipitates or intensifies the crisis. The guy's a tough nut, but he can be a bit too hard-headed, especially when it comes to Berlin. The city and our role there are near and dear to the old guy's heart. In fact, I think he believes that he alone pretty much saved the city from the Soviets."

"Which is understandable, seeing the role he played personally in defending it in the late 40s."

"Yeah, I just hope he can adjust to the changing situation," Baier said. "It could require more guile then hardware."

"Well, I'm afraid our own leader demonstrated little of the former earlier this year when he met Khrushchev in Vienna."

"You're right, Frank. I just hope the Kremlin doesn't get overly confident this time around."

Carberry leaned back and let the Roman sun bathe his face for several seconds. "Man, I love this city," he said. "The people, too." The waiter delivered another bottle of Pellegrino to the table. Then Carberry sat forward, pushing his glass of mineral water aside. "Now that we've settled the world's problems, Karl, let me pass along some of the information you requested."

Baier bent over the table in turn. "Great. Thanks. What have you found out?"

"Well, for openers, your Russian friend is definitely here. The Italians were able to find a record of someone they believe is this Chernov guy who entered two days ago."

"He's not traveling in true name, I assume."

Carberry shook his head. "No way. He has a French passport now, and he's traveling under the name of Pierre Rouget."

"That must have been the package, or at least part of it, that the other guy passed him in Paris. Their brush pass was good, but not that good. I guess they didn't think anyone was following them in the park that day." Baier thought for a second. "Funny, but I've never heard him speak French. He must have one hell of an accent."

"Be that as it may," Carberry continued, "it suggests that your Russian friend has tapped into a Soviet support network in Europe. And that, Karl, is not good news for you."

"Yeah, I know." Baier sighed. "Any idea where he's staying?"

Carberry shook his head and sipped some espresso. "I'll give that to you in a minute. As is the custom in most places, he was required to list a residence for his stay. Our Italian friends are trying to run down any additional information that might be out there. I should have something for you tomorrow, if they find anything."

"Well, shit then, I'll have to wait. That means eating more delicious pasta. What about the guy he's supposed to be hunting?"

Carberry sat back and shook his head again. "Nothing there, I'm afraid."

"How much do you trust the Italians, Frank?"

Carberry leaned back in. "Quite a bit, actually. They're generally open and friendly toward me. It's like they really want to help, even to please. But they didn't have a whole lot to go on with this other guy. The picture from Paris wasn't much help. Are you sure he's here and that your buddy is really hunting him?"

Baier sat in silence for a moment. He stared hard at the empty cup to his front and the green bottle of sparkling mineral water beside it. Even the spoon resting on the saucer against the cup held his attention for several seconds. Murmurs swept around them as the crowds sailed past.

"Yeah, I'm pretty sure the guy is here and that 'my Russian friend,' as you call him, is after him. That's got to be the only reason he would have come to Rome."

"And you're certain of this based on what, Karl?"

"Based on instinct. And a report I picked up while in Paris."

"A report? One of our sources?"

Baier shook his head. "No. I really can't go into it, Frank. Not yet at least." Baier paused to study his colleague. "Frank, you know how it is when you're ready to make the pitch to someone."

"Are we talking about this new source, the one that claims the hunt has moved to Rome?"

Baier shook his head. "No, no. I'm back on the Russian. But you know how you get a feeling for the individual, for what makes him tick, and whether or not you can trust him."

"Sure, Karl, but all that's based on the interactions you've had and the material you've gotten up to that point."

Baier looked up at the local Station Chief. "That's right, Frank. And I've had years of experience with this Russian. I'm pretty sure I know the guy and what drives him."

"Well I hope you're right, Karl. But I've got some other news for you."

"What's that?"

"This German guy that grabbed you. He's here as well. And he's traveling in true name." Carberry paused and studied Baier's face. "That wouldn't be the source of this report you mentioned, would it?" Baier was silent. "If so," Carberry continued, "I'd be very careful trusting any information you've gotten. It's more than likely a set up."

"I'll keep that in mind, Frank."

"Sorry, Karl. But you have to admit this has gotten more than a little hairy."

"True, I'll give you that. I take it the Italians came up with that bit of additional information."

"Yes, they did. They asked me on a hunch if we were interested in this guy as well. And it turns out he has a pretty suspicious past. I don't know what story he fed you, but this new character is hardly what we would like to think of as a 'good German.'"

"How so?"

"Well, for one thing, the fact that he travels in true name is a surprise and pretty unprofessional. It's like he doesn't give a damn who knows where he's going and what he's up to."

"Which is?"

Carberry sat back and laughed. "Hell if I know. That's another fun fact you're going to have to dig out, my friend. But the Italians were none too happy to see him on their turf again."

"What do you mean? I thought he had spent the war on the Eastern Front."

"That may have been what he told you, but his resume reads a bit differently. He did start the war as part of the Krauts' big *blitzkriegs* in France and Russia, but then he was sent to North Africa as part of Rommel's *Afrika Korps*. After that he came north a bit. The Italians were upset to discover that he had been here during the fighting in southern Italy and at Anzio. Once Rome fell, he got shipped north to France when we made our landings at Normandy and the long battle to break out from the beachhead began. He fought some more in the west until the collapse of their Ardennes offensive. Then he was sent back to fight the Red Army. That's where he ended his part in the war."

"Yeah, he left all that out of the biography he gave me. They do tend to leave out any parts about fighting against us Americans."

"The Italian records indicate that he was taken prisoner by the Soviets during the capture of Koenigsburg in East Prussia. I gather he was lucky to have survived that slaughterhouse. Wasn't it one of Hitler's fortress cities?"

"Yeah, it was. Which suggests he was one those German soldiers who took their oath to the Fuehrer seriously. But that would have put him in a Soviet POW camp, like he said."

"Sure, I guess so. But you're right. He sounds like one of these guys who want to tell us that they spent the whole war fighting the Bolsheviks, not the good guys like us."

"Well, thanks for all that anyway. It will help if I run into him again."

"Oh, I suspect that will happen if you stay in this particular game, Karl."

"Why do you say that, Frank?"

"Because the East Germans are clearly interested in how this story with your Russian pal plays out, too. Maybe you need to ask yourself why they are so interested. I mean what's the relationship like between the KGB and the Stasi?"

"Let's say that they are allies, but not the best of friends. At times, it's not all that good. The Soviets don't trust the Stasi because, they are, after all, Germans, and they'd like to keep a tight leash on those guys. Which they've been able to do, pretty much anyway. For their part, the East Germans appear to resent the condescending attitude they get from their Russian brethren, and they resent the constraints. One source told us the Soviets are keeping all the American operations to themselves."

"Interesting. Especially in that it raises new questions about their own interest in whatever game you and your Russian are playing." Carberry said, nodding. "So, do you know where this Russian is staying?"

Baier shook his head, studying the bottom of his empty cappuccino cup. He frowned at the thought of ordering a macchiato.

Carberry pulled a slip of paper from his outer jacket pocket and handed it to Baier. "Here's the address of a hotel he gave at passport control. It's in the part of town on the other side of the river known as Trastevere. It has some interesting historical sites that should make your surveillance stints a little more enjoyable."

Baier took the slip and read. He looked up at his colleague. "Oh, really? Like what?"

"Well, you may get to walk alongside some remnants of the Aurelian Wall, built back during the time of the Roman Empire. The third century, to be exact. Or at least I think that's when it was."

"It didn't do them much good against the barbarians, did it?"

"Actually, the wall was pretty solid and stood up well against the hordes of Goths descending on the city, as well as some later invaders like the Normans and the French. It seems the invaders kept slipping in thanks to someone betraying the city by opening the gates or letting them know which parts were undefended."

"Bastards." Baier smiled. "Anything else?"

"As a matter of fact, yes, there is. If you get the chance, try to visit the Santa Maria church there. Interestingly, it was built on the site of an earlier church built by Pope Innocent II, who demolished the one before it because it was associated with one of his rivals, Pope Anacletus II."

"Doesn't sound very religious or pious."

"You're surprised?"

"Not really. But such pettiness and self-centeredness certainly won't help restore the faith of my childhood." Baier stood. "Besides, you getting to sound a lot like Pittman up in Paris."

"How so?"

"He, too, is doubling as a tour guide these days for visitors like myself."

"Well, Karl, it's hard not to when you live in cities like these." He stood and reached out his hand for Baier to take. "I suppose you'll be doing the same thing in Berlin someday. Let's just hope it's for the entire city, and not just half. Be sure to let me know if you need anything else. In any case, let's talk before you leave. I want to be able to send Washington a complete report on your time here."

"I will, Frank, and thanks."

As he walked away, Baier just hoped he'd have the chance to play tour guide back in Berlin someday.

• • •

In the end, Baier did not have the time or the opportunity to visit old churches or ancient walls, regardless of their importance to the history of the Papacy or the safety of classical Rome. It was only the second day of his surveillance against Chernov, who had remained in the Trastevere district. The Russian, however, did not go to Mass, nor did he inspect the ancient stonework that once protected Rome. On the first day he did stroll along the banks of the Tiber until he reached the Palazzo Salviati, where he pulled a U-turn and took a path that brought him past the Palazzo Corsini. Baier thought perhaps the Bolshevik admired the ruins of pre-capitalist wealth or perhaps he was picking out and surveying properties for when he joined the decadent West. Then he remembered that Chernov was anything but a Bolshevik. The real question was rather just what sort of label fit Chernov these days, and what the name of his game was as he wandered the capitals of Europe allegedly in search of this elusive killer.

One thing was certain, though. The Russian was still meeting someone from whatever network he had penetrated, or with whom he was cooperating. First, there was the short, thin stranger, whom Chernov met outside the first villa, the one that belonged to the Salviati family. They chatted briefly, then had a nicely executed brush pass that Baier would have missed if he hadn't been looking for something just like that. He did not, however, get a good enough look to guess at just what had been passed. A weapon, perhaps?

The second was the same rotund bastard Chernov had met in Paris at the restaurant that one evening. Those two were much more amiable, although Baier did see Chernov slide an envelope inside the other man's jacket during their initial hug. At the same time, the fat one stuffed another envelope in the side pocket of Chernov's jacket. Expenses, maybe? Although Baier doubted Chernov was on some sort of *per diem*. Or a payoff perhaps, or more false documentation?

So just who the hell were these people that Chernov kept meeting here in Western Europe, and under the very noses of the Americans and their French and Italian allies? Were they helping Chernov track his brother's killer, or was Chernov still happily employed by his KGB masters? Speaking of which, Baier had yet to see any of that crew, unless, of course, these clowns Chernov kept running into were active members of that very organization. Had 'the fucking Russian' thoroughly bamboozled Baier into helping him escape to the West so he could run some KGB operation while all American eyes and efforts were trained on Berlin and the crisis underway there that threatened to erupt into World War III?

The irony behind Baier's anger over a possible betrayal by this KGB agent who had worked so successfully with Baier on and off over the last 15 years was that the American never got to brace the Russian, as he had hoped and planned to do. Instead, it was Chernov who ambushed Baier. It must have been the long walk along the Tiber that did it, Baier reasoned. It was actually a very smart move by Chernov because it forced Baier—or anyone else working a tail—to expose himself in the open space along the riverbank. Baier had tried to keep some distance between himself and Chernov, but he could only fall so far back before losing sight of his quarry. He was pretty sure that he had mingled well with the small crowds at both villas to avoid having been made at those spots. No, it must have been along the damned riverbank.

It happened the very next morning, as Baier sipped his cappuccino—well within the accepted hour for the drink—at a café, or bar, about a block and a half from Chernov's hotel, a modest establishment with a baroque imitation façade that appeared to be quite common in the Eternal City. Chernov must have risen much earlier than usual, because Baier had just taken his seat and gotten his coffee a little after eight o'clock, when he received his unexpected visitor.

"Herr Baier, I must congratulate you on your persistence and capability." The Russian slid into one of the two vacant, narrow metal chairs at the little round table facing Baier. "You tracked me down, not once but twice."

"I was wondering when we were going to have this confrontation."

"Would you prefer that we have our talk in my hotel?"

Baier smiled. "I'd rather keep our meeting here in the open, if that's alright with you."

Chernov signaled for the waiter and pointed to Baier's cup. "It looks like you could use a refill, Herr Baier. And I have not had my morning coffee yet. You see, I had to arise much earlier than I like today."

"All to meet me?"

"Of course. Now tell me why you are pursuing me."

Baier finished his cappuccino and set the cup back on the saucer. He stared at the Russian for half a minute or more before continuing. "Seriously? You give us the slip in Berlin despite all we did to get you out of that hellhole in the East, break our agreement, go on your grand tour of European capitals, and you have the nerve to pose that question?"

"I have done nothing of the sort. You knew full well that I had a purpose and a mission of mine to achieve. After that I would put myself at your disposal, which I might add, your side badly needs, seeing how things are going back in Berlin." His ingratiating smile lit up his face in a particularly annoying way. "In fact, your team has had a string of embarrassments lately." Chernov started to count on his fingers. "Let me see, there was that U-2 shoot down, then the Bay of Pigs fiasco, the Vienna Summit, not to mention Sputnik several years ago. Need I go on?"

"Can it, Sergei. Tell me, why the slip? Imagine our surprise when we found your accommodations empty the following morning."

"Herr Baier, can you be serious? You should know that I would be much more effective and successful if I operated on my own. I certainly do not need any assistance from your people. In fact, I would much rather do this part of my work alone. And I suspect your side would rather not be involved."

Baier leaned in close over the table, his face and voice hard. "But damn it, Sergei, I needed to know. You cannot run off and leave me in the dark. Even you can imagine how suspicious this makes both of us look among my superiors back in Washington." He glanced up at the waiter who stood at the table with a tray on which sat two more coffees. "And let's leave Berlin out of it for the moment."

"Perhaps we should not. Berlin is very much a part of the story."

These words seemed to escape from behind the waiter. When he bent over the deliver the two coffees, Baier saw the tall gaunt figure of Joachim Hoehn, who had sneaked up on their table behind the waiter. He pointed to the coffees, then to himself and nodded at the waiter.

"Jesus, I should have rented an auditorium. Is anyone else coming?" Baier asked. "That prick Gracchus perhaps?"

The German pulled the remaining chair at their table to his side, which he then set between the American and the Russian. "Oh, heavens no. This city is far too decadent—and enjoyable—for a man like Gracchus."

"You should know," Baier replied. "I gather you spent some time here a few years ago, although under less favorable circumstances." The German stared at Baier, who continued. "Yeah, I know you fed me a line of real bullshit in Paris." He noticed a look of confusion on the German's face. "It's an American expression, but it translates easily enough. Think of *Kuhmist*."

"Oh, I understand, Herr Baier. You do not need to explain any of your American witticisms. I am just confused by your reference to my past activities. I have nothing to hide. Where did you acquire this additional information? And what does it mean exactly?"

"We'll leave that for now. What I find even more interesting is how intent you are on pursuing me and my colleague here."

"Yes, just why are you here, and why have you joined us?" Chernov asked.

Hoehn took the cup and saucer when the waiter brought them, then waited for the man to disappear before continuing. "I could hardly stand aside when I saw the two objects of my visit to this city in close consultations. How do I know that you are not both conspiring to gang up on me?"

"Why would we do that?" Chernov asked. "I, for one, do not even know who you are. But the name Gracchus does raise certain concerns. I am sure you can understand that as well."

"Ah, but surely you understand my confusion when I find representatives of the two superpowers battling over the future of my capital enjoying a morning coffee in Rome together. Is there some sort of deal being made that my superiors in Berlin should know about? Is one of you working for the other side? And if so, to what purpose? And these are questions of great importance, since the game in Europe is about to undergo a radical change." The German turned to Baier. "Especially for your side, Herr Baier."

"What do you mean?"

Hoehn smiled as he stirred the milky foam that sat atop his coffee. "You Americans and your West German friends have had an easy time of it, using Berlin as your meeting place, your *Treffpunkt,* as we say, for your agents in our country. There will be no more easy access for these people to meet you in Berlin. That venue is disappearing."

"And why should that upset or even interest me?" Chernov asked.

The German turned to face the Russian. "Perhaps not at all, Herr Chernov. But that really depends on the game you are playing now. I suspect it is not one your bosses in the KGB are aware of."

"Perhaps it's time we all took a walk among the ancient ruins of this once great city," Baier said as he stood. He tossed a pocketful of lira on the table. "This should cover the cost of our coffees." Hoehn stared at his recently arrived coffee with disappointment. He seized the cup handle, drained as much of his drink as possible in two gulps, then set the cup back on the saucer with a light clang and a satisfied look on his face.

"What do you propose, Herr Baier?" Chernov asked. "More Roman history and church visits." He turned to the German. "Our American friend can be quite the Catholic, you know. He must feel very much at home here. I think he has us at his advantage."

"Ah, how so?" Hoehn replied. "Our file mentions his parents' Social Democratic background, but it says nothing about him being so devout. So, where does that come from, Herr Baier?'

Baier sighed. "You people need to do a better job at your homework. My parents also came from Baden, which as you should know, Herr Hoehn, is a Catholic region."

"But they did not find that at odds with their political beliefs?"

Baier sighed once more, only louder this time. "Not all Social Democrats are atheists. In fact, in my experience few were or are. My parents found a similarity in the beliefs and perspectives of both creeds. Despite what our Russian friend here says, I am no longer particularly devout. Mass at Christmas and Easter is about the size of it. But I do like to think I have learned certain principles to help guide my life."

"Then which cathedral would you choose? And will it serve all our purposes?"

"No churches today, gentlemen," Baier replied. "The weather is far too pleasant, and I think we need to clear the air here and tell our stories."

"Then who will go first?" Hoehn asked. "Why not you?'

Baier shook his head as they walked into the via della Scala. "No, you two already know my story, or enough of it. I want to hear more about your purposes here."

"Then where are we going?" the German asked.

"Let's head to the Forum. I've always wanted to see the center of ancient Rome. It should be a fitting setting for the three of us. After all, we represent three of the modern empires." He stopped and looked over at his German companion. "Although yours has gone the way of Rome's apparently. And rather quickly."

"But why do you get to choose who goes first?" the German pressed.

"Because I paid for the coffee. We could begin with Sergei here. After all, he's the reason we're enjoying this late summer morning in the Eternal City. But I'd rather begin with you, Herr Hoehn. Your presence is the one that needs an explanation the most."

"Alas, I'm afraid I will have to bow out," Hoehn said. "I do not want to become too closely associated with either of you. Nor do I wish to reveal too much so early. Meeting the both of you here and seeing the uncertainty that underlies your movements has served my purpose. Not that much has been said, but I can see from your behavior that my initial concerns were unwarranted. I believe I have enough to report back to my superiors. At least as much as I see is necessary." He held an index finger in the air. "I can always fill in the rest with my own speculations."

"You mean your imagination?" Baier asked.

"Whatever."

"But why should you care in the first place?" Baier pressed.

"Because his bosses don't trust either of us, any more than we trust them. Isn't that right, my German friend?"

Hoehn only smiled. He paused in mid-step and waited for the Russian and American to stop and turn. "You are right, of course, Herr Chernov. Plus, I am sure you can both imagine how much difficulty it could create if my companions saw me engaged in close conversations with both of you simultaneously." He glanced around. "Unlike like either of you, I have companions here. Fortunately, I allowed them to do some shopping for their wives and children this morning."

"Please…" Chernov said, a pained expression spreading across his face.

"Yes, I shall leave it that. At least for now." The German studied the skyline before returning his gaze to his two companions. "But I would add one more thought for you both to ponder. A parting gift, as you will."

"And that would be?" Baier asked.

"Your Soviet assassin. I understand he has a new mission now, a new target."

"And that would be someone we know?" Baier pressed.

"I wish I knew, but I have nothing more specific. In any event, I beg you both to be very, very careful."

CHAPTER TEN

September 9-10, 1961

"So, what do you think? Do you trust him?" Chernov asked.

"Who? The German?" Chernov nodded. "I'm not sure," Baier continued. "I don't know him well enough to decide either way, and I keep learning new things about his past."

Chernov frowned, his lips wrinkled as though he had tasted something sour. "I do not trust him. I do not like him either. But mostly, I do not trust him."

"How well do you know him? I take it you've met before, in Berlin perhaps?" Baier said.

Chernov shrugged and shook his head. "No, I've never met him before." He noticed the puzzled look on Baier's face. The American had even stopped walking. "I do not need to know him," Chernov continued. "He is German. That is enough."

"Well that's a convenient pigeonhole." Baier resumed walking.

"You mean that I am prejudiced?" Baier nodded. "Of course, I am. At least toward Germans. Have you forgotten what they did in my country? The suffering, the deaths?"

"And yet you were willing to work with them in Berlin. And for them during the war."

"A momentary lapse in judgment, Herr Baier. I have not made the same mistake with the people running East Germany. Or have you not noticed?"

"I'm not sure at this point what I've noticed and what I've missed, Sergei."

Chernov paused to study the street ahead and behind them, and he spent what seemed like several minutes inspecting the shop windows along Via Garibaldi. Baier guessed that he was looking for a possible tail and wondered if the Russian had been fighting surveillance for his entire jaunt in Western Europe. And what that meant for his quest and mission. If so, what did this say about his activities, his plans and intentions, his relationship with the Soviets he appeared to be meeting in Paris and Rome? And what were their roles in all this?

"It's how we think about each other and have for years," Chernov added. "There is simply too much history between Russians and Germans to do otherwise."

Baier reached out to grab Chernov's sleeve, as though to hold him up, to interrupt their walk. "My first question does not involve the German, Sergei. I'll figure him out soon enough. My real concern is whether I can trust you."

"I see."

"So, tell me, just what have you been up to?"

Chernov stopped and turned on the American with a look of disappointment, disbelieve almost. "You should know the answer to that. I told you my original purpose for coming out at the very outset. Surely you remember back to that night in the dismal room you were using for a safe house in East Berlin. My God, I should hope so, Herr Baier. It is depressing even to think about that place. I explained it all there."

Baier stepped in close. "But you disappeared without a word. You made no attempt to establish contact."

"Of course not. I have been busy. And we had no communication plan in any case."

"We would have if you had stayed put in Berlin for another day or two."

Chernov smiled and shrugged. "I was afraid you would keep me there until I had completed my debriefing and told you everything I know." The smile broadened. "I did not have much to say yet. I know much more now."

"Like what? I thought you already had some hot scoop on Berlin." Baier did not bother to hide his skepticism.

"Well, for one thing, Herr Baier, I know much more about the illegal network the KGB has established in Europe."

"You mean the network of sleeper agents?" Chernov nodded. "And how is that?"

"They are the ones providing support to an assassin like Marchenko and others like him."

"Who?"

"Oleg Ivanovich Marchenko. The man who killed my brother. That was an illegal you saw me meeting in Paris outside the Louvre. He lives in the Rue de Grenelle just off the Parc du Champ de Mars, appropriately enough. You can give his description to your people in Paris.

"I already have."

"Once they set up their surveillance, they may be able to wrap up many of the illegals working in Paris for us." He smiled again and spread his arms wide. "You see, you are already benefiting from my escape."

"What did you tell the fat man in Paris about your appearance there?"

"I told him that I had been sent to monitor the movements of Marchenko because he was suspected of planning to defect."

"Is he?"

Chernov shrugged. "I do not really care. It is all the same to me. I will see to it that he does not live long enough to enjoy his life either way."

"And this Marchenko fellow is in Rome?"

"Yes, I tracked him here. It is why I came, of course."

"How did you do that? Where is your information coming from?'

"In this case, it came from my friend in Paris. The one you saw me with in the Tulieries."

"And?"

Chernov studied the pavement for a few moments before looking up into Baier's eyes. His own had grown suddenly sad. "I have not been able to act here in Rome. He has too much surveillance on him."

"Other than you?" Chernov nodded. "But why? Do they always do that? Don't they trust him? Aren't your people taking a chance of drawing attention to him that way? What if the Italians are monitoring your people here? I'm sure they're trying to."

"Of course, they are." Chernov looked off in the distance in the direction of Saint Peter's. "Ah, I do not know the whole story yet. I was not able to identify everyone. There were too many. Perhaps your people were present as well. All I know is that it has prevented me from killing him." Chernov sighed and shrugged. "And as for my people, I understand that they have their own doubts as to the man's reliability. They suspect he may have gone rogue."

"Rogue? You mean like some kind of free agent?"

"Yes, something like that. And if that is the case, then they will want to eliminate him as well."

"Which is probably a tall order in any case. I doubt he's an easy man to bring down."

"Of course not. But I must try all the same. If they are also in the hunt, then one of us should be able to get him."

"Maybe your KGB pals suspect him of trying to defect. He'd probably have some interesting stories to tell. What can you tell me about him? Do you know him at all?"

The two men resumed their walk, Baier's gaze darting along the sidewalk and streets for any tell-tale signs of a Soviet presence. Others as well, but mostly Baier was concerned about a KGB presence. If they were following this assassin, he guessed, they were probably trying to keep tabs on Chernov as well. Probably more so, if Chernov was the one who had gone rogue. His disappearance had to have been noticed by now. If that's what it really was.

"Yes, I know him. Our paths have crossed before. During the war and even in Budapest."

Baier involuntarily sucked in his breath, remembering how he and Chernov had worked together in Budapest and the warnings the Russian had tried to give about the impending Soviet crackdown. Had Baier missed ones about the presence of a predator like this Marchenko, who may have been on the hunt for a high-level source among the Hungarians like the one he had been running? He shuddered again at the thought. But at least Baier had gotten his man out to freedom. For a little while, anyway.

"He is Ukrainian. Which is odd, because he has killed several leaders and journalists associated with the Ukrainian independence movement."

"You mean like Stephan Bandera and his group?"

"Yes, and others as well. You know that the Ukrainians enjoyed a short-lived independence after the First World War. At least, as long as the Germans remained through 1918 and later, even until 1921, I believe, when the Bolsheviks reconquered the territory."

"Yes, of course. And there was some ongoing guerilla warfare in the 1920s and 1930s. And beyond that as well, up into the 1950s."

Chernov nodded enthusiastically. His focus seemed to have shifted from the street to the past. "That's right. And many greeted the Nazis as liberators with a very warm welcome in '41, hoping to regain their independence. Of course, Stalin did not help with the purges and the famines. So, people like Khrushchev have never been comfortable with any sign of a separate Ukrainian national identity. He was scared by his time as party leader there during the war and right after."

"Has this killer only targeted Ukrainians?"

"No. no, of course not. He has also killed at least one defector in Paris and one in London."

"Sounds like a nice guy."

Chernov raised his finger. "Ah, but remember, he only acts on orders from the Kremlin."

"Until now, anyway. Or some suspect. So, what is your plan now?" Baier pressed.

"I will continue to watch him and wait for my chance. I have no other option at the moment. And you must realize that this remains my priority."

"Has he contacted illegals here in Rome?"

Chernov shook his head. "Not that I've noticed. And that

puzzles me." He stopped as though struck by a brilliant idea. "You can watch him as well. Perhaps this will give you a chance to find your own illegals all by yourself. Think of how happy that will make your superiors back in Washington."

Which I may need to keep support or at least tolerance for this operation alive, Baier thought. "I just might do that, Sergei. It will also give me a chance to keep tabs on you."

"Good. He is staying at a hotel near the Vatican. It's in the Via Crecsenzio across from the castle of Saint Angela. The Palazzio de Roma. Perhaps I'll see you tomorrow."

Let's hope not, Baier thought. If you do, then I won't be doing my job.

• • •

The good thing about the Via Crescenzio and the proximity to the Castle of Saint Angela—a former residence of the Popes built during the reign of Emperor Marcus Aurelius and hence, a tourist attraction—was the presence of so many cafes, bars, and people. So, it was easy for Baier to hide himself among this crowd as a perfectly ordinary Italian or tourist sipping his cappuccino on a bright September morning just across the street from the Palazzio de Roma. He had the photograph from Paris that purportedly showed the face of the man he was seeking, and Chernov had told him that the assassin almost always wore a full-length coat regardless of the weather. It was as though the man had something eternally to hide.

Baier did not have to wait long. He was making his way slowly and enjoyably through his second cappuccino when a tall, heavy-set man who looked very much like the face in the photograph nestled in Baier's shirt pocket emerged from the front door of the hotel. Baier quickly pulled the picture from his pocket to check and was surprised to see that in person the assassin had a harder, more muscular face, the eyes almost hidden under a set of heavy eyebrows and a forehead that reminded Baier of shrubbery on a mountainside, hardy enough to survive nearly anything. But what was even more convincing was the long and heavy coat that shrouded the man like old drapery. My God, Baier thought, the man looks like someone who has just escaped from a displaced persons camp. Lord knows, Baier had seen enough of those people wandering around Berlin and Germany right after the war. But this one looked to be much better fed, almost like a man trying to transform himself into a bear, the better to terrify and overwhelm his opponents.

Bear-man stood at the hotel entrance for a moment, then swept the doorman aside with a wave of his paw when the latter approached to offer assistance. He stood on the sidewalk at the hotel's front for several more minutes surveying the human forest before strolling off in the direction that led away from Baier's bar, a look of smug satisfaction filling the bulging cheeks and the heavy black eyebrows. The Ukrainian's day, at any rate, appeared to have gotten off to a good start.

Baier tossed a fistful of lira on the table and bolted for the door. Once on the sidewalk he slowed to a more normal, almost leisurely pace, hoping to avoid drawing attention to himself. As yet, there was no sign of Chernov.

Marchenko, if that's indeed who he was, rambled like some kind of unstoppable force across the Tiber and roamed the streets of Rome for about twenty minutes. Baier had to wonder at the man's control over his body temperature, like it was simply a matter of controlling a peculiar body chemistry by sheer force of will. He showed no signs of exhaustion or discomfort from the weather and his wardrobe during what must have been a tough sweat-inducing exercise. It was almost as though the man was incapable of generating normal human warmth, as though his body was fueled by ice water.

When he reached the Pantheon, a Roman temple that became the first Christian church in Imperial Rome, Marchenko took a seat in one of the cafes, at one of the sidewalk tables, in the plaza surrounding the church. Even here, he chose a table in the sun, rejecting the comfort offered by a place in the shade. Maybe he was still thawing out after all those Ukrainian and Russian winters. Baier settled in a nearby locale for his third cappuccino of the morning, hoping he'd be able to find time for a bathroom stop.

Almost as soon as he sat down, the dodging shafts of sunlight caught Baier's attention. The rays sliced the Roman architecture as they danced, separating the ages of the Eternal City into the distinct yet merging epochs of its history. From Imperial to Medieval to Renaissance and Baroque, before settling the visitor's attention on the city's modern eras of its republican, Fascist, and finally its post-war restoration periods. It had been an incredible—and for much of its time, a successful—history, inspiring European development and aspirations, its dreams of glory and legacies. So where would Baier and his work, his career, his country's role fit into all this, he wondered. Was Washington truly the Rome of our times? Baier certainly hoped so. And if it was, how long would that last? Was Berlin a test we would pass?

It was then that Baier first found Chernov. The Russian looked as though he needed a toilet stop of his own. Chernov was dressed in a beige summer suit that offered a marked contrast to the Ukrainian. Chernov could not keep still, apparently driven by a wave of anxiety and nervousness. Baier was struck by how unprofessional it all made him look, as though he had become chilled by the Roman air and the thought of his self-appointed mission. This much movement was sure to draw the bear-man's attention. Chernov never took a seat anywhere. He simply paced and glared periodically from his corner of the square in the direction of the Ukrainian, who sipped from his espresso in apparent comfort. Every once in a while, Chernov would disappear around the corner of the church before re-emerging with a more tortured look on his face. Baier wondered if he was about to witness the Russian's moment of revenge.

He realized then that he should never have taken his eyes off the Ukrainian. It was probably a foolish thing to do with a real bear in his natural habitat—or anywhere else, for that matter. Baier was suddenly aware of a large figure looming in front of him at his table. This close the dimensions of the bear-man changed from that of a black bear to an angry grizzly.

"Why you smile?" the Ukrainian asked.

Baier stared into the dark, penetrating eyes that seemed to measure him as it would any other piece of prey. "Oh, it's just something I remembered."

"From when?"

"From before I saw you or knew of you."

"You know who I am?"

"Yes, I believe I do. You're Marchenko, aren't you?"

"*Da*. And I know you. Baier." He paused to let the revelation sink in. "Why you follow me?"

"To get to know you better and what you're up to in Rome?"

The bear-man nodded. "I see." He leaned forward, coming about two feet from Baier's face. Two huge hands with fingers like branches from a large tree gripped the edges of the table. "I see. That is good. Now we know each other better and what must be done. My time in Rome is over. I think we meet again in Berlin. It will be my pleasure then."

"So, your work here is done, you say? Just what have you been doing?"

The Ukrainian beast smiled. It was a look that was more a threat than a reassurance. "What was necessary," he said. "Now I know what I needed to know."

The Ukrainian stood up straight. Perhaps it was Baier's imagination, but the man seemed to block the sun. The smile grew slowly across thick lips scared by time and experience. It was the look of a predator, pure and simple. Baier stared back at the man, hoping the pounding of his heart was not too loud.

"You are returning to Berlin? Can you tell me why?"

A smile spread across Marchenko's face, revealing a series of yellow teeth that resembled weathered stones. "You can learn that for yourself, Baier. It should not be difficult. We are interested in the same man. I will finish there."

"Yes, I see."

So, for Baier, it would bring him back to Berlin. It was almost inevitable. That was his personal Rome. For him, all roads led to that former German capital and nowhere else. Or so it seemed.

And it all made sense, given his personal history, his family, and the course of the twentieth century.

As the Ukrainian moved off, Baier turned to find Chernov. He had half expected to hear a shot, Chernov fulfilling his dream of closing the chapter on his brother's death. Instead, the Russian stood there with a smile of his own. This one, however, looked just silly, as though he was a man who posed a threat to no one.

Just why the hell is everyone smiling here but me, Baier asked himself. Just who is playing what game and with what goals? He turned to find Chernov again, but the Russian had disappeared once more. So had the Ukrainian.

• • •

The following morning Baier met Carberry across the street from the American embassy in a local restaurant along the Via Veneto. Rumor had it that the Embassy was located on the spot of a villa Julius Caesar had purchased for one of his mistresses. If so, it had certainly changed. But it still made a great story.

"I think I've had my fill of cappuccinos here in Rome," Baier proclaimed.

"Miss the beer, do you?"

"Of course." Carberry was outfitted in a more suitable dark blue suit for an American diplomat this morning, complete with a white shirt and a striped tie. "Meeting with the Ambassador today?"

Carberry nodded. "Just about every day, in fact. You know, the usual: daily intelligence brief and discussion of what we're up to—in a vague and general manner, of course—to avoid unpleasant surprises. Speaking of which...." He signaled the waiter for another plate of rolls and some more jam.

"Yes? I hope it's not something unpleasant from Washington."

"Well, actually there are two messages. The first one is also kind of general, but I think you should be aware of it. Headquarters is pretty much done with this Russian operation of yours. They don't see it leading anywhere, since you haven't been able to rein this KGB defector in and obtain any kind of debriefing. They think he is leading you on the proverbial goose chase, especially since nothing damaging has been given over yet from your interactions this time around. All that appears to have happened is that we got him out from behind the Curtain, and he's been running all over Europe doing God knows what."

"Damn it, Frank. What about the illegals network in Paris? Has the fat man Chernov exposed turned up back there?"

Carberry shook his head. "Not yet, apparently. But Paris is looking for him. I certainly hope he does, for your sake, Karl. Frankly, from my position it does not look good. It looks as though this Russian friend of yours has sold you a false bill of goods."

"Well, that chubby guy was here in Rome as well, but he should have headed back to France. Let the Station know, will you?"

"Sure thing, Karl. I hope it helps."

Baier sat back, angry and disappointed in Washington, Chernov, and especially himself. "Son of a bitch," he muttered. He found that he had grabbed one of the new rolls the waiter had delivered and crushed it in his hands. "Sorry, Frank. Have they used the word 'recall' or anything similar?"

Carberry shook his head again and selected one of the surviving rolls. "No, they haven't. Can you tell me just what this Russian guy is doing?"

"Frank, I've been trying to spare everyone some very difficult decisions. Can this remain strictly between us?"

Carberry paused and stared at Baier. It was as though he was expecting some unpleasant news. "You know better than to ask me that, Karl."

"Then look." Baier checked to make sure the neighboring tables were empty, then leaned in close. "I agreed to let the Russian take care of a personal matter first. I won't say anymore. But it seems he's come crossways with some kind of KGB or GRU operation because of it, and that has complicated things. It has also dragged the entire affair out longer than either of us expected."

"Does this refer to the 'hunting' you mentioned the other day?"

Baier nodded. "Yes, it does. That is the 'personal' side of this whole operation. The Russian is on a mission of revenge."

"I'll leave it at that, Karl. Have you told anyone else of this 'complicating' factor?"

"I let Pittman up in Paris in on some of it."

Carberry nodded. "I see. And you still trust the Russian?"

Baier leaned back. "I…I think so."

"Hardly a ringing endorsement, Karl. In any case, the other message is from Berlin. Sabina wants you back there right away. Something to do with her parents."

"What is it? They haven't been snatched by those pricks in the East, have they? I thought we had an escape plan all worked out."

The local chief spread strawberry jam across the insides of his breakfast roll. "Not that they've said. Actually, she did not say anything specific. Just that she needs you home to help sort something out."

Baier was silent for a moment. God, but he hoped nothing had gone horribly wrong. He had left his wife there in the belief that the exfiltration of her parents would be a relatively simple operation. Now this, too, appeared to have run off the rails. If only he hadn't had to stay away for this long. It made him even madder than before at Chernov, that 'fucking Russian.'

"I was planning to head back there today anyway. I'll check in with Tom just as soon as I find out what has gone wrong with Sabine."

Carberry nodded as he chewed on the roll and jam. "Good idea. I just hope they leave you enough time to sort things out."

CHAPTER ELEVEN

September 11, 1961

"My God, Karl, why did you take so long?" Sabine Baier embraced her husband the minute he walked in the door. It felt as though she had been waiting at the front entrance almost since he had left. "It seemed like you were away forever. I was starting to get worried."

She released Baier, and he followed her through the passage from the dining room into the kitchen. She stood there, leaning against the sink with her back to the window. Her eyes stayed focused on her husband. Worry and disappointment lined her forehead and surrounded her hazel eyes. It was early in the afternoon, and Sabine was dressed in casual cotton slacks and a white blouse with its buttons undone low enough to reveal her cleavage. He wondered if she had done this as punishment for what he missed by staying away for so long. Baier stepped forward and pulled his wife close for several seconds before answering.

Seeing her there, back in Berlin, dressed as she was and as appealing as she was, despite the dish towel in her left hand and frown on her face, brought back memories of their early days together after the war in this very neighborhood. It was not the same house, but at least it was on the same street. This one sat a couple blocks away, covered in white plaster rather than the red brick of their original home. But it, too, was surrounded by the tall pines that grew so well in this area of the city, less than half a mile from the eastern border of the Gruenewald. She had followed his career and his moves, all of which had brought them back to this place, a different moment but still a time and challenge they faced together.

"I am sorry, Sabine, but one thing led to another." He rested his chin on top her head and let his gaze wander along the back of her hair and down along her spine while his hands pressed her closer. "I had to follow my visit to Paris with a stop in Rome. I had no way to communicate with you since I wanted to keep my distance from our stations. I also did not think it was safe enough for me to call you on an open line."

"Did you find Chernov?"

"Yes, I did. And more. I'm afraid it's far from over."

"Not over yet?" She pushed herself away from Baier, and her hand slapped the dish towel against her thigh. "When will it ever be over? There's always something else."

Baier sighed and relaxed his hold. He wanted to reassure his wife, let her know that somehow it would all work out. But he didn't know where to find the right words. "I wish I knew. There are just so many questions still. And our Russian friend is being even more cagey than usual."

Sabine took another step away and held her husband's gaze for a moment. Then she dropped her arms, took his hand and led him into the living room. She pulled him down next to her on the sofa. Grabbing his head on both sides in her hands, she drew him to her, leaving a long, lingering kiss and pressing her body against his. Memories of the past flooded back once more for Baier. The last thing he was going to do was argue with her. She must have felt the same way.

"That's okay, Karl. I understand. I'm so glad you're finally back. I feel better. But so much has happened."

He pulled back. "What is it? Is it your parents? How are they? More to the point, where are your parents?"

"Karl, you've been away too many days. I need your help here."

"Tell me, Sabine. What's wrong? Have they made it out yet? I almost expected to see them here with you."

She took both his hands in hers. "No, Karl. The attempt was never made. Your asset, that Syrian diplomat, was arrested before we could try. I guess it was fortunate that something didn't happen with my parents in his car."

He stood. "Arrested? How can that be? The man's an accredited diplomat."

"Well, not exactly arrested, although he may be just that in his home country by now. Apparently, he liked to drink and party too much. And all that led to him talking too much. Someone over there reported what he said—more than once, I might add—to the authorities. They brought him in for questioning, and he's been expelled back to Damascus."

"Damn. Does Hendricks know?"

"He must. He's the one who told me."

"Well, I don't envy the poor sap. His days are certainly numbered."

"Didn't your people warn this man? About the appropriate behavior, I mean? The need for discretion?"

Baier shifted his weight closer so that he was sitting tight up against his wife. He wanted to bring himself as close as possible, as though that would make things easier. "Of course, Sabine. But you can't make a man change his character. I suppose we would have eventually found out what he had been doing and cut him loose. Or depending on how valuable he had been, brought him out. Which, of course, probably would have created a whole new set of problems. But it's obviously too late for any of that now."

"Is there any chance, Karl that you could try to bring my parents across?" She took his hands in hers and squeezed them tight enough to leave an impression. "I mean you yourself."

Baier squeezed his wife's hands in return and kissed her forehead. "Sabine, you know that wouldn't work. They know me too well over there."

"But you've made the trip over there before and always driven back. You're an accredited diplomat here now—again—and they wouldn't be allowed to stop you."

"Sabine, I'm afraid that those sorts of diplomatic niceties won't matter much to those bastards. True, they couldn't hold me, at least not for long. But they wouldn't care about that as long as they grabbed your parents. I'm afraid we wouldn't have much to stand on in that case."

Sabine let her hands fall and moved in close, circling her husband's shoulders with her arms. "I was afraid you'd say that." She paused while she studied the floor, her head resting on his chest, before looking up at her husband. "That's why I've re-established contact with some of my old partners from right after the war."

"The people you worked your smuggling and black market activities with? Before I knew you?"

"That's right."

Baier leaned backed so he could look down at his wife's face. "But how? My God, you didn't go into the East on your own, I hope."

"Oh, Karl, it wasn't that hard. Nobody is looking for me."

"But they'll recognize the name. Baier."

"It isn't all that uncommon here, in this part of Germany. I obviously made it back."

"How many times did you go over?"

"Just the once."

"And that's all it took to find your compatriots in the old business?"

She smiled and nodded. "Yes, just the once. But that's because I had help here in the West. There is one of my old companions still there in the East, and he lives at the same address as all those years ago, which is not unusual. The big difference for me is that his brother lives here in the West, and he told me where to find my old colleague. I don't know if you remember, but they used to work together. And, Karl…" She backed off and put her right hand on his chest. "…They still do. They have resumed their people smuggling. As you can imagine, they have quite a few customers these days."

"Two brothers, you said? I think I do remember them. Are they the two men who later worked for us when we had that original stable of people from your old black market network? I thought they had retired. What good will that do?"

Sabine nodded vigorously. "Yes, yes, that's right. His brother Hans was one of those who ran for the West when that part of the network started to break apart. But his brother stayed behind. He couldn't leave his old home and neighborhood in Prenslauer Berg. Once this wall started going up, they decided to resume their work moving people back and forth. Only now, no one is going back and forth. There is no smuggling into the Soviet zone. Everyone is coming out. And Hans works the western end of the business. I'm told they've made a lot of money so far."

"So far? They couldn't have been in business all that long."

"No, of course not. And one can't be sure how much longer they'll stay at it. The authorities over there are very clever, Karl."

"Yes, I'm aware of that. How are they doing it?"

"Well, the methods change, of course. They have to adapt as the authorities get wise to each method. First, they were helping people with false identifications and forged documents. There's still some of that, of course."

"Of course."

"And they've helped people swim across the Spree and the canals. They also used the subway. At least they did until the regime cracked down on attempts to ride and jump or leap out when they still made stops in the West. They've also used ropes to swing or glide over the construction from buildings along to sector boundary into the West."

"That means they must have accomplices here in West Berlin."

Sabine was growing more excited and enthusiastic as she expanded on her story. She jumped from the sofa, bent over and grabbed Baier's hands again. "Of course, they do. That's why I said Hans arranges things on this end. There are hundreds willing to help, even in the police. But don't you see the benefits of that? We can work with them. We don't need to go over all the time."

"But your parents are too old to be jumping from trains or gliding along tightropes."

"You're right, of course. But they've turned to building tunnels now. The East Germans are already blocking up the windows and doors in the buildings that border the new wall. And they are creating a border zone, what some people are calling a death strip. So, the best chances now are to go under it, Armin said."

"Armin who? Hans's brother?"

"That's right. Armin Ruggersfeld. That's my old contact and partner. Yours, too. You must remember him? You once told me they were very useful."

"Yes, yes, I remember now. But what does Armin, the one still in the east, do when he's not smuggling people to freedom?"

"He's a construction worker. So, he's got just the right experience for something like this. It means he also knows where there's construction work being done by the regime and where it would be safe to dig a tunnel."

"How so?"

"Because he knows where there's good cover and where the best buildings are located for the shortest and safest routes. They need those to cover their tunneling work. He's also familiar with the topography in the city. You know, the water levels and soil and that sort of thing."

"And this is how you plan to get your parents out?"

Sabine dropped her husband's hands and stood up straight. Baier couldn't help himself from admiring how well his wife had held her figure over the years. She had aged extremely well over the 15 years of their marriage, despite all she had been through. A kidnapping in East Germany, a prison and escape in Budapest, a coup in Turkey, and now this, a wall being built to split the former German capital in half, separating her from her parents.

"What is it, Karl?"

Sabine's words brought him back to the moment.

"I was just wondering how safe it really is. Where are your parents now?"

"They had to go back to Erfurt. They didn't have a good reason to stay in Berlin, if the police asked."

"Do they still have the documents we gave them?"

Sabine shook her head. "No, your colleague, what's his name, Robert, the Polish kid from Chicago, took them back when the

Syrian thing fell through." She put her hands on her hips. "But that's okay. They won't need them to get through the tunnel."

"*The* tunnel? This Armin has already started one?"

She nodded. "Yes. He began work on it almost right after the wall started going up. He said it was obvious something like this would be necessary. He thinks it will be ready in about a week. Maybe a few days longer."

"How will you contact your parents?"

"On the phone, silly. I will call them from the post office or Armin's house, like any daughter would. Many people are doing something similar since the regime cut off telephone connections from this part of Berlin. But they can't stop everything. Even this regime can't do that."

Baier stood and placed his hands on Sabine's shoulders before kissing her forehead. "Well, not yet, they haven't. But be careful about what you say, and for God's sake, speak cryptically. You never know how safe your parent's telephone is."

They broke apart when the doorbell rang. Both looked automatically in the direction of the front door.

"Now, who the hell can that be?" Baier asked himself, more than anyone else.

When he opened the door, Baier met the frowning face of Tom Hendricks.

"Glad to see you're finally back," Hendricks said. "Carberry said you were on your way home. Did you have a nice train ride from Rome? I hear the trains still run on time there. Did you bring me anything?"

"On time? Hardly. But come on in, Tom. And no, I did not bring you a present from France or Italy. You're one of those men who already has everything."

"Hardly, but I do have a Russian defector."

Baier stopped in mid-step and turned. "Say what? Another one? Don't tell me a line is forming over there."

"No, not yet anyway. It's just the original. Your buddy is back."

"So where is he hiding this time?"

"He's where he should have been all along. The house on

Mexicoplatz." He grabbed Baier's shirt sleeve and turned back toward the front door. "Let's go see what he has to say for himself."

• • •

"I'm sorry about the mix-up with Sabine's parents," Hendricks said. His white Mercedes drifted through the late morning traffic that left the streets of Dahlem nearly empty. "You've noticed the lack of traffic today, I'm guessing. It's been like this for a while now."

"Too bad there aren't more people to see your nice new car. How long have you had this one?"

"Just a week now. And I have to say I really like it. You're not the only one who gets to ride in semi-luxury around here."

Baier glanced out his window at the nearly empty sidewalks. "I take it everyone is still rushing down to the see the new wall going up."

Hendricks nodded. "Pretty much. But they're also going to cheer on the escapees, and maybe even help if they can." Hendricks glanced over at Baier. "By the way, we were as surprised as anyone by the Syrian's detainment."

Baier looked over at his colleague. "You mean you guys weren't aware of his behavior before this? The guy sounds like a walking counterintelligence invitation."

"No, Karl, we hadn't recruited him that long ago, as you may remember. You signed off on the cable, in case you've forgotten."

"Sorry. A lot has been going on lately."

"Yes, I know. But you may recall that we were in a rush to get some kind of insight into developments on that side of the city, given all the pressure from Washington for information on what our late allies in Moscow are up to over there. This is not exactly the first crisis in this city over the past 15 years, as you well know."

"I really am sorry, Tom. I know what pressure you've been under. Hell, we've been passing much of that pressure along as it falls on us back home. There's so much uncertainty as to what the Soviets have planned for this city. That's why I think we need to press on this Russian operation. I mean, can you imagine what we would gain if his claim about insight into Soviet planning for Berlin is true?"

Hendricks nodded and shrugged, clearly ambivalent. "Yeah, sure. If it isn't a load of bullshit to pull us in."

"Well, there's only one way to find out. Besides, I'm just frustrated by a number of things, including trying to figure out what to do about Sabine's parents." Baier sighed. "It's doubly frustrating, since they could have left at any time in the past decade with little trouble. But they had to wait for this damn wall to go up first."

"Like just about everyone else over there. Any ideas where to go from here?"

"Sabine's talking about one of the tunnel projects that are starting up over there."

"Yeah, but that takes time. How long do you have for your stay in Berlin?"

"I think I can extend it a little longer. I mean, this operation is not about to wrap up anytime soon." Baier smiled and shook his head. "Unless, of course, our Russian defector gets himself killed or decides he's been playing us long enough."

"So, what do think he's actually up to?"

"I'm still leaning toward the notion that he really does want out. I think he's overplayed his hand on his side of the fence, and that he really does want—and need—to get out. And he's got some goods to sell to us to ensure a welcome reception."

"Then why all the running around? Headquarters is getting very suspicious, Karl."

Baier paused to consider his next few words very carefully. "Tom, can I tell you something that I've been holding back?"

Hendricks's head shot around to take in Baier's look, to try to gauge his seriousness or anxiety. But his colleague remained a sphinx, a true professional. "Karl, that's a helluva thing to do. You know full well that nothing good ever comes from that kind of nonsense." He gripped the steering wheel as his focus returned to the road. "I would have thought you trusted me enough to be more transparent. I just hope you haven't put me in an impossible situation."

"I am truly sorry, Tom, but it explains the Russian's jaunts through Paris and Rome."

"Go ahead. But I'm making no promises."

Baier paused as they pulled up in front of the house where Chernov had returned. Baier studied his colleague's face for several moments before continuing.

"Chernov is on a mission of revenge. He wants the assassin that killed his brother. If he succeeds, there is no way he returns behind the Curtain. And that very character has shown up. He's now a part of this game."

"When did this happen?"

"In Rome. He even confronted me. And he knew my name."

"Goddamit, Karl, how did that happen?"

"I think we've got a leak or a KGB or GRU source working in the Mission, Tom. And I just hope it isn't someone in the Base."

"Well, fuck me." Hendricks right hand slammed the steering wheel. Twice. He shook his head and glared straight ahead.

"You mean, fuck all of us," Baier responded. "That is, if it's true."

Hendricks drew in a deep breath that Baier thought might have moved a few trees in the Gruenewald if the two men hadn't been sitting inside the base chief's car. "About the assassin, though. Is the Russian planning to kill him?"

"Yes. But I'm hoping to grab the guy. Can you imagine the stuff we would get from holding and debriefing him?"

"What sort of chance is there for that?"

"A small one, I'll admit. But it's worth the try."

"Well, this has been one hell of a morning. Let's see what your Russian pal has to say."

The house on Mexicoplatz loomed as large as ever. Although Baier had only been away for about a week, he had forgotten how huge some of the Allied housing was in occupied Berlin. This was especially the case after his time in Paris and Rome, cities that were filled with rows of apartment blocks, although many had been built in a range of impressive architectural styles over the centuries. Well, at least Rome's urban landscape reflected the long periods of its prosperity and power. Paris's was more recent, having been rebuilt by the legendary architect Hausmann on Napoleon III's orders. Basically, in Berlin the Allies had seized the homes of Nazis who had expropriated them from political dissidents and Jews and were holding them until the original owners returned. If they ever did. That was the theory at least. Baier had heard of numerous cases where the Allied authorities simply grabbed whatever house looked nice—and still relatively complete after the bombing and the battle—leaving the occupants on the street. The justice of the victors, apparently. *Siegerrecht*, the Germans called it. Well, they had hailed their own *Sieg* often enough, so too bad. At least that was how the Allies saw it back in '45.

This particular German house still had its *faux* Bavarian exterior, spread over three floors that rose from the property like a small mountain. But the house also ran far enough back into a huge yard and had enough space for about half a dozen bedrooms, never mind all the bathrooms it must be hiding. The front door swung open as the two Americans ascended the long staircase leading to the front porch.

"Welcome, my friends," a beaming Chernov announced, framed by an elaborate front door entrance that spread like an invitation. Baier almost felt as though he should be crossing a moat. "It's so nice to see you two again."

"Likewise," Hendricks replied. "We're so happy you decided to return our favor of getting you out by actually coming back to talk to us." The forced smile did little to hide his displeasure.

"Come inside, gentlemen. I have a bottle of fine red Italian wine, a Borolo, in fact, that I brought back from Rome. I realize it may be a bit early for you Americans, but hopefully, we can still share a glass or two to discuss our next steps."

The three men marched through the front corridor and into a square den in the corner of the first floor and off to the side of a long dining room that could seat a dozen guests, at least. Three deer heads, antlers and all, adorned the back wall. In the den, three glasses half full of a rich, dark red wine sat on end tables next to three plump armchairs that were covered in a green silk-like fabric. Baier had no idea if it was real silk. Nor did he really care. Otherwise, the walls in this room were bare, except for a large portrait of Queen Sophie Charlotte, the wife of Frederick the Great.

"Please sit, my friends. I think you will find the wine to be excellent."

Baier moved over to the far chair set against a bay window that looked out on a street that ran in a half moon inside an impressive residential circle. He raised his glass and sipped. The wine was indeed excellent, at least as far as he could tell. Baier remained more of a beer man, given his many years in Germany and Austria. The raised eyebrows of Hendricks suggested he felt the same about the wine. Chernov's beam grew wider and brighter.

"When did you get back?" Baier asked.

"Last night. I must have grabbed an earlier train you, Herr Baier."

"You must have had less to think about and take care of. And your Ukrainian friend?"

Chernov sipped his wine, and it sounded as though he had smacked his lips in appreciation. All three men settled into their chairs. Hendricks had been sure to take the one nearest the entrance to the room.

"It seems he, too, has returned to Berlin. I believe he had to depart Rome rather suddenly. He seems to have left a corpse behind."

"One of yours, I hope," Hendricks added.

Chernov took another sip of wine, then replaced his glass on the table. "Oh, of course. It seems another one of our officers was planning to defect. You see, there is great uncertainty on our side of the Curtain at the moment, and a number of KGB officers are looking for a more secure future in the West." He paused to consider his wine but decided not to take another drink. "There was no one in Paris, however. That stop was to receive new orders."

"For the Rome killing?" Baier asked.

Chernov smiled. "No, no. He already had those."

"And how do you know this?" Baier asked.

Chernov let his gaze rest on Baier as he mulled a mouthful of his wine in thought. "I told you that I still have friends in my service. There are any number of favors I can call in, you see." He held up his hand. "You will forgive me if I do not elaborate. At least not yet."

"Then who or what? Do you know the next target?" Hendricks pressed. "Is it someone we can help or protect? More to the point, is it someone we would want to protect?"

"You mean to bring them over to you, another feather in your cap, as you like to say?"

"Well, yes. Of course, we would try to use this opportunity."

"Exploit it, you mean?"

"Let's not get buried in semantic games, Sergei," Baier interrupted. "At least he'd still be alive and with a whole new set of friends. Do you know who the next target is or not?"

"As a matter of fact, I do." Chernov paused, as though for effect. "It happens to be me."

"Jesus," Hendricks gasped. It took a moment for him to recover his breath. "How can you be sure?"

"That's one of the things the man I contacted in Paris told me, Karl." Chernov turned toward Hendricks. "Your colleague Herr Baier trailed me expertly in Paris and discovered one of my contacts." He returned his attention to Baier. "Have your people there contacted him yet? He's been back for a few days now."

"Let's leave that for now," Hendricks said. "What more can you tell us about this latest directive to the killer?"

"Not much more, I'm afraid. Of course, the details will be left to him. The man's a true professional, you know."

"So we've gathered," Baier said. "Why didn't he just carry out this assignment in Rome?"

This time the smile on Chernov's face grew much wider and brighter. "Because he did not know I was there. You see, I am not such an amateur as you seem to believe, Herr Baier."

"Okay then, what do you plan to do about it, now that you are apparently hunting each other?"

"Well, I'm afraid I'll have to cross back over into the East."

"What?" Hendricks shouted. "That's absurd. After all we did to get you out, now you tell us you want to go back. That's bullshit." Hendricks did not bother to lower his voice.

Baier stood. "Tom, please. A little softer. I understand your anger, and I'm as surprised as you." He turned toward Chernov. "Just what do you hope to accomplish by going back, Sergei? Certainly, you realize how difficult that is, not to mention dangerous."

Chernov stood in turn. He lifted his glass and drained the remaining Borolo in one long gulp, as though he was drinking vodka. "Of course, I know how difficult and dangerous it is. Do you think I am foolish, Herr Baier? Have you learned so little about me over the years?" He threw the wine glass against the wall to their right. "Just what do you expect me to do? Sit here and wait for the mad Ukrainian to show up on my doorstep?"

Hendricks and Baier were silent. Hendricks stared at the Russian, his mouth open. Baier looked at the floor, shaking his head.

"Well, I refuse," Chernov continued. "No, instead, I go on the offensive and take the fight to him, just like that general you and the Germans all admired so much, Rommel. It's what he would have done." Then in more of a murmur than a declaration, he mumbled, "Although he never fought on the eastern front against us."

"No, instead you had to contend with the likes of von Manstein and Guderian. How fortunate for you. But just how do you suggest we go about this? Do you plan to return in your true name, as though everything will be forgiven? That this execution order will somehow be lifted?"

Chernov scoffed and sat back down. "Of course not. What do you take me for? I still have the passport that I used to travel to France."

"The one that says you're a Czech?" Baier asked. "How well do you speak the language? And just where did you get that?"

"Well enough. Remember, Herr Baier, I was stationed in

Prague before the war." He shrugged. "As for the origin of the document, that must remain my own little secret."

"I suppose that came from some of these old friends you claim to have. And do you plan to simply walk back across the sector boundary?" Hendricks asked.

"No, not that. That would be inviting arrest, since they have no record of me leaving. And certainly not under this name. No, that would invite too much scrutiny. This document would be simply for back up, as you say." He rose and walked over to Baier's chair, handing him the passport for inspection. "No, instead, you can sneak me back over in your car."

"Shit," Baier mumbled. He couldn't think of anything else to say at that moment. This was a new take on things. Carrying people back rather than out.

• • •

"Do you still trust him?" Hendricks asked. The car crawled through the streets of Dahlem to give the two Americans time to discuss the latest twist in their operation.

"I have no other option right now."

"Even though that puts him back in their hands? If he is a dangle, he'll be back in the safety of their arms, Karl. And he'll have picked up some valuable information on our infiltration and exfiltration methods."

"I know, I know. But we've gotten little ourselves thus far. And don't forget, he did turn over that link to their illegal network in Paris. Have we picked up on that yet?"

"I'll try to find out from Pittman. You're right, though, that could be valuable. But we don't know yet how extensive the network is and how much we'll be able to pick up. It could be a lot and very damaging to the KGB, or it could be just crumbs."

"Yes. Only time will tell. And in the meantime, they could be wrapping that particular network up, if they're aware of Chernov's contact with us."

"Well, they're aware of something, if he really is on a hit list. I mean, we also have to consider that if they've ordered his killing, that group or any of its members could be bait they'd simply be throwing away." Hendricks paused. "Or the claim that he's now a target could be just a line of crap he's throwing at us."

"And in that case, they're all useless anyway. No, you could be right, of course. But I feel I have to play along at this point. You have to remember, Tom, in some ways I owe my life to this man."

"Remember? It's news to me. How so?"

"If it wasn't for him, I could be rotting in a Hungarian prison right now. He was instrumental in keeping me out of the clutches of the Hungarians and the KGB back in Budapest. He and a colleague sprung me. Twice, as a matter of fact."

"Well then I guess that settles it. How do you want to go on this? And what about Sabine's parents?"

"She'll have to take care of that herself for now. At least the details. Lord knows she's capable enough, and she certainly knows the landscape. Besides, she's worked with some of the people before."

"After the war? When you first met her?"

Baier nodded, his eyes searching the sidewalks and street corners, as though a solution could be found there. "That's right."

"And you? What are your next steps?"

"I guess I'll have to see what I can do to keep track of my 'fucking Russian.'"

"That means more time in the east. Are you ready for that? Do you really want to sneak him back over. Washington will have a shit storm if you do."

"No, I do not, not really. I mean, talk about going back into the lion's den, as it were. And there are people over there just waiting for me to show my face again. At that point Washington will be the least of my worries."

He thought of the Gracchus character, who had threatened to kill him. That sounded like an extreme threat to make, the kind one throws out in anger. But who was to say what sort of man this particular East German was? He certainly came across as a serious Stasi officer, dedicated to the cause of his half-baked country and prepared to do whatever it took to protect its interests, its survival. Moreover, it was a dedication reinforced by a difficult and troubled family history. And then there was the Ukrainian. Baier thought back to their encounter in Rome. God knew that guy was threatening enough. He almost felt sorry for Chernov, wondering if he would be a match for the giant. Then again, maybe he didn't intend to follow through on his own threat. Maybe he was just playing Baier and had been turned at some point after the Budapest adventure.

"I guess I have to go back over to follow this through. Otherwise I won't be able to sleep at night. There are just too many loose ends, Tom."

"I don't see how you can sleep as it is," Hendricks answered. He paused and studied the street ahead for several seconds before turning to Baier in the passenger seat. "What do we know about this brother of your Russian? I mean, anything more than that he was simply this guy's sibling?"

Baier turned and looked over at his colleague, his eyes wide with a revelation. "My God, Tom, why the hell didn't I ever think of that? All I know is that he allegedly escaped, along with their sister, after the Revolution. The family had been pretty well-to-do, I believe. Upper middle class with the father a pretty successful merchant. Even dabbled in sable furs from what I remember. They weren't exactly enamored of the Bolshevik revolution."

"So how did your guy get involved in all that?"

"A student radical from his days at the university in St. Petersburg, or so the British file claimed." Baier saw the question marks in Hendricks's eyes. "They shared a file on the man when he was a high-level counter-intelligence officer for the NKVD in Berlin after the war. The Brits had been keeping tabs on him for some time."

"Why? How did they come to know about him?"

"You know, they never really explained that. I guess it was just a part of the job. You know, identifying the opposition and searching for their vulnerabilities. In any case, they did a pretty good job of it. They had him down to the proverbial T."

"And the siblings?"

"Well, the rest is a long story, but the brother and sister

supposedly fled to Paris, and then on to South America. That was Chernov's first defection."

"His first? How many are there. And how has he survived this far?"

"Oh, the man is quite capable, as you've no doubt figured out. But he fled with a group of Germans associated with Sabine's first husband…"

"Your *doppleganger,* as it were?"

Baier smiled. "Yes, I suppose you could call him that. Anyway, Chernov returned when he discovered they had both died. Or so he claimed."

"And how is it he never ended up in Siberia or in a hangman's noose?"

"Ah, well, there the story gets really interesting. It seems he got lucky with his timing. Stalin's purges and those that followed Papa Joe's demise appear to have wiped out those with a memory and a grudge from Chernov's desertion. He was supposedly able to fend any detractors off with a story about a wild goose chase to find his siblings and run down some German gold in the bargain." Baier laughed, remembering his first encounters with Sabine and her family. "Which actually is partially true."

"And now?"

"Well, now he claims that the brother never died. Instead, he was in Paris the whole time, but was recently bumped off."

"By this Soviet assassin?" Baier nodded. "And the sister?"

Baier shrugged and returned his gaze to the road ahead. "Who knows? I wouldn't be surprised if she suddenly appears as well. This 'fucking Russian' is surrounded in mystery and calculation."

"Then I think you'd better look into this brother to try to remove some of the mystery and reduce his room for calculation."

"I think you're right, Tom. And I think I know where to look."

"You mean our German friend from the Schuhmacher group?"

Baier smiled and sat back in his passenger seat while Hendricks pulled into the driveway of the house where Baier and Sabine were staying. "Yeah, the guy who spent those years in the concentration camp with the Soviet spies."

CHAPTER TWELVE

September 12, 1961

Wolfgang Hohrmann lived in the Schoeneberg district of Berlin, an area that had grown in importance with the city's division because that was where the Allies had set up the municipal government for West Berlin, in the Schoeneberg *Rathaus*, or city hall. The district was also not very far from Tempelhof airport, and Baier could hear the airplanes that approached the city as they flew low over the residential areas surrounding the runways for their landings. It was also an area he remembered well from his tour in the city after the war, particularly as one of those that had been more heavily bombed, with the residents finding what shelter they could in the ruins that lined the streets.

A lot had changed, though, over the last sixteen years, including on the left wing of German politics. According to Hendricks, Hohrmann lived in Sedanstrasse, a short walk from the Schoeneburg U-Bahn stop and not very far from the Schoeneberg *Rathaus*, where he worked in the administration of West Berlin's Social Democratic, or SPD, mayor Willy Brandt. Hendricks had gotten to know Hohrmann as a local contact and sometime informant, who worked closely with the Americans at the behest of Brandt. The mayor, who had fled to Norway and who had reportedly been active in the anti-Nazi resistance, recognized the value of establishing a close working relationship with the Western Allies and their various agencies active in Berlin if Germany was ever to establish a working and effective democracy. Not to mention a reunification under liberal and democratic auspices. And this was especially true for the American ones.

Hohrmann himself was an old-time SPD member and activist, having worked in the anti-Nazi resistance as well. Hohrmann also sat in the more conservative wing of the party, among the group known as the *Kanalarbeiter*, or 'sewage workers,' an homage of sorts for their background as true working-class adherents who recognized the threat posed by Communism in the East and the need for a close alliance with the more powerful Americans and their Western allies. But especially the Americans, and in this they mirrored their young and popular new leader. Accordingly, Hohrmann was also active in the Social Democratic faction known as the *Schumacheragenten,* or the Schumacher agents, named for the first postwar leader of the SPD, an inveterate anti-Communist. He had also been a firm anti-Nazi, which earned him years in a concentration camp.

The Schumacher group ran a network of Social Democratic assets who had stayed behind in the Soviet Zone after the forced merger of the Communist Party, or KPD, and Social Democrats, which together formed the SED, or *Socialistische Einheits Partei*, the Socialist Unity Party. It was anything but, of course, and the merger occasioned a massive flight of SPD members west. Still, Schumacher had succeeded in keeping some party members in place in the East, where they formed an active network that reported on developments and plans within the SED and the East German government more broadly. Unfortunately, the building of the new wall was making it more and more difficult to run those agents. And the prospects only looked worse, because of the restrictions on travel and contact the new system was creating.

Hohrmann had been lucky, Baier thought, to have landed in the city's western end after the war and to have found an apartment in one of the rebuilt apartment blocks along this street. Rather than the square, faceless structures thrown up to meet the drastic housing shortage that presented a tedious and squat façade, Hohrmann's building had been rebuilt on the ruins of one of those solid housing units that had sprouted during Berlin's imperial period in the second half of the last century, when Berlin had grown in political, economic, and cultural importance as a major European capital. The building had four stories and an exterior that harked back decades with its solid limestone front and carved stone window frames and doorways. This particular building had apparently survived the war with its foundation and walls still strong and intact. Or at least, Baier hoped so for the well-being of the residents there. But given the impressive foundation and thick walls, he figured they had little to worry about.

He also wondered what the interior would look like. When Hohrmann met him at the door of his third-floor flat, Baier encountered something of a disappointment. Rather than the old-world elegance he had imagined, something akin to what the Germans had known as *Biedermeier* and what the pictures of Baier's parents' childhood homes had resembled, Hohmann inhabited a clean and almost vacant space that had been created inside these magnificent old buildings. The carved wooden moldings so common that had lined the ceilings and doorways in decades past were gone, replaced by little more than a coat of paint. The plain walls and squared living spaces had probably been built according to a restructured interior that the city fathers had thrown up inside the shells of these older places, also in a hurry to accommodate the need for living space. Baier laughed inwardly at how the Nazi concept of *Lebensraum* had been recast on a much smaller and less grandiose scale to take care of single families and homeowners.

"What's so funny?" Hohrmann asked.

"Oh, nothing." Baier answered. "I was just thinking of one of the ironies of recent German history."

"Yes, I see," Hohrmnann said, motioning toward a sofa set against a tall bay window that looked out onto the street. "There have been quite a few of those in recent years."

Baier sat down and looked over a setting for an afternoon coffee so typical in German homes, what was known as the *Kaffeestunde,* or 'coffee hour.' The cups, saucers, and pot looked like an authentic set of Dresden porcelain, along with the mandatory cream and sugar bowls. There were also slices of German cheesecake and what looked to be a marzipan concoction as well. Baier had already set his sights on the latter.

"Please, help yourself, Herr Baier," Hohrmann offered, pouring a cup of coffee for himself and one for his guest. Baier did just that, reaching for a slice of the tempting marzipan treat. Hohrmann took a seat in a chair at the corner of the sofa where Baier sat, balancing a slice of the marzipan cake on a plate of the Dresden china resting on his lap. Hohrmann sat holding only a cup of coffee. The rest of the cakes looked to be present primarily for decoration or to provide Baier alone with a wide choice. It was then that Baier noticed the withered left arm that acted more as a balancing rod than a functioning appendage on Hohrmann. Most of the hospitality work had been performed by the right arm, with Hohrmann's left serving a supporting role that required no lifting, tucked as it was close to his waist. The skin of the hand also looked unusually pale and stretched over the bones of the hand, as though Hohrmann had to apply it each morning after he got up.

"What can I do for you? Herr Hendricks was not very forthcoming when he called this morning requesting that we meet. I assume there is a reason for his reluctance."

Baier nodded and tried to speak between bites. "You'll understand, of course, that there is not a lot I can say about the details of the case. But I was hoping you might be able to steer me towards someone who can speak to the Soviet, or more precisely, the Russian émigré communities that sprouted in Europe after the Bolshevik Revolution in 1917."

"Are you interested in the one that was established here in Berlin during our Weimar Republic? It was quite extensive, you know."

"Yes, perhaps that would help. But I was actually hoping for some information and leads elsewhere. For example, in Paris."

"Ah, I see. That will be more difficult, of course. And may I ask the reason for this?"

Baier paused to consider his response. The marzipan provided a convenient excuse, as Baier did not have to fake the pleasure he was experiencing eating this particular piece of cake. It took about a minute to finish. Hohrmann sat motionless and without expression, his visage broken only by the periodic sips from his coffee cup, which he moved to refill as Baier finished his own rich treat.

"Well, I have been following a Soviet officer, who has a family history here in Europe. It seems he lost touch with some siblings who fled the Revolution. I suspect at least one may have settled in Paris, but I am uncertain about the rest."

"How many were there?"

Baier held up his fingers. "Two that I'm aware of. There may have been more family members, but those are the only two I've ever heard mentioned."

"I see. And do you know the dates of their flight or what they did once they had escaped?"

Baier shook his head and set the plate back on the table to his front. He picked up his coffee cup, added just a dash of cream, and took a sip. "No, I'm afraid I do not have anything that specific. At least nothing beyond 1919 as their time of flight from the Soviet Union. The two siblings I am aware of may have traveled further to South America at some point, but that has not been confirmed. For all I know, the brother at least never left Paris. That is certainly where he ended up."

"Is he still alive?"

Baier sat back against the cushions and stared at the floor for a moment. "I don't think so. But I'm not sure."

"And what do you hope to do with this information?"

Baier looked into the eyes of the German. "I need to check on the Soviet officer's background, to establish his *bona fides*, as it were."

"And learning of the man's lost family members will do that?"

Baier continued to probe the German's face, his eyes. But his visage was that of a true professional, giving nothing away. Baier was relieved to notice that at least there was nothing hostile or skeptical in Hohrmann's look. "Yes, I believe it will." Baier paused and broke his stare to look out the window. "At least in part. It's a strange case."

Hohrmann replaced his own cup and saucer on the table. "Yes, it certainly appears to be." He looked up from the table at

Baier, who had returned his gaze to his host. "Is there anything else you can tell me about this Soviet officer? I assume he is KGB."

"I'd rather not say," Baier answered. But then he reconsidered. Like any intelligence professional, Baier was trained to keep information about an operation as close to his chest as possible. But there were times when he realized he would have to be a little more forthcoming. This was one of those. The man sitting across from him had lived a life that had almost certainly been more difficult and more challenging than that of just about anyone Baier had worked with in the past. And according to Hendricks, he had proven his partnership with the Americans and what they were trying to do in postwar Germany on numerous occasions. He had also shown himself to be a man of discretion. Still, Baier would share as little as possible. "I can give you that much, though. He is an active KGB officer, who is currently here in Berlin."

"Well, then, I might be able to help."

"That would be great. I would really appreciate any assistance you can give me."

Hohrmann sat back and crossed his legs. A cigarette appeared in his right hand, a quick and deft move from pocket to fingertips that spoke of years of practice. "Do you smoke, Herr Baier?"

Baier shook his head. "No, thank you."

"Then I hope you don't mind if I indulge." Baier shook his head again and smiled. "Thank you. Would you mind opening the window behind you?" Hohrmann asked.

Baier rose and walked to the window, which he opened with a shove after unlocking the latch. The sounds of Berlin's urban traffic rose through the opened space, mostly the occasional horn but also the roar of engines racing under the hands of German drivers. They were easily the most aggressive drivers Baier had ever known. Many could move through all four gears in the space of a single city block. And they often did.

Hohrmann continued. "I don't think there is much that I myself can do for you. The emigres and their work have not been something I have concerned myself with. Not directly, in any case. But I could introduce you to a colleague who is much better versed in these matters."

"Is he also an SPD member, one of the *Kanalarbeiter*?"

"Not exactly. But he is one of colleagues who stayed behind in the East."

"A *Schumacheragent*?"

Hohrmann smiled and nodded. "Yes, you might say that. But he has a different and much more interesting history. You see, he is one of the Volga Germans by birth who ended up here in Berlin after the war. In fact, his personal history in Germany extends to well before the war, but this is the city where he has lived since about 1949."

"I thought all of the Volga Germans were shipped further east by Stalin after the German invasion. He didn't think he could trust their loyalty with the *Wehrmacht* rolling eastwards so rapidly."

Hohrmann nodded. "Yes, they were. But this fellow was already here in Berlin at that point. You see, because of his language capability and German heritage he was sent here by the NKVD to work with the *Rote Kapelle*. You've heard of them, I am sure."

"Absolutely. The network of Communist agents working in Berlin. They were a very successful bunch, if I remember correctly."

"Yes, they were. But the Nazis were eventually able to capture most of them and break up the ring. This man, Ludwig Volkmann, was arrested and spent the last three years of the war in a concentration camp. However, because he had been arrested and imprisoned here, the Stalinists no longer trusted him. Many like him were treated just like the Soviet soldiers who surrendered to our forces or to you and the British. After the war they were all shipped to Siberia. In effect, they were betrayed by the Western Allies, who acceded to Soviet demands for their repatriation."

"Yes, I'm aware of that particular chapter in our postwar history. But it's not like they had an easy time living under the Nazi regime either. Weren't most of them used as slave labor?"

"No, you're correct, they did not. And, yes, most were exploited in that way. Those that did not starve to death. I guess you could say they were betrayed by all sides. In any case, Volkmann escaped and fled back to Germany. His family did not survive the forced expulsion to the east. Like so many others, his parents died during the journey, and his siblings passed away in captivity. So you see, he had nothing to stay behind for. He came to Germany to start a new life, as it were."

"But why settle in the East? I mean, after all that happened to him and his family in the Soviet Union?"

Horhmann smiled and gave Baier a condescending look. "Because he still believed in a Socialist future. Or he did at the time."

"So, I take it his commitment has wavered or weakened over the years."

The smile remained, but the look shifted to one more of understanding. "Yes, you could say that. He has had a difficult time in the East."

"What does he do there? How does he support himself?"

"Ludwig works as a journalist, independently. Or as much as he can. He does provide some articles for the party newspaper and government press, but periodically he also sends articles to the West. Under a pseudonym, of course. It has allowed him to earn some west Marks, as it were. We keep those funds in an account here in the West that he draws on periodically."

"I see. And how do you know him?"

Hohrmann leaned forward. "We were together in the Sachsenhausen concentration camp."

Baier hissed loudly as he inhaled. "I'm sorry. Hendricks did not tell me about that part of your past."

Hohrmann sat back and waved his right hand. Baier noticed that at this point, the left hand quivered slightly. "He probably did not think it was important for this meeting. But Volkmann and I became like brothers. We kept each other alive, and we have stayed in touch ever since. Socially and professionally."

Baier motioned toward Hohrmann's left arm that had remained nearly useless at his side throughout the conversation. "Is that where that happened?"

Hohrmann glanced to his side then back up at his guest. "Yes.

It would have been worse, and I probably would have lost the arm, perhaps even my life, if not for Ludwig. An SS guard had broken my arm during a beating one day, and Ludwig reset it and took care of me so that I did not starve or miss out on my work details, which would have led to a slow and agonizing death, probably by starvation if not an actual execution, as I am sure you are aware."

Baier sat back and blew out a breath that felt like it had been stuck inside his chest for minutes. "I am so sorry."

"That is over now. Fortunately, I have been able to do useful and productive work for Germany and a future that is free and democratic."

"And how would this man be able to help, if I may ask."

"I think he will be able to help because of his past work. If he does not have the information you seek, he may know someone who does. As a former espionage agent, Ludwig may have some knowledge of what was going on among the Russian emigres in Europe. Of course, that sort of thing was probably heavily compartmented, but in my experience, the Soviets can be quite careless. He also has some contacts among the KGB and Stasi today still. Not everyone considers men like Ludwig to have been traitors to the cause of Mother Russia and the Revolution."

"And you trust this man? Despite his past of working for Soviet intelligence?"

"With my life. And he has never let me down."

"Well, that's good to know."

Hohrmann stood. "Yes, it is. Because we will have to do it again. He lives in the East, and we will have to meet with him there."

"We?"

"Yes, he probably will not talk to you otherwise. After all, you are nonetheless an American. He dislikes your side only a bit less than he dislikes the Soviets."

"The lesser of two evils?"

"Exactly."

CHAPTER THIRTEEN

"Do you really think this will work?"

Baier glanced over at Hohrmann, who occupied the passenger seat in the blue Mercedes he had taken for the day's trip to the East. He had wanted something different in appearance from the car he had been driving on the other side, and this blue model was the best he could do. It didn't have to be perfect. It was just in case the likes of Gracchus were still on the lookout for him after his absence of a little over two weeks. Once, they checked his diplomatic passport, of course, they would be well-informed of his presence. That is, if the border guards had been instructed to inform their Stasi superiors as soon as they saw him. Baier hoped the check would be filed away in some anonymous drawer—or better yet, a waste basket or shredder. But even if they did inform the higher-ups, Baier and Hohrmann would still have a head start on any surveillance they might send out—time enough, he hoped, to get to the SPD safe house Hohrmann had selected for his meeting with the mysterious Herr Volkmann. If that was even the guy's true name.

"I think it will work just fine." Baier said. He took in his passenger, who leaned nonchalantly against the door on his side of the car. "As long as you keep your cool."

Baier had made sure to acquire a false set of documents for his passenger, since West Berliners were not permitted, at the moment, to visit the city's eastern half. Apparently, the regime considered this too much of a risk. Lord knows, Baier thought, just where this would all end.

"That sort of thing is important to you Americans, is it not?"

Baier laughed. "Well, it certainly is today. And especially for something like this."

The East German border guard and his Soviet companion gave the American and the West German, who squirmed just a bit as they studied his passport, little more than a condescending smirk. It was almost as though they couldn't care less, because their side had stolen a march on the stupid Americans and their German allies by acting so quickly and forcefully to separate the city's halves and solidify East German rule in this part of Berlin. It was something Khrushchev and Ulbricht, the East German leader, had been pushing for years, at least since the Kremlin's ultimatum about a separate peace treaty with the German Democratic Republic in 1958. And even earlier, like in 1948 when Stalin tried to force the Allies out of their western sectors in the city by cutting off their rail and road access.

"Enjoy your visit to the capital of the German Democratic Republic." The guard tossed the phrase almost perfunctorily at them in the bewildering Berliner dialect. The Soviet looked bored. He was already studying the car behind them.

"Up yours," Baier mumbled in his own American Midwestern slang.

To avoid any potential surveillance choke points, Baier sped down Friedrichstrasse to get to the other side of Unter den Linden and Alexanderplatz. Someone had once told him that during the height of the Imperial period, the former had been considered by many as a more beautiful promenade than even the Champs d'Elysee. That certainly did not apply now, Baier thought, and probably never would as long as the same crew was in charge over here. Building shells and littered sidewalks lined the once grand avenue and the streets behind. Maybe someday, though, he thought.

Although he was traveling away from the meeting site, Baier drove further out until he caught Elsasserstrasse and used that avenue to create a big loop back toward their starting point. He then found Frankfurter Allee and headed out towards Lichtenberg and Friedrichsfelde, two sections where the regime was throwing up huge apartment blocks to create some new housing for the proletariat. Along the way, Baier passed through more ruined neighborhoods that still looked as though they were nothing more than discarded shells and heaps of rubble. The newer buildings under construction did not look like much of an improvement, and he wondered how long they would survive since the regime didn't appear to bother with anything like maintenance in its five-year economic plans.

"Over here. Down this street," Hohrmann said. One side of the avenue had been razed, presumably for one of the new structures. The first street still had the old street sign, though, which said that this was Wagnerstrasse. Some bureaucrat must have missed his assignment on the street-name purification job, Baier thought. The second turn he took brought them to Hagenstrasse, where Hohrmann had him pull in behind one of the few structures that had survived the bombing and, thus far, at least, further demolition. The two men hustled inside, and Hohrmann led the way up a back set of stairs that brought them to a dark and damp flat that smelled as though someone has just applied a fresh coat of mold. The building also looked to be deserted.

Volkmann sat in a back corner, hidden almost entirely by a late afternoon shadow that escaped the border of sunlight breaking through the dirty glass in the window at his side. Baier was struck almost immediately by the man's small size and wafer-like thinness. At times he seemed to float on the fetid air in the room. That is, when he wasn't fading into the background behind him. It seemed as though Volkmann had yet to recover his health from those years in the concentration camp and the deprivation of life under Communist rule ever since. In fact, the most noticeable physical marker on the man was the mane of silvery, almost white, hair that spread back from his temples like a worn carpet. Baier asked himself if this almost invisible physical appearance had helped him hide so well in the years since the war. For people in power, it would be remarkably easy to forget someone like this. Then again, to survive for this long took more than physical skill alone.

There was no other furniture in the flat, so the two visitors remained standing in the center of the room, but out of line of sight from the window.

"Wolfgang said you needed my help," Volkmann stated. "I must admit that I had second thoughts about helping the Americans. I still do."

There, in that voice, Baier discovered the strength of this man, the inner confidence and resolve one needed to last for so long as a prisoner in the history of this city and this nation. First the Nazis, and now the Communists had persecuted but never defeated him. That much was clear.

"Why is that?"

"Because you represent to new Imperium, but it is one based on capitalist wealth."

"There's more to it than that. We have our own history and legacy, our own ideals. It's what gives us our appeal, our power."

"And yet, you still need my help."

"Yes." Baier glanced at Hohrmann, who nodded for him to continue. "I was hoping you could enlighten me on some Soviet or Russian refugees who fled to the West after the Bolshevik victory, and how they might have remained active in the politics and goals of either the Reds or the Whites."

The man smiled and then laughed with a strength Baier did not think the body possessed. "Is that all?"

"Yes, I know that is what we Americans call a 'tall order.' But any information you can give me will be of great assistance."

"Assistance for what?"

Baier looked over at Hohrmann with a question on his face, wondering what or how little his German companion had passed along. When he turned back to Volkmann, the Schuhmacher agent was shaking his head. "There is only so much one should divulge in a brief radio communication like ours. Surely, people from your organization are aware of that."

Baier nodded and shrugged. "Yes, yes, of course. I am sorry. You see, I'm trying to get a better picture of the actions and motivations of a Soviet KGB officer."

"A KGB officer? That would be difficult, if also impressive."

Again, Baier faced the dilemma of how much to divulge to a virtual stranger. It was clearly more of a risk that it had been with Hohrmann, a West German who had been cooperating with the Americans and Baier's own organization for many of the postwar years. This man had a slightly different pedigree, but he was still someone for whom Hohrmann vouched. And he did so with conviction. Plus, he already knew for whom Baier worked. Hell, Baier thought, in for a dime, in for a dollar. "I agree. It is impressive, or can be. He has offered to work with us."

"And you don't know much about this man or what motivates him? That's not a very promising start."

"Well, I have worked with him some in the past…"

"Then what can be the problem? Are you telling me you still don't know whether to trust him?"

"I thought I did know him and trust him. I mean, he even saved my life at one point."

A 'harrumph' erupted from the German host. "There could be any number of reasons to explain that. Perhaps it was simply convenient for him at the time."

"Yes, it certainly was. But I believe there was more to it. That wasn't the only time we cooperated."

"And you are still uncertain?"

"He is prepared to make it a more permanent arrangement, but something new has come up, and it involves the history of one of his siblings who supposedly fled to Paris in 1919 and was recently murdered by a Soviet assassin. Or so this KGB officer claims. It was his brother."

Volkmann leaned forward enough to bring his head and shoulders out of the shadows. "There were many Soviet citizens who fled to the West after the revolution, and a good many of them to Paris. But I am sure you are already aware of that."

"Yes, I am aware of that. But my problem goes further than that."

"And that would be?"

"I need to know what one of them in particular did, something that might have carried its repercussions through to our time."

"You are aware, of course, that many of them were also not truly fleeing. That they had been sent there to infiltrate the White counterrevolutionary groups. Dzerzhinsky was a master at creating counterespionage operations. The Soviets were able to penetrate all those groups and effectively destroy them. They and their money were ultimately manipulated for Soviet ends."

"Yes, I understand that. And I am well aware of Dzerzhinsky's abilities. That's why the crack East German border regiment has been honored with his name for their unit."

Volkmann smiled. "Yes, that is true."

"But what about after that? What happened to the few Whites who survived or may have wanted to travel onward to get further away from their Red enemies?"

Volkmann sat back in the darkness again. "Well that depends, of course, on the individual's history. What is the name of this KGB officer and his brother?"

Baier hesitated. Now, this was a step much farther along. To provide the true name of his contact would break every rule in the proverbial book about protecting your sources and methods. This was not the sort of thing you bragged about or even let slip if you could ever help it. It was why operations of this sort were so heavily compartmented, the information provided to only a select few with the ominous 'need to know' label. It was why assets like Chernov were given pseudonyms. And why even these were closely guarded.

Then again, this German, with all his history, all that he had experienced and survived, surely knew this. What secrets had he been privy to? What had he withheld during the years of torture and deprivation? If this man could not be trusted, what hope did Baier have to discover the truth behind Chernov's actions, his plans and intentions? Baier knew that there was a clear reason for his question, that he needed the information without which he could be of no assistance. And it was also a test for Baier, to determine how far the German could trust him, whether they would be working here as partners, as equals in the search for truth. If Baier could not trust Volkmann, as well as Hohrmann, that he would never unravel this new layer in the enigma of his 'fucking Russian.'

"His family name is Chernov."

A hiss broke from the darkness as though a snake had escaped. "What did you say? What was that name?"

"Chernov. Have you heard it before?'

After what felt like a full minute of silence, the voice whispered. "Yes."

It was all Baier heard for another minute.

"You say you have worked with this KGB officer before?" Volkmann continued.

"Yes." Baier could not think of anything else to say at that moment.

"And your KGB officer never spoke of his family's history?'

"Only once. Right after the war. My KGB friend was working in Berlin for his organizations predecessor..."

"The NKVD. Yes, I know it well. Too well, in fact."

"Yes, well, this particular Chernov fled to the West when he thought he had come into a large sum of money and wanted to reconnect with his siblings, who he believed had fled to South America."

"Which was not true, of course."

"No, apparently not. You know of them?"

Another minute of silence followed. Volkmann stared at the floor, as though weighing just what to divulge to the American and how to say it.

"Yes, I know of him. The brother in Paris, I mean. He worked for Dzerzhinsky's group, infiltrating the Whites. Paris was probably the main target of Soviet espionage back then."

"Not Germany or London?"

"No. no." Volkmann's head shook back and forth hard enough to shift his meager body weight. "True, Germany was one of the crippled losers from the war, and the Soviet leadership saw the future success of the world revolution hinging on Germany's emergence as the true source of Communist change. Most of the work there, at least in the early years, was to prepare for the German revolution, which they felt was sure to come. And when that failed after 1923, the focus was on stealing Germany's industrial and scientific secrets. No, after that Paris became the main focus for political and military espionage. That was where the real threat came from. Or so the Kremlin believed."

"But wouldn't Chernov have known of his brother's work?"

Another laugh broke from the corner. "That was all very well protected, of course. Surely your organization follows similar rules. The Kremlin would not let anything jeopardize the cover of their people in a place like Paris."

"Then how did you know?"

"Because I was in Berlin for many of those years between the wars."

"Until you were captured by the Nazis."

"That's correct. The Nazis were very affective at breaking up our networks. Even the famous *Rote Kapelle* only lasted until 1942."

"But why would you know of these operations in Paris?"

"Because Berlin was still the central place for communications back to Moscow. The communications systems were so much more primitive then. Direct links to the Kremlin were unheard of. So, everything went through Berlin, and there were a few of us who were aware of these operations because of our place as intermediaries. We also oversaw the flow of money to these agents."

Baier found himself pacing the room. This was all so much in so little time. The humid air in the room did not help either, and he could feel the patches of moisture under his armpits along with a line of sweat across his forehead. He moved in closer to Volkmann.

"So, what happened? Did the Chernov brother stay in Paris? Did he continue working for the Soviets?"

"Yes, he did. But once the Whites had been taken out of the picture, he helped run some of the student and journalist networks that provided reports on French industry and science. The Soviets were desperate, you see. They knew how far behind the West the

Soviet Union was, and they believed the only way to catch up to defend the Revolution from its enemies in the West was to steal those sorts of secrets…"

"Even though many of them were not actually secrets."

Volkmann smiled again, as though amused by this American's naiveté.

"There is little that the Soviets do not see as a secret, especially when it comes to the West. They feel very inferior, you know." He paused as though to rediscover the point in his narrative. "But I doubt the brother found this all very adventurous or exciting. Especially not since he taken up with the wife of a White general."

"What? The guy fell prey to an affair of the heart?"

"I think it was more an affair of the pants, or the groin, to be exact. She was very beautiful. Rumor had it that the Chernov sibling was completely smitten, and that she convinced him to betray his contacts in the network first to the French police and then to the Germans after 1940."

"Do you believe that?"

Volkmann shook his head. "I am not sure what to believe in this story. The network was most certainly betrayed, but just what this Chernov's role in it was remains a mystery to me. The White general's wife may have been the culprit after some irresponsible pillow talk. She may even have been what you Americans refer to as a 'honey trap,' sent to seduce someone like this innocent Russian boy."

"He was surely a good bit older by then," Baier said.

"Yes, but perhaps still a boy in these kinds of matters."

Baier paced some more, looking at Hohrmann, who had remained motionless throughout the session, standing off to the side, his right hand thrust deep into his pockets, while his left dangled by his side. Baier then turned to Volkmann, who was once more leaning forward.

"But that was quite a while ago," Baier continued. "Surely, it would not take this long for a Soviet assassin to find the alleged traitor."

"Not if the traitor was working and living alone, without any help."

"So, you're saying that Chernov's brother had help?"

"I cannot say for certain, but he would have been connected to some of those working as illegals."

"Illegals? But don't they surface only when they have their own sources of information or people they've recruited. They wouldn't work in a support function, would they?"

Volkmann shrugged. "That depends on what the needs of Moscow Center are. If it was a matter of support for someone who was himself deep under cover, an illegal of his own, as it were, then that's what they would do. Who would be better placed to keep in contact with these people and not betray their presence?"

"So, you think there was an illegal who may have helped the Chernov brother hide from his former Soviet masters."

"Not exactly."

Baier sighed in exasperation. "Please, no riddles."

"I apologize. But you see, I know that this Chernov became active in Soviet intelligence after the war once again. And I believe it was an illegal in Paris who helped."

"So, he stayed in France throughout? He never went to South America?"

Volkmann shrugged again. It seemed take most his energy to make such a simple movement. "That I cannot say. I cannot speak to all his time and movements."

"So, what can you speak to?"

"I can tell you that it was recently discovered that a certain illegal operating in Paris had been close to this Chernov sibling and provided much assistance in helping him contact the NKVD. He also resisted instructions—no, orders—to betray Chernov's location." Volkmann smiled again. "It seems the KGB does not forgive and forget so easily. And they found him in any case."

"And who was this illegal in Paris?" A chill moved up Baier's spine before traveling to settle in his stomach in a flutter of nausea. He was afraid he already knew the answer.

Volkmann smiled, but this was not the result of condescension or wonder at the American's lack of insight or experience. It was a product of anticipation, a sense that he was about to betray a secret that would confuse the American all the more, as though everything that had come before had been little more than a prelude.

"Ah, this is where it gets truly interesting," Volkmann announced.

"How so? What can you tell me of this other man?'

"I do not know his name. But he is a large, overweight individual, someone who moves ponderously slow. He is not a very ambitious or effective intelligence officer. More of a plodder, who survives by keeping his head low."

Baier thought back to the individual he had seen with Chernov in Paris and Rome, deep in discussion, exchanging brush passes. And it fit. Yes, it did. This must be the man who had helped Chernov stay on the move and perhaps even locate the Ukrainian killer, just the sort of assistance Chernov would have needed. And he had gotten this help from an active Soviet illegal.

"How is it that you know so much about these men now?"

"Our Soviet allies are not nearly as discreet as they should be nowadays. And I still have friends here in the East, including among the Stasi, people who were also active in the underground during the war." Volkmann paused as he studied Baier. "My guess, though is that the fat man's days are numbered, if they are not indeed already over."

Baier had resumed his pacing as he thought the whole scenario through. He halted at these words, however, and glanced at the German over his shoulder. "Why do you say that?"

"Because the death sentence is still hanging over the head of this illegal in Paris despite the death of the younger Chernov brother." Here, Volkmann paused to magnify the impact of the words that would follow. "And your KGB friend Chernov is the one with the order to execute the man."

Now that did not fit in with the scenario Baier had developed.

• • •

That evening Baier sat on the back patio of the temporary residence where he and Sabine were staying. Their chairs were close together, and the two were holding hands. Sabine had said that she felt a slight chill in the air, a warning of autumn perhaps. Baier had stepped inside and returned with a shawl that he spread over her shoulders. He reclaimed his seat next to her. After a minute or so, he reached for her hand. He had not said a word since they had moved outside. Baier simply stared at the line of tall pine trees that circled the back of their yard.

His thoughts were interrupted by the ringing of the telephone. Sabine rose and went inside to answer it. She returned with the phone in her hand, a long extension cord running from the socket in the living room just outside the patio door.

"It's Tom. It does not sound like good news."

"How do you mean?" Baier asked.

"He doesn't sound very happy." She handed the receiver to her husband.

"Karl," Tom Hendricks said, "your friend has done it again."

For whatever reason, Baier was not surprised by the news. "You mean he's back in the East?"

"That's right. Apparently, he couldn't wait for you to take him. But he did leave some contact instructions. For tomorrow. I can show them to you in the morning."

Son of a bitch, Baier thought. I wonder who else the Russian prick has shown them to.

"Any word from Paris yet on the information we got from this so-called Russian friend of ours?" Baier asked.

Baier could almost feel Hendrick's head shaking through the line. "Nope. That particular fellow appears to have disappeared."

"Thanks, Tom. I'll be in your office tomorrow early. Eight o'clock."

"Sure thing, Karl. And sorry about this. Try to get some sleep. It could be a long day tomorrow. Give my best to Sabine."

Just one more fucking surprise from this fucking Russian, Baier thought. He could feel the heat rise to his cheeks as the muscles in his chest tightened. He swore to himself in a half whisper that even Sabine may have heard. If he has been playing me and if this whole operation all goes belly up, I'll kill the son of a bitch.

CHAPTER FOURTEEN

Chernov's note called for a meeting at Alexanderplatz. He had left it lying under a jar of strawberry preserves on the kitchen table at the safe house in Mexicoplatz. He had written it for a meeting in Potsdamerplatz, which as Baier and just about every other living person in Berlin was aware, was a virtual impossibility, since Potsdamerplatz, once the busiest traffic circle in Europe, was now split between the city's two halves. But there was space on the western side of the wall to observe the construction underway, which, of course, was hardly possible when one of the two parties was stuck in the eastern half. Chernov and Baier had long ago agreed that this would simply mean they should look for each other in Alexanderplatz, which had become the traffic and pedestrian center of East Berlin. That made the square an ideal place to meet. Unfortunately, that also made it difficult to pick out possible surveillance. The two men had also agreed that the time of the meeting—listed as 10:00 in the note—would actually be an hour and a half later. So Baier knew he should be at the square no later than 11:00 to do what observation he could with time to spare before meeting his Russian renegade. Given his recent suspicions about Chernov, Baier decided to aim for 10:30 this time around. Which also meant, of course, that he should put in a good hour or so of countersurveillance on his way to the meeting. If so, he had to get an early move on for the drive east, do some countersurveillance, find a safe place to leave his car, and so on.

As he had expected, Baier found Alexanderplatz crowded and somber. There were even more people wandering through the patch of concrete and blacktop than usual, almost all of them dressed in light plaids and solid shirts made of thin cotton, and almost all with downcast eyes, jaws firmly set, and furrowed brows. Since they were now well into the second week of September, many wore thin windbreakers or jackets made of grey or brown polyester. It was not that cold yet, but most appeared to do so more out of habit than comfort. Couples whispered to each other through the sides of their mouths, their gazes darting among the many faces that surrounded them. One could never be sure who was there on official business and who was there to take a morning stroll or get in some shopping. Not that there was a whole lot available. A good number, more than half, strolled in the direction of the new wall, as though on their way to study a new curiosity. But they walked very slowly, afraid to push their pace toward newly forbidden territory. It was as if they knew they had lost an important part of their city, their history, and for many, their families.

Baier strolled around the square for what seemed like thirty to forty minutes, but then took his position at the corner of a sausage stand that was selling bratwurst and the Berliner specialty, *curry wurst*. He had never understood the Germans', and especially the Berliners', fascination with this odd mixture of curry powder and ketchup that they would tuck their sausages into with such dedication and seeming delight. Granted, it was a post-war invention and one that took off during the country's occupation several years after the end of the war. So, the Americans were partly to blame. And it could be found elsewhere in Germany, even the Rhineland. But it had become a Berlin specialty, and why would anyone, he wondered, substitute that mash for good old German mustard? And how could so many Germans come to like it? What the hell, he concluded, and ordered one. Besides, it might help his cover.

With people and faces swarming around him, Baier actually found it difficult to distinguish one individual from the other, and, more important, to remember those features that would separate the repeat encounters from the innocent passersby. Once, he moved to the edge of the square and all the way to Breitestrasse to see if he had any tails, but no familiar faces or memorably clothed pedestrians crossed or followed his paths. No cars repeated themselves either as he strolled along the sidewalk.

He had settled into the corner near the sausage stand and worked his way through the *wurst* with as little of the curry concoction as possible. At least the French fries—or *pommes frites*, as they were known here—tasted good. After about 15 minutes Baier noticed the Russian walking towards him. He was moderately late, as usual, but by no more than another 15 or 20 minutes, as though operating on a quickened Moscow clock. But this time, he also acted oddly. Rather than the normal, arrogant smile, his face was set in a deep frown, his mouth and eyes pulled wide with anxiety. Not only that, but he was dressed in a long tan raincoat that looked like it had come from a Burberry's store somewhere in the West, one that covered a nice maroon V-neck sweater that appeared smooth enough to be cashmere. What the hell was he playing at, Baier wondered. This was not exactly one what one would call a discreet sense of fashion, not in this neighborhood. And why the funny face?

When he was about 20 yards from Baier, Chernov glanced to either side and shook his head. The American turned to go, dumping his remnants of curry *wurst* into a trash bin and making his way through the throng of idle civilians towards Unter den Linden, where he hoped the slow moving mass would give him the time and opportunity to escape. After about ten steps, however, Baier felt the barrel of one of those ubiquitous Makarov semi-automatics in the small of his back. The standard Soviet military pistol was also the favorite of the KGB and their henchmen behind the Curtain. And he hated the damn things. Too many memories, and none of them pleasant.

Baier spun, sweeping his arm behind him to deflect the weapon and free himself from his pursuer, who he hoped would certainly not fire in such a crowded environment. As it turned out, he didn't have to. Another Makarov pistol rammed itself hard into his stomach, and Baier doubled over from the pain and shock as his breath felt like it had just blown itself across the square and as far as the Brandenburg Gate. Baier dropped to his knees, and an arm that felt as though it was made of concrete slammed against the back of his neck. That sent Baier rolling down even further, landing on the ground and spread eagle. He started to pull himself up on his knees to make another attempt at escape, when a pointed leather shoe caught him in the ribs and ended the battle. Such as it was.

When Baier looked up, he saw Chernov standing over him, each arm in the firm grip of men in long, black leather coats. They wore fedoras to hide their faces, but the grim visages looked familiar enough after Paris. And once again, he was down on the ground and aching.

"You bastard," Baier breathed. He meant it mostly for Chernov, but these two creeps would do just as well.

Chernov simply swung his head back and forth, a look of sorrow and shame covering his face. His mouth started to move, but a sudden jerk on his arm by one of thugs ended that effort.

"I warned you, you American son of a bitch." The words stormed at Baier in a stream of spittle from a face he had hoped to forget. He had hoped never to see this Stasi prick again, but that now seemed so futile. It was the cruel and hard visage of Johann Gracchus, who had bent himself almost double to bring his own face close to Baier's. And he wore a look of total triumph.

• • •

He collapsed in the back seat of the Wartburg and leaned with his head against the window on the passenger side. For some reason, Baier kept trying to remember if the car's color was brown or simply a dirt-covered shade of something similar, as though that might be important at some point. It did help him shove the pain further away from the present, though. For brief moments at least. The route they were taking was eerily familiar, as the car sped down Frankfurter Allee. When the Wartburg turned onto Wagnerstrasse and then once more to Hagenstrasse, Baier's stomach clinched and then turned, as a wave of nausea churned deep inside his body and soul. Had they known all along? Oh Lord, he prayed, please let us enter this building alone and not have anyone waiting for us in the apartment. Volkmann deserves better than this, he thought.

His prayers were answered, at least initially. It was the first thing that had gone right all morning. All in all, the day was turning out to be a disaster. First, the parking had been a bitch, then the *currywurst*, and now this. The flat was empty, except for a set of chairs, the one in the center of the room looking as though it had been there since Baier's last meeting here. But it also had three companions now. A single light bulb dangled from a lonely chord that ran across the ceiling and then down about eight feet shy of the floor in the center of the room. Baier did not remember the light from the last time he had been in this flat. In fact, he did not remember any illumination at all, except for the thin streams of sunlight that had made their way through the window—still crusted with the same dirt, presumably—from the street outside. Even that light seemed weaker and more desperate. There was no other sign of occupancy, of life even, in the entire flat. The desolation was so overpowering that Baier wondered for the second time if there were even other people in the building, or if it was occupied by anything other than a crowd of rats. The animal kind. We brought the human ones, he conceded.

The two thugs from Alexanderplatz and the car dragged Baier up the stairs, and the black-coated heavyweight on his right threw Baier into one of the chairs. He thought it was probably the one Volkmann had sat in when he was here last. Now that he could see them clearly, the two thugs were most definitely those from the encounter in Paris and a couple earlier ones in Berlin as well. Baier wondered if these two men had been assigned as part of his personal detail. He swiveled his head for a quick search to see if his other acquaintance in the Stasi, Joachim Hoehn, was also present. Baier did not see him, but he was unsure if this was a good or a bad thing.

Gracchus approached slowly, the better to draw out his victory. When his face appeared to be no more than inches away from Baier's Gracchus reached up, grabbed a tuft of Baier's hair, and pulled Baier's head back away from his own.

"Does this look familiar, Herr Baier? I would think so."

"What the hell are you playing at Gracchus?"

"This is our way of letting you know that we are on to you and that bastard Volkmann. We've discovered your little game, and we mean to end it. Today."

"I think you're shy a few people and quite a few facts, asshole."

"No, you are right. We do not have that traitorous bastard Volkmann yet. But we will."

"Piss off. I don't know what you're talking about."

"Oh, but I am sure that you do. Would you care to tell us how we can find him? It might convince us to go easier on you."

Baier swallowed as he struggled to catch his breath. "Why call him a traitor? If he ever met with the likes of me he's the one who's remained true to his principles. You're the bastard who let himself get sucked in by Stalin's charms. Was that life in the horrors of the Hotel Lux really so charming and luxurious?"

"What would a capitalist, imperialist bastard like you know of the sacrifices we made back then? What it all means today, and why we are not going to let you destroy what we have achieved thus far here in Germany?"

Baier let his head rotate slowly from side to side before looking Gracchus in the face. "Achieved? You haven't done a damn thing worth saving."

Gracchus's face held the smile of a man who considered himself infallible. He dropped his grip on Baier's hair, swung his arm to the side, then brought it hard across his prisoner's mouth. Baier could taste the blood as it pooled along the side of the teeth in his lower jaw. He worked it into a bullet of spittle, then spat the entire load in Gracchus's face.

That brought help to the Stasi officer in the form of his two companions, who threw Baier on the floor and proceeded to kick his legs, buttocks, and ribs.

"That's enough," Gracchus said. The two East German sidekicks lifted Baier back into his chair. Then they jerked his arms behind the back of the chair and tied his wrists together. "It's too bad your friend Hohrmann didn't come with you today," Gracchus continued. "My colleagues and I would enjoy interrogating him as well."

Baier looked up at his captor, a move that brought immediate pain on his right side and down along the lower back. He tried to shift his weight but the new constraints made that nearly impossible. And now, along with the threat that his immediate predicament held, there was a new mystery, one that loomed in the back of Baier's mind as possibly even more portentous. Just how did this bastard know about Volkmann and Hohrmann? First the encounters in Paris and Rome, and now here?

"You are going to pay for this, you asshole," Baier spluttered. "You cannot treat an American diplomat in this way."

Gracchus leaned back and a burst of laughter erupted from his face. He glanced at his companions, smiling broadly as he pointed his right index finger at the American. "Diplomat? That's a good one, Mister CIA agent. You've been apprehended on an illegal voyage of sabotage in the German Democratic Republic, demonstrating precisely why we need to build our protective barrier to seal off your half of our capital until you leave."

"That's quite a speech. Have you been rehearsing it for long?"

Gracchus drew back his hand again but then seemed to think better of it. Instead, he leaned in close. "Long enough. Most of this summer, in fact."

Gracchus sat back in one of the chairs opposite Baier and seemed to consider his position and that of his captive before speaking again. "If you want to live, if you ever want to see your lovely wife again, you will tell us where we can find your friend Volkmann."

"What makes you think I know where that man is?"

Again, Gracchus looked at his colleagues before studying Baier's face. "We know you Americans are running people like him here in the East. It's the only way they can survive."

Baier used what little strength he had to shake his head in disgust and disbelief. "You really are a fool, Gracchus. You and the rest of your gang. You are simple, ideological fools."

"Oh, come now. Surely you do not want to die in a hovel like this. What a disappointment for a lackey like yourself. Have you thought about how poorly you've been served, about how they've abandoned you and left your fate in our hands? I mean, look at this place."

"No, and why should I? Hell, I'm the one who gets to drive the Mercedes. Besides, this pathetic hole of a room is on your turf. Have you forgotten where we are? I've never even met this man Volkmann, you fool. But I wish I had. Especially if he's as courageous as you make him out to be. Do you want to know why people like him cooperate with people like me?"

The smile had not moved. "Why?'

"Because they realize what pigs you and your sidekicks are and how little hope there is for this country as long as you are in charge. That you will never build a truly socialist state here, or anywhere else. It's all about power with you pricks. It has nothing to do with justice or equality."

Gracchus turned away slowly and motioned in Baier's direction to his two colleagues. For some reason they untied his hands. Probably to make it easier to toss him around without breaking anything. They threw Baier to the floor and set themselves upon the American with a relish that astonished even Gracchus, who grabbed them by the arms to restrain them after what was probably less than a minute. To Baier, it felt like over an hour.

Baier uncupped his hands from his groin and hugged his midsection. He lifted his head about two inches off the floor and looked into the eyes of his captors. They seemed to have become bored. He realized they never really expected him to reveal the whereabouts of Volkmann, or that he even knew where the man was. They had simply wanted to deliver a message to the interloping American. If Baier had revealed anything, then that would have been an unexpected treat, dessert, as it were.

"If you really want to find out what you need to know, why not ask your friend, the Russian."

Gracchus paced the room before approaching Baier. "You mean Chernov?"

Baier started to nod but then caught himself. He simply let his head drop back to the floor.

"That Russian bastard is probably in Karlshorst by now. And he's going to get a lot worse once he arrives than you ever did today."

Baier rotated his head without lifting it off the ground. "What do you mean?"

"That traitor will be lucky to last five minutes before they put a bullet into the back of his skull."

"How did you find him?"

"He stumbled into our path. The man got overconfident and careless. Just like you."

"What do you mean?"

"We traced his movements after he crossed back over. Once he led us to you, we gave him to our Soviet comrades." Gracchus rose to his full height, hands planted on either side of his waist. "We're wrapping up all your western operations on our soil now and taking control of the game on our home turf. You'll see."

"Taking control from whom?" Baier asked.

"From everyone," Gracchus replied.

"From the Soviets?"

Gracchus stared at Baier for a moment before answering. "From everybody."

CHAPTER FIFTEEN

September 14, 1961

The rest of that day and the night that followed was more like a blur than reality for Baier. He wasn't sure how long he had slept, but he did remember waking up to watch the sun set as it casts shadows across the dimly lit room that seemed to dance with the weak yellow glow from the ceiling fixture. His captors had probably left the light on to make his sleep as uncomfortable as possible. But at least they did not replace the bonds on his hands or arms, which allowed him to wriggle on the floor for some small bit of comfort, despite the pain each and every movement caused. He also managed to get a ride, crammed in the back seat of one of those new Trabants while the couple in the front periodically looked back in awe and suspicion.

"A mugging, you say," the driver muttered. "Maybe we do need this new wall, like our government says."

"*Nein,*" Baier replied through a swollen jaw. "*Diese waren unser.*" These were ours. Baier explained that he had gotten too close to the construction, and the border guards had responded immediately, despite his cries of innocence. He also laid on his best imitation of a Saxon accent to give his report some credibility.

"*Mein Gott,*" the woman in the passenger seat exclaimed. "What is happening to us? Will the Americans invade, do you think?" she asked, her eyes wide in anxiety and anticipation.

"*Wenn wir Glueck haben,*" Baier slurred, as his lips began to bleed again. If we're lucky.

The driver shrugged, while the woman nodded.

Once he got to his car by Alexanderplatz, Baier sat inside for a few minutes, collecting his strength and going back over the evening. He was pretty sure no one would bother him anymore. The message had been delivered to Baier, and now it was his place to spread it further in the western half, especially among his American colleagues. Gracchus he could figure out. That guy had his own reality, his own sense of purpose, to which Baier's repeated presence on the eastern side posed a real threat. And his own words had only infuriated the man. So, the bastard had dealt with it in the best and most gratifying way he knew how. If he couldn't run an operation to expose the Americans' perfidy and wrap up his sources, then a good, old fashioned thrashing would have to do the trick. Along with some threats about future action as well. And there was no way he would ever see the world through Baier's eyes and vision of what was right and wrong.

But what about Chernov? Had he betrayed the meeting and its location, as Gracchus suggested? But if so, then why? If it was a professional operation—which is what Baier would expect of the Russians and even the East Germans, whether they were working together or not—why not continue the charade and get what he could from the Americans until he ran them dry? Baier could not be certain that this was what exactly was going on, but in light of the day's events, it did make some amount of sense. Now that the eastern side had secured Berlin—or at least it's eastern half, while making access to the western part for East Germans all but impossible—they could undercut the vast array of operations run throughout East Germany by the Western Allies and their West German friends. Jesus, he exclaimed, the son of a bitch Gracchus had actually bragged about it. Baier imagined that the prisons were filling up already with the reporters and assets that had been run so successfully for the last fifteen years by simply bringing them to the openness of Berlin for their debriefings and assignments. So, did this mean they had completed their work, and that now it was time to even the proverbial score with the Americans, as well as the Brits and any others they worked with?

But what was he to make of Cheronov's worried and anxious appearance at Alexanderplatz when the net was dropped? And his sudden disappearance? And the ominous words of Gracchus about what Chernov could expect once he got to Karlshorst? Or was it all simply part of the charade?

Screw it, Baier thought. I've had enough for one night. He fired up the Mercedes, which some lout had scraped with his key, leaving a long trail of contempt along the driver's side of the car. I guess he wanted to make sure I saw it, Baier concluded. He drove straight home, not even bothering to stop at the check point. Instead, he just flipped the bird to the East German border guard when he approached. Yellow and white rubber barriers scattered as Baier crashed through and sped away into the western night.

• • •

"My God, Karl, what have they done to you?" Sabine stood unmoving inside the front door of their quarters in Dahlem. She was too shocked to move, but after about half a minute, she rushed forward and took her husband in her arms. "Do you need to go to the hospital?"

Baier threw his right arm around her shoulder and moved toward the stairs. He pressed the soft, thick cotton of her robe against his shoulder. For some reason this felt so reassuring. "No, I'd rather just go upstairs and lie down for about a year. I think I'll be all right."

"Are you sure?" Together they navigated the stairs and stepped into the bedroom. "Please, Karl, let me get a warm towel or something to clean you up."

Baier laid down on the bed and kicked off his shoes. "Yes, thank you, Sabine. That would be nice." The room began to swim around him, so Baier propped himself on his left arm and leaned toward the bathroom, where he could hear his wife gathering towels and medicines while the water tap ran. She returned with her arms full of succor.

"Here, let me undress you."

Sabine pulled his jacket off, then unbuckled his pants and unbuttoned his shirt. Within about twenty minutes she had Baier clean, in his pajamas, and tucked in under the covers. "Who did this to you? And why?"

"The Stasi."

"Not the KGB?"

Baier shook his head as lightly as he could. "No, they weren't even there. I'm pretty sure now that this was an East German operation from the start."

"But what did they want?" She leaned back for a moment. "And why didn't you give it to them? They could have killed you."

"No, they only wanted to use me as an envelope."

"What? Karl, I think you're delirious."

"No, Sabine. You see, they had a message to deliver. That the game has changed. That this is their town now. That the game as it's been played for the last decade and a half is over. They want to set the new rules."

"But then why even play at all?"

"Because this town, this spot on the map is too important. It's where our two sides meet, face-to-face. It's where we've been fighting the Cold War, and where we've worked the hardest to get the information we need to read Soviet plans and intentions."

"But surely not only here, Karl."

"No, of course not. But it's been the one place where we are in direct contact. And it's been a very advantageous place for us thus far. So, we've got to find some new rules of our own. We can't let them push us out. It's not right. And there would be hell to pay in the future if we did. You see, that's why Chernov could be so important, to give us a heads-up on what sorts of things the Kremlin has planned."

"And the East Germans? Can Chernov help there?"

"No, I doubt it. That's something we're going to have to prepare for on our own."

Sabine patted her husband's head and stroked his arm. "That's okay, Karl. That's enough for now. You've made your point. To me, at least." She stood. "But before you fall asleep, you need to call Tom Hendricks."

Baier looked at the clock on his night table. "But it's after ten o'clock, Sabine. Can't it wait?"

She shook her head. "Not according to Tom, it can't. He's been worried sick and even sent some officers out to look for you in the East. He said you should call the minute you get back."

"But before I do that that, Sabine, you must tell me what is happening with your parents?"

"I'll explain all that tomorrow. There's been some good news. First, talk to Tom."

Baier rolled from the mattress and stood on shaky legs. Sabine helped him into a bathrobe, and then down the stairs to the telephone in the living room by the bay window that looked out on the tree-shaded street running past the front of the house.

"So, what the hell happened to you, Karl?" Hendricks asked. "And are you all right?"

Baier explained his night's adventure to the local chief of base. "But I'm okay. Or I should say I don't think there's any lasting damage."

"Well, we'll get you to a hospital in the morning to make sure. And we'll find a way to make those bastards pay."

"Both sound like pretty good ideas to me, Tom. But right now, I just need a good night's rest. Can we make an appointment for later in the morning, or even the afternoon?"

Baier could hear Hendricks breathing through the line. It lasted for ten, maybe fifteen seconds. "What is it you're not telling me, Tom?"

"Karl, we're having a visitor tomorrow. Your boss. Well, actually both our boss. But yours more immediately."

"Who? Fred Hagerty, the division chief?"

Baier could almost see Hendricks nodding at the other end of the line. "That's right. He flew out here today from Washington, and he wants to meet with you first thing. I'll delay as long as I can. Maybe we can even come by your place rather than make you drive in here to the office."

"What does he want to talk about?"

"Can't you guess? Karl, be sure you've lined up your ducks

on this operation, why you've persisted, and what your buddy over there can bring us. That is, if you still think he's playing it straight with us." Hendricks paused, as though he was thinking of something for the first time. "By the way, where was he when all this was going down? I take it he was not at Alexanderplatz."

"Oh, he was there all right. At least at the beginning."

"Then what? He waved goodbye and sailed off into a red sunset?"

"Not exactly. According to my new East German best friend, our man is in loads of trouble of his own with his superiors and has been arrested."

"Do you believe him?"

"Tom, at this point and the way I feel, I'm not sure what to think. He may have led the East Germans to our meeting at Alexanderplatz, but I only have Gracchus's word for that. The only thing I believe in right now is the benefit of a good night's sleep. I'll sort it out at some point."

"As the heroine said in a movie once, Karl, tomorrow's another day. You can worry about it tomorrow."

"Well, it's been a while since I've seen that film, and I think that's not what she said exactly. But you're close enough."

CHAPTER SIXTEEN

September 15, 1961

If anything, Baier felt worse the next morning. Maybe it was the lack of sleep. The clock read 8:15 when he awoke. He couldn't remember how long he had lain in bed before falling asleep. More likely, though, he was pretty sure it must be the soreness and pain from the night before settling in throughout his body. His ribs ached, and all his leg and arm muscles—which had absorbed the bulk of his beating—felt stiff and sore. But that was nothing compared to his head. That felt like it was stuck in a vise, and he could barely stand to move his jaw. The inside of his mouth felt as though it was edged in sandpaper whenever he moved his tongue. At least none of the teeth were broken. As best he could tell.

The only sign of relief came when Sabine sat on the edge of the mattress with a cup of coffee and a pair of aspirin. Those he gulped down with about a third of his coffee, black. Then he let his head nestle gently back into the soft, warm folds of his pillow.

"Are you still against a trip to the hospital?" Sabine asked.

"No, not really. But I need to see what my schedule today looks like. Apparently, there's a visitor from Washington in town."

"I know. Mister Hagerty. Tom called a little while ago. They're going to come over here to make it all a little easier on you."

"When? Did he say?"

Sabine nodded and reached for his mug. "Yes, he did. Around ten. So, you don't have a lot of time. I'm guessing you'll be moving rather slowly today. Do you think you can handle some breakfast?"

Baier propped himself against the pillows and headboard. "Not really." He drank another mouthful of coffee, then passed the cup to Sabine. He pushed the covers down to his legs and started what looked to be a long, difficult process of getting out of bed.

"Just a minute, Karl." Sabine placed a hand on his arm. "I want to bring you up to date on my parents."

Baier laid back down. "My God, that's right. I'm so sorry, Sabine. Please. How are they? And where are they?"

Sabine cradled the empty coffee mug in her lap. "They are here in Berlin. In the East still. Staying with some friends of mine from the postwar days."

"How did you arrange that?"

"I've been in touch with the man I mentioned before, the one organizing escapes from the east, through his brother here in the West. He agreed to take them in temporarily."

"Temporarily? How does that help? Just what is going on, Sabine?"

"Karl, they are ready to come out. This man began working on a tunnel as soon as the barriers went up."

"That can't be more than a month ago." Baier thought for a moment. Thinking was hard enough, let alone doing math. "God, it's just September 15, and the wall started going up on the 13th last month. Jesus, Sabine, that's just over a month ago. Did he start the very same day? And how the hell did he escape notice?"

"Because he's what you might call a professional, Karl. They only work at night, of course. Most of them, anyway. The people who live in the house they're using can do some more during the day, but only a little. And they can only dig so much because they have to distribute the dirt around the city. Take too much out or leave too much collecting nearby, and the police will know that something is up. Then they start inspecting all the buildings in the neighborhood."

Baier wiped his forehead with a bare hand and pushed his hair back. "Of course. That does make sense. But then wouldn't he need more time?"

"Normally, yes. But they chose a site close to the new wall and at a spot where they won't have to go under the River Spree, so they don't have to dig too far down. Plus, the people who live there in the house and are helping will be coming out with them. They also did not have to dig very far. And it's not in the city center. It's to the southwest, not far from Potsdam."

"And your parents?"

"He's agreed to let my parents join the group coming out. That's why they're staying with him temporarily."

"But aren't they afraid that could draw attention? I mean, won't someone like the neighbors notice the extra people?'

"They haven't been there that long. They only arrived two days ago. And if they stayed somewhere else, a neighbor there might raise an alarm when my parents leave suddenly."

"Either that, or your parents' friends would probably get arrested for aiding 'flight from the Republic.' God, *Republikflucht*. Only a regime like the one over there could create such a word." He shifted the position of his head to take in Sabine. "When do they go?"

"In two days."

"Holy Jesus, Sabine. That's pretty damned soon. Is everything really ready?"

"They have to move quickly, Karl. The longer you wait, the greater the chance of discovery."

"But are you ready, Sabine? Is there anything you want me to do?"

Sabine stood. "I want you to be there with me in case anything happens." She held out her hand when Baier started to protest. "I know you can only do so much in a situation like this. But one never knows what unexpected challenges will arise, Karl. Things rarely go according to plan. You of all people should be aware of that."

Baier slid his legs over the side of the mattress and stood slowly, warily. When he realized he could keep his balance, Baier looked into his wife's eyes and sat back down on the edge of the bed. "You're right, Sabine. Whatever you need. I'll be there. Regardless."

• • •

When his visitors arrived, Baier was seated in the living room in an armchair at the end of the sofa and near an open window. Baier heard the car drive up and the doors open and slam shut. Neither man wore a topcoat, only the jackets to their dark suits, as though they had arrived for a funeral. The faces of both men were hardened and glum, looking like they had bad news to deliver. Very bad news. About a minute later Sabine led Baier's two colleagues, Hendricks and Hagerty, in from the front door. Both men thanked her and took seats on the sofa after Sabine had pointed to the furniture near her husband. Hagerty set his light brown homburg on the table to his front.

Hendricks nodded at the hot water bottles on either side of Baier's ribs. "Heat?" Baier nodded. "Ice would be better, even if doesn't feel as good at first. It's better for keeping the swelling down."

"Thanks, Tom. But right now my concern is more for the pain and discomfort. And this certainly helps with that."

"Along with a good dose of aspirin," Hagerty added. "Have you been to see a doctor yet?"

Baier shook his head. "No, not yet. I'm hoping to go this afternoon. But I did begin with the aspirin this morning, thanks to Doctor Sabine over there." Baier nodded at his wife and smiled. She waved at her husband, as though to dismiss him, then left the room.

"Good for her." Hagerty did not say anything else for a moment. Instead he crossed his legs and studied Baier's face, then looked over at his chief of base. "Tom?"

Hendricks looked at the division chief from Headquarters, nodded, then glanced over at Baier. "Karl, could you bring Fred here up to speed on where things stand with your operation and the Russian? I've given Fred a broad outline, but you're clearly more familiar with the people involved and the details."

"Yes, please, Karl," Hagerty added. "I feel like I've got a good grip on what's been happening from the cable traffic you and Tom have been sending in, plus the odd bits from Paris and Rome. But I'd like to know where you see this going from here. Especially in light of what happened last night."

Baier shifted his weight slightly to get settled for what he knew was going to be a tough conversation. "Fred, I'm not going to try to sugarcoat anything. The Russian has been a big disappointment thus far. You're aware of his family's history and how that is motivating him?"

Hagerty nodded. "I am now. Although you took your time in letting us know how big a part that played in all this. Especially his plans for revenge."

"You're absolutely right, Fred. And I apologize for withholding that information at the outset. But I wanted to check on his story to make sure it was the truth."

"And is it?"

"Yes, I believe so. At least, I do now. I've learned a great deal from various sources here in Berlin, as well as from our contacts with the local services in Rome and Paris. The problem is that there's a lot of extraneous involvement that comes with that background, which has complicated the case and made our Russian friend, well, frankly, unprofessional at times. So, as you can probably imagine, things have not gone as smoothly as I would have liked or anticipated."

"How so?" Hagerty asked.

"Other people in the KGB and Stasi network are involved, not all of which is a negative from our standpoint."

"Explain."

Well, it's created a larger target pool, as well as some insights into the Soviets' operational methods and objectives."

"I can see the latter benefit, although I'm not sure how much we're actually gaining there. But you also mentioned targets. Targets for what? Recruitments?

"Yes, that's right."

"You mean the illegals network."

Baier nodded more vigorously than he would have liked. It sent a wave of pain riding from the back to the front of his skull. He paused to massage his forehead. "Yes, primarily. It's a lead we haven't had before. It's also put us on to the presence of one of those assassins the Soviets use, who, if we can grab him, could give us all kinds of information on Soviet aims and methods here in Europe. Not to mention where the fissures and tensions are in their European operations. There must be some. After all, he's been pretty busy of late."

"I see. Anything else?"

"It has also given us some insight into what the Stasi's plans are for their operations here in Germany, and how this new wall of theirs fits into everything they want to do and accomplish. Basically, Fred, they believe they can roll up our entire network here—not only in the east—and seize the momentum. And we need to plan on how we're going to fight that."

Baier hesitated for a moment, trying to decide how far to take this without raising expectations too far. "There may also be a contact we could pursue among the East Germans."

"A contact?" Hendricks asked. "Do you think he can be recruited?"

"I'm not sure at this point. It's still early. But I do believe he's willing to talk and even provide some information periodically. He's a tough one to read, though, and we'll have to proceed with a lot of caution."

"And the negatives?" Hagerty asked, as though to bring the conversation back into focus.

"Well, it has obviously created some new challenges. People like this Gracchus fellow look to be pretty competent. I'd expect them to continue giving us problems on this case and more in the future. That may make this other East German even more valuable as a contact, even if we don't recruit him as a full asset."

"Just where does this Gracchus fellow stand in relation to the other East German you mentioned?" Hagerty asked.

"He's the other one's boss." Baier paused to consider his next words. "Unfortunately, the whole operation has also led to some questionable—and uncooperative—behavior on our Russian's part. Even I've had to question his motives and plans at times."

"Like now?" Hagerty asked.

"Yes, like now. His role in the events of last night is still not clear to me."

"So where is he now?"

"Well, he disappeared soon after I was grabbed at Alexanderplatz, and the clowns who took me yesterday claimed that he was under arrest and being taken to Karlshorst for a KGB interrogation that they did not expect him to survive."

"Do you believe them?" Hagerty pressed.

"I'm not really sure. You can read what happened and his role either way right now. But I'd like to find out for sure before we go any farther."

"And you think you can actually find out for sure?"

"Yes, eventually."

Hagerty stood and paced the room. Hendricks, who had been sitting forward on the edge of the sofa throughout the conversation, leaned back, as though the great denouement was about to arrive. He glanced over at Baier with a look of solid, stony indifference. Baier expected nothing more and nothing less. It's what he would have done. And it did not harbor good news.

Hagerty stood at the bay window for about a minute, his hand on his chin, as though weighing an important decision. Then he returned to the sofa and sat down, his knees together and body weight far forward to make this as easy and personable as possible. His hands were clasped together, hanging between his legs. He looked Baier in the eyes.

"Eventually, Karl? That's a troublesome word."

Baier pointed to himself. "Well, Fred, as you can see, I'm a bit hobbled at the moment."

"Still, I think it's time to give this up." He held up his hand when Baier opened his mouth to protest. "Karl, I really think it's for the best. There is simply too much uncertainty and risk right now."

"But, Fred, there is always a risk, especially when you're situated this close to the sort of changes that are underway right now. And what about this new East German possibility."

"I realize all that, Karl. It's why we were willing to have you initiate and continue this operation, despite the doubts. And I know you've had a long and somewhat fruitful cooperation with this man in the past."

"He saved my life, as well as Sabine's."

Hagerty nodded. "Yes, I realize that. But I believe it has also gotten you too involved emotionally in his case. I think your man has played you on this one, Karl." He paused. "As for this new Stasi officer, the one you think would make a good contact and possibly an asset, well, we can have Tom here explore that particular case. But very cautiously."

Baier remembered the look on Chernov's face when he was seized the night before, the attempt to warn him away from the square. "Okay, I'm sure Tom and his people can handle that one. But I clearly disagree about the Russian. I know this guy. Just let me confirm what's happened to him."

"Karl, I respect your concern, and I understand your position. But given what has happened, even if he is still alive, and should the improbable happen where he actually returns to the west, we can no longer trust him. You have to let it go. I've seen too many operations like this one go bad eventually. I will not let that happen on my watch."

"I think you are making a big mistake, Fred. I hope you won't object if I file a dissenting cable on this call."

Hagerty did not respond immediately. He watched Baier's face to see if his deputy was going to relent. Baier's face was unmoving.

"You have that right, of course. And I will not block it. But it could hurt your career, Karl. I do not want to see that happen, especially over this operation. It was well conceived but ran into some difficulties that are understandable in light of what has been happening in this city and in Europe generally."

"Thank you, Fred."

Hagerty and Hendricks stood. "Take a few days to rest up and get yourself able to travel, Karl. I need you back in Washington. Your familiarity with Berlin and Germany more broadly are sorely missed in our building at the moment. We are going to be very busy for the foreseeable future."

"And get to a doctor's, or a hospital," Hendricks added. "I'll send a car over so Sabine doesn't have to drag you along all by herself."

"Thanks, Tom. I appreciate that."

Hagerty stood and stepped over to Baier, his hand out. He held his hat in his left hand. "Thanks again for all your efforts on this case, Karl. You've done all that could be expected of you in light of what you were up against."

"Thank you, Fred, for being so understanding. I'm sure we'll continue to work together well back in Washington. Our country needs us to do so."

Hagerty smiled and nodded. "Absolutely."

As the two visitors moved to the front door, Baier saw Sabine in the hallway just outside the kitchen and only a few feet from the living room. She stood stiffly, her hands together at her front. Her face said it all for Baier, the muscles tense and the jaw set, while her eyes were wide with anxiety. Her look was a combination of sorrow and protest, caution and even fear for her husband. Baier assumed she had heard it all and remained as unconvinced as he was. She, of all people, was probably the last person in Berlin willing to trust Chernov. But she also knew how much this operation and the fate of the 'fucking Russian,' as she had anointed him so many years ago, meant to her husband. It would be very hard for him to let it all go. And it would eat at him for the rest of his days in Washington.

CHAPTER SEVENTEEN

Two days of rest—but without the relaxation—was enough for Baier to feel a little better. The doctors had given him a clean bill of health, sort of. There were no broken bones at least—Baier had worried most about his ribs—although his body was covered in bruises. At least the pain had shrunk enough for him to move around with only a modest limp, and he could lift his arms above his shoulders again. Even the bruises had started to fade a little, patches turning from blue to a yellowish green. When Baier contemplated those markings in the shower, he thought about how unprofessional they looked. Not on him so much as the product of his assailants. It was as though there had been too much emotion behind their attack, as though they were intent on leaving a lasting message and warning, as it were. They will need to learn how to leave their attacks without any external damage or, more important, evidence. He did not doubt that they would learn quickly enough. Hell, given this country's recent history, they probably were already aware of that and had simply enjoyed beating the shit out of him.

"Seventy-two hours," Hagerty had said. "I want you back at your desk in three days, Karl."

Baier had agreed, of course, at least initially. But he had then gotten his chief to relent and extend the deadline an extra two days. After all, he was pretty banged up. He had an airline reservation on Pan Am for early in the morning the day after tomorrow, which would put him, theoretically at least, in the U.S. sometime in the afternoon. That is, if he made the connecting flight out of Frankfurt. That way, Baier could claim that he had met his commitment to Hagerty and the top brass at Headquarters.

This schedule would also give him time to give what help he could to Sabine for the escape of her parents. That was supposed to occur tonight, well after dark for the obvious cover they would need, but not too late to mess up his travel orders to return home. Not that that had had anything to do with the timing, of course. That was driven solely by the concerns and schedule of the tunnel diggers in the east, and they had decided that now was the best time to move.

The tunnel had been completed in pretty short order, as far as Baier could tell. Of course, this sort of thing was a new adventure for Berlin, so there wasn't any real or accepted standard yet. Baier smiled when he thought of the war movies out of Hollywood that included some sort of POW escape from a camp guarded only by bewildered Germans straight from the eastern front. The guards must have been stunned and overjoyed to find themselves out of the endless winter and artillery barrages from the Red Army. The Americans would disperse the dirt from the tunnels as they marched around the prison yard, shaking their trouser legs to spread the excess dirt in a somewhat even and random pattern.

That should not have been that much of a problem in this case. And maybe that helped with the speed of the digging and construction. The site for the tunnel was in the city's southwest, in an open and forested spot that stretched between Potsdam and the Dahlem and Zehlendorf neighborhoods in the American zone. For one thing, it was not in the city center, where so much of the regime's and the world's attention was riveted. For another, there were no water barriers like the Spree River or the Landwehr Canal that would require a much deeper penetration. The diggers had wisely chosen a spot far enough away from the Wannsee, the infamous lake nearby where the villa stood that was the site of the planning for the Final Solution, or *Endloesung*, as it was so coldly labelled by the Nazi regime. The isolation from the prying eyes of neighbors and constant border guard activity, not to mention construction workers who were busy navigating urban streets and housing, also made it much easier to get rid of the dirt. Hell, much of it, at least initially, could be left inside the house. And it had certainly helped that the chief tunnel-digger—Sabine's old companion in her smuggling ring after the war—had been assigned to the wall construction underway in this sector of Berlin, as the regime rushed to complete the encirclement of West Berlin with an 81-mile long barrier that would shut the free city off from the surrounding countryside. There was also the added attraction for Karl and Sabine Baier in that the site was almost just down the road, an easy drive.

As they waited in their car down the street on the forested outskirts in Zehlendorf, Baier admired his wife. She had coordinated her parents' involvement from the western side of this operation from her perch in Dahlem through a revitalized contact with the western half of this new and active escape business via the brother now resident in Wedding, an old working-class neighborhood on the western side of the city. It was adjacent to the new wall, which at times made the escape planning a little easier. Not tonight, however. This was an entirely new adventure in its type and scope.

In any case, it would have been far too risky to involve the American Mission in such a thing. While the American Government and its representatives in Berlin were more than happy to welcome the escapees from the east and provide whatever assistance they could once in the west, it was diplomatically—and probably legally—impossible to take an active hand in the escape itself. Probably, Baier thought, because this was all new ground for the occupying powers in so many ways. That was the one thing that gave Baier hope should his presence and participation become necessary. He could always plead ignorance and an open heart to explain whatever role he might have to assume.

But the chances of that, he believed, were minimal. Thanks to Sabine. She had used her former connections to the old postwar smuggling ring to help maintain and oversee what work and cover were necessary on the western side, while keeping herself informed of the progress on the escape plan. She was also able to stable her parents and protect her sources of information and assistance in the east. The schedule and the instructions necessary for her parents had all gone fairly smoothly, as best Baier could see, probably through the two brothers' connection with Sabine, as well as their own experience from those immediate postwar years. It would have been far too risky, for example, to try to make telephone calls from the city's western side now that the regime had restricted those calls and was monitoring those that remained. He only hoped that successful communication would continue through the night. There was maybe an hour to go before the group's estimated arrival, but one could never be sure how the schedule and plan would work. It wasn't like they were taking in the opera or a new Hollywood film.

The Baiers had parked their car in a slight curve of the road and away from a streetlight in the hopes that this would make them less easily recognized or even seen from the eastern side of the wall. A few minutes after ten o'clock, Baier heard a commotion on the other side, roughly at the spot where he and Sabine believed the tunnel was supposed to begin. It was in the basement of an older two-story farm house built in the first years of the century, where descendants of the original owners still lived. Naturally, they were in on the plot and demanded that the organizers see to it that they would escape as well. Their allegiance to the Communist regime had evaporated when their ownership of the property and surrounding fields had been taken over by the state. They also figured that the structure's time was limited, given its location so close to a wall that was sure to expand with a wider spread of barbed wire and maybe even some watch towers and a no-man's land separating the surrounding countryside from this western enclave. At least, that was the story Karl and Sabine had heard from the brother in Wedding.

The noise, however, was worrisome. Karl and Sabine had no way of knowing just what that meant and who might be involved. Until they heard the shots. That clearly indicated either the police, the damned *Vopos*, or possibly the East German military had appeared on the scene. Sabine was out of the car and running down the street to the tunnel's exit in seconds. Baier started the engine, then pulled ahead and parked directly across the street.

Not only did he want to get to the spot as quickly as possible, but he also wanted to park as close as possible in case they needed to make a quick departure. His heart was pounding, and he all but forgot the pain in his sides and legs as he swung himself from the car.

Sabine rushed up behind him, nearly out of breath. She grabbed Baier's arm. "Karl, what is it? What can be happening?"

"Hell, Sabine, I wish I knew."

"Should we go over?"

"Go over? How?"

"Karl, I don't know. Just push our way through barbed wire and climb over the wall. We should be able to avoid being seen. Things are so new here."

"No, no. That would only make matters worse. I don't think there's anything we can do."

"Karl, please."

Baier looked into his wife's face, tears streaming down her cheeks. She jerked his sleeve down towards the barrier and the commotion, sending a shot of pain up through his shoulder.

Fuck it, he thought. He broke from his wife's grasp and ran toward the area where the tunnel exit was supposed to be, next to a row of shrubbery that extended along a property line in a small residential neighborhood. Faces appeared at the windows of several houses in the west, obviously awakened by the noise form the other side of the wall. At this point, there wasn't much of a barrier in place just yet. The concrete blocks stretched about seven or eight feet into the air with a stretch of wire running along the top to discourage would-be climbers. Rough splotches of mortar ran out between the rows of bricks, a sign, Baier assumed, of hasty construction and not much in the way of professional oversight. That was probably the result of the workers' militias that been drummed together to work on building the wall. The groups included men from all walks of life, few of them actual masons, or even construction workers. That was probably one thing that made Sabine's partner in the east so valuable. For some odd reason, it gave Baier a bit of reassurance that the organizers had chosen the right spot to make their escape. But now? With the shots?

Baier found a stump from a tree that must have been cut down to make way for the wall about ten yards away from the hedge and in a clearing with about five yards of open space to either side. As with the wall's construction in the city center, there was actually a space of several yards on the western perimeter that was still in the Soviet zone, the better to allow and aid the work underway.

Baier climbed up and peered over the top of the wall, which now ran up just shy of his neck. He saw a small clutch of humanity gathered outside the house and collected by the side under what looked like a kitchen window. There were two guards and about half a dozen civilians standing stock still, most of them looking at the ground. The soldiers must have stumbled across the group during a routine patrol. He doubted they were moving at regular intervals, though. More likely the patrols were now on an irregular schedule, the better to maintain an air of uncertainty for would-be escapees. Which meant that the members of this particular group had been horribly unlucky. But they had been uncovered, whatever the circumstances, and theirs was a natural reaction. They no doubt felt helpless and lost, and they clearly wanted to avoid the eyes of their captors and probable recognition. Not that it would do any good.

Baier's heart sank. He saw Sabine's parents at the center of the civilian grouping, their dreams of joining their daughter in the west fading like so many others among the lost populations in this part of the world.

He shouted at the guards to stand back and let the people pass. It was their right in a city occupied and administered by the four victorious and occupying powers. It was futile, of course, but he didn't know what else to say or do. One of the guards turned his head slowly and looked to see where the noise was coming from. Baier again had the odd thought that it was good thing he spoke fluent German; at least the creep could understand what he had to say. When he found Baier's face, the guard smiled. He slowly raised his rifle, as though he intended to shoot Baier. Instead, all he did was shout in reply, "Bang, bang." He then motioned toward the would-be escapees, and a thin smile of cruelty and contempt spread across his face.

Baier held his arm aloft and flipped the bastard the bird. He felt good about that. Powerless, but good, nonetheless.

Then he heard something much more encouraging. It was another gunshot. But this one did not come from the East German border guards. In fact, one of them crumpled to the ground. The other's smile disappeared, replaced immediately by a look of panic. Baier was afraid he might spray the civilians with gunfire in response, which would undoubtedly win him an award from the regime. "Get down," he shouted, first in English before he even thought about what he was saying, then repeating it in German.

At that moment another, larger figure came running around the corner of the house, his trench coat flapping behind him like some superhero's cape. His right hand held a pistol that he waved at the other guard, who was raising his rifle. It did not get very far, however. Sabine's father leaped from the crowd and brought both fists down hard on the soldier's neck and head in two crushing blows that Baier never thought the old man had in him still. Strange times make strange heroes, he thought.

"*Jetzt*," Baier shouted. 'Now.' And then, "*Schnell, schnell.*"

The entire crew responded just as he would have hoped. They quickly disappeared inside the house, and Baier scrambled around the area nearby, searching for the exit spot. Once he found it, Baier flung the sod-covered door to the sky.

Minutes later, East Germans of varying age and condition crawled from the ground. The first were two teenagers, a boy and a girl, who turned to help the older escapees up from the earth. The first couple after them looked to be the parents, and Baier assumed they must have been the occupants of the house where the tunnel began. Then came a middle-aged couple and a single male who looked to be in his late twenties or early thirties. It was hard to tell given the dirt and darkness that surrounded everyone and everything there. That and the sheer joy in the faces that emerged from a dirt-covered hole in the ground. And last came Sabine's parents, who hobbled forth, assisted by the man who proceeded them.

Baier hadn't even noticed that Sabine had appeared as though by magic at his side. She ran to her parents, who let out muffled cries of joy and surprise. The middle-aged couple looked on with a joy of their own, and Baier hoped they were on their way to meet family as well. Baier stepped up to his wife's father and took his hand. "*Gut gemacht, Friedrich,*" Baier congratulated him. 'Well done.' Once more, he felt at a loss for words during such an emotional time. But the old man saw the meaning behind the words and embraced his son-in-law.

When he walked over to close the lid to the tunnel, the single male, who had remained kneeling at the edge, reached up touched his arm. "Wait a minute, there is one more coming. He is moving more slowly, because he appears to have been wounded or beaten."

At that point Baier remembered the lone ranger with the pistol who had made the final success of the escape possible. He stuck his head down into the tunnel exit and saw a shadow moving slowly forward. Baier knelt by the side and reached down to help the savior up. When the man's head emerged, Baier's heart nearly stopped.

"You fucking Russian," he said.

Chernov climbed out and saluted his American companion. Then he turned and saluted Sabine and her parents. Sabine leaned on both her parents, her jaw open and her eyes wide. "My God," she whispered. "I don't believe it."

"First, Herr Baier, let me apologize for the other day in Alexanderplatz." Chernov shook his entire body like a large furry dog in an effort to rid himself of the dirt from the tunnel. Also, perhaps, the air of East Berlin. "I was not in control of the situation, as you might have guessed. I was already a captive and no longer in control of things from my end. And I did try to warn you. But it was too late." He stood back and waved his hand at himself. "As you can see, I had to suffer an interrogation as well."

Chernov nodded and smiled. "Here," he said, as he handed the pistol, yet another Makarov, to Baier. He also gripped an automatic weapon in his left hand, something resembling the AK-47s that were mass-produced in the east, to the American. Baier was no weapons expert, so he could only guess at the exact type of weapon. "And another gift," he said. "I liberated this one from the guard that the old man there disabled."

Baier noticed the burn marks that spotted his right arm and ran from the wrist up and under the shirt sleeve of the Russian's right arm. "Yes," Chernov continued, "they used cigarettes to burn me in an effort to get me to talk about our relationship."

"My God, Sergei, I never thought I'd say this, but it is good to see you. But what happened? I thought you were as good as dead. I never expected to see you again, and certainly not tonight."

"As you can see, Karl, I was not that cooperative during my interrogations. So, I was being transported to another prison at the barracks in Potsdam for more interrogations, when I was able to overpower my escorts and escape."

"How the hell did that happen?"

"Well, they were quite careless. They let me sit alone in the back. I jumped the driver and forced the car into a ditch. I then stole his weapon—that Makarov there—and forced both men into the same ditch. I'm afraid I had to shoot them both in the legs to prevent them from making their way to the barracks. I took the car and was heading for the west when I heard the commotion here. I had planned to try to ram my way through, but then thought better of it when I saw this group. I had no idea…"

"Okay, okay," Baier said. "Apology accepted. But let's talk about it later. Come to the house for some celebratory champagne, or *Sekt*. I'm afraid all we could find tonight was some German stuff. Appropriately enough, it's a rose champagne from Saxony."

Chernov smiled. "Let's save the celebration for another night. I have to leave right away."

"Oh, come now, Sergei. Not this again."

"Yes, yes, I am afraid so. My quarry has returned to Paris. And I must follow him. I will explain it when I get the chance. I assume you will be following as well?"

"Yes, I suppose so," Baier replied. "Same place tomorrow?"

"I think the day after would be better. It would give me more time to get the lay of the land, as you Americans say."

Baier nodded. "Of, course." Seventy-two hours and back at my desk? Yeah right, he thought. This operation was far from over.

CHAPTER EIGHTEEN

September 19, 1961

So, Pittman had been right after all; Baier had come back to Paris. Just like everyone else.

"I don't know, Ralph. Meeting across from Notre Dame again? I love the site of that grand cathedral, but isn't this getting a little predictable?"

The local chief of station smiled and sat back against the bent rattan and wicker chair at the same café the two Americans had visited the last time Baier was in the City of Light. Baier had spent a day waiting in Berlin, cooling his proverbial heels, sending and responding to cables with Washington and Paris. That was the sort of thing any case officer dreaded, the bureaucratic give and take with the entourage of colleagues and superiors in Headquarters. Then he spent the next day getting back to what most operations officers considered the real work of espionage, becoming active in the field. He spent that time much more constructively, in his view, traveling and contacting Pittman and arranging this meeting, laying the groundwork for the conclusion of his operation.

"I have to say I was surprised and even a bit flustered by your call, so I did not have a lot of time to think of someplace new for our morning meeting. And I wasn't sure how well you know this wonderful city and can find your way around. In any case, I don't think twice makes for a pattern, Karl. So, you can relax." Pittman raised his cup of *café au lait*. "Besides, this is a natural place for visitors to our city to come when they're in town. Have you been back to the book stalls?"

"Of course. And I did not see any tail. We should be okay." Baier smiled. "I also passed on the books again."

Pittman leaned over the table. "Good. Because we need to talk about what you think is going to go down here. This case of yours has got people in an uproar. Well, some people at least."

"You mean Hagerty?"

Pittman nodded before taking some more coffee. "Among others. Why not give it up, Karl? Lord knows there are enough improbabilities and risks that, in my humble view, far outweigh whatever gains you can hope to accrue. Given all that has happened, I wonder if a lot of what he knows is already pretty dated."

It was Baier's turn to lean back. He studied the façade of Paris's famous cathedral for a long moment before looking back over at his host. One of what was probably the last of the summer tourist barges floating along the Seine passed by, its decks swarming with visitors.

"Frank, you know how subjective this work can be at times, right? I mean, you've experienced things like this before, I'm sure." Pittman nodded, his eyes focused on Baier's face. "Well, then maybe this is an extreme case of just that. For better or worse, I've found my own work and career in Europe tied irrevocably to this Russian. Not just him, of course, but he's been a big part of my efforts—and my success—here. I can't just walk away. Not now. Not after that last meeting in Berlin two nights ago." Baier sipped some of his coffee in turn. "And there is the prospect of learning more about Soviet planning for Berlin. He had to shoot his way out of Soviet control back there, you know."

"I did not know that. But can you be certain his escape wasn't arranged by his alleged captors?"

"I was there, Ralph. I believe him."

"Well, when I consider everything that's happened it still looks to me like he's sold you down the proverbial river. And it can only get worse. I don't mean to question your judgment, Karl..."

"Which you're doing."

"...But his escape sounds a bit improbable to me. And what

has he delivered in this operation that truly established his bona fides, his sincerity?"

Baier sighed, more out of concession than frustration. "I can see your point, Frank. But let's not forget the illegal he exposed."

"Who has disappeared. Which, as you've explained, may well be your Russian buddy's doing."

"As far as I'm concerned, the verdict is still out on that one. I will get you an address, and I do mean more than a neighborhood, that you and your French friends can look into. And even if there is no nugget of gold on Berlin, there's all he can tell us about the inner workings and structure and the chief personalities of the KGB. That would be invaluable."

"Fair enough. It is, after all, your call. Do you think your new German buddies will show?"

"I don't see why. And that's probably a good thing, since the scales are already weighted against us, as it is. Although I have to confess that I wouldn't mind the chance for some payback. Do you think your French colleagues would be able to help if needed?"

"What, give the French an opportunity to sweat some Germans? They'd be slobbering all over themselves at the prospect. But where do we go from here now that the whole crowd appears to be reassembling in Paris?"

"We?"

Pittman looked hard at his colleague, his mouth set. "Of course, 'we.' If you need anything, Karl, it's a wingman. I'm not letting you walk into a potential ambush alone."

"Thanks, Frank. I appreciate that."

Both men stood. Pittman tossed a handful of francs on the table, followed by several coins that rattled as they settled on the bills.

"I'm supposed to meet my 'fucking Russian' near the Louvre in an hour. Will you have my back?" Baier asked.

"You bet. Should I draw us each a weapon?'

Baier blew out his breath again and glanced over at the cathedral. "I suppose so. It wouldn't hurt. Brownings?"

Pittman followed Baier's gaze. "Yes. And I'll bring some extra clips. Just in case."

"That's probably a good idea, too. Those monsters will probably be just what we need, if anything goes wrong."

"Tell me, Karl, are you expecting trouble?"

"Well, if we do come across any trouble all that stopping power could come in handy. And seeing how things have been going, it's probably best to prepare for the worst."

"Well," Pittman added, "let's swing by the office first. I just hope they're not needed, but you're right. It is no doubt best to be prepared."

"Amen to that, my friend."

• • •

Chernov was waiting for Baier on a park bench in the Tuileries, just off the path they had taken during their last meeting here. He appeared to be oddly calm, relaxed even. He was also wearing the long grey overcoat his compatriot, the 'illegal,' had been wearing when Baier last saw the two Russians together. Baier took a seat at the opposite corner of the bench from Chernov. The Russian stared straight ahead, as though afraid to look Baier in the eyes.

"That coat looks familiar. A trophy of sorts?"

Chernov let a small laugh escape. "Hardly, Herr Baier. I am sure you remember this coat from my compatriot. I had two purposes today in wearing it."

"And those are?"

"One, I wanted to be sure you would recognize me from a distance and know that I am alone here, that the man who wore this before is not here with me, hiding somewhere."

"He could still be hiding somewhere, Sergei, only wearing something else. A better disguise."

Chernov smiled as he nodded, staring straight ahead. "That is true. But if you saw this from a distance, you would have plenty of time and space to look for him. He is not an easy man to hide. Which brings me to my second purpose."

"And that is?"

"To let you know—and anyone else you may have brought— that this man has disappeared."

"That sounds ominous, Sergei."

"But it is actually not, Herr Baier. He is gone, and I helped him depart."

"That sounds even more ominous, given what I heard about an assignment you had. Why don't you tell me exactly what has happened?"

Chernov looked over at Baier for the first time since his arrival. "He has gone into hiding. He was a marked man for helping my brother. You will forgive me if I do not tell you just where he has gone and how he got there."

Baier waited a moment to see if the Russian had anything more to say. "I had heard that it was supposed to play out differently. That you had a specific assignment regarding this man. You were, in fact, supposed to shoot him."

Chernov slid his arm along the back of the bench and leaned towards the American. "You have good sources, Herr Baier. But they had only partial information. I assume you mean I was supposed to kill him." Baier nodded. "That is not quite correct."

"Not quite?"

"Yes, that is right. I was supposed to spot him, as it were. Set him up for the real assassin. This is one way our bosses in Moscow test our loyalty. It is how I know that Marchenko, the assassin, is here in Paris."

"I was wondering about that. Odd that you would have been given an assignment like that, and to work with that particular killer."

"It is much the same mentality there now that ruled during Stalin's purges. Dedication to the cause of the Soviet state first and foremost. It is also the main reason that I believe Minister Khrushchev had for agreeing to have the wall built in Berlin. He was under great pressure in the Kremlin and elsewhere to do something to preserve our biggest gain from the Great Patriotic War."

"By elsewhere you mean the other Warsaw Pact capitals?"

Chernov nodded. "Yes. But as you can see, I am a poor subject. It is why I became a target myself."

"Can I really see that, Sergei? There have been numerous riddles throughout this operation. And they still haven't been answered."

Chernov leaned back into his own corner on the bench. "Ah, yes, Alexanderplatz. I tried to warn you, you know. I did not want those East German bastards to catch you."

"You still let me come there. And they still got the meeting site and time from you. Once that happened, I had little chance."

Chernov's fist slammed against his thigh. "Do you think I was a free man myself? Do you think I had the opportunity to warn you beforehand?" He slid the sleeve of the coat and the shirt underneath it back to reveal an arm still black and blue, spotted with patches of red. "You saw these the other night, did you not? You know what these are?" He pointed to the red markings. "These are where my KGB colleagues burned me with their cigarettes. The other arm is worse."

"Yes, I did see those, Sergei, and I am truly sorry to see that you have suffered. But you were held first by the Stasi."

"And they are much worse that my countrymen. Those bastards dislocated all my fingers to get me to give up that information." He glanced down at his hands that Baier noticed for the first time were covered by brown leather gloves. "Yes, the swelling has not down completely. And they actually dislocated only eight fingers."

"Only?"

"Yes, eight. They had started on the ninth when I broke. At least they pushed the others back once they had what they wanted. Our East German colleagues probably did not want to show signs of torture on me when they turned me over to the KGB."

"I am truly sorry, Sergei. But you also have slipped away repeatedly. And there has been no way I could ever be sure of what you've been up to."

Chernov rubbed his face with his hands, then ran those through his hair, pushing the grey and black mop away from his forehead. He stood. "Do you really think I could have been able to track a man as cunning and as dangerous as the Ukrainian with you and your colleagues at my side? Were you and I supposed to stroll through Europe hand in hand to find him?" He stood. "And didn't I always come back?'

Baier stared up at the Russian, who seemed to tower over him.

"Yes, you did, Sergei. But that can be explained any number of ways."

"Such as?'

"Such as the need to re-establish contact, to maintain your own operation, to get all that you could from me."

"All? About what?"

"About our operations and methods, about our officers, about what we know and don't know, about what our own requirements are. Anything that might help the Kremlin look ahead as to what our response will be to the events in Berlin."

Chernov waved his hands at the air between the two men. "But you've given me nothing of the sort. And I knew you would not. I have been honest with you throughout this entire time, even before, back when we first met in Berlin years ago. You should have trusted me."

"I do trust you, Sergei. I have come to that conclusion. That's why I am here now, against my superior's wishes and against my own better judgment."

"Good. Because you will need to trust me even more. We are going to meet the assassin. I am not sure he will be alone, so we must trust each other if we are to survive."

Baier stood. "Now?"

Chernov turned to go. "Yes, now. The time has come."

Baier glanced around the park. He saw no sign of Pittman. That meant either that his colleague was very, very good—or that things were about to go downhill very, very fast.

CHAPTER NINETEEN

September 19, 1961

He would have sworn that they walked for hours. When Baier checked his watch, he was stunned to discover that it only been one. Their route took them across Paris and up the slow, grinding hill of Montmarte, the haunt of artists and tourists. They moved at a cautious and deliberate pace. Chernov paused every once in a while, apparently in need of catching his breath, which allowed Baier to look for some sign of Pittman. There may have been a sighting or two, but he could not be sure.

"You look worried, Herr Baier. Have you not found your colleagues?"

"What do you mean?"

"Oh, come now. I surely did not expect you to act alone here. That would be foolish. And I hope you do find them. That would be of help to my purposes as well."

"Your purposes?"

"Enough, Herr Baier. Let us not squabble now. At least you have that weapon." He motioned with his head towards the inside pocket of Baier's jacket. "You might want to hide it better before we arrive. Perhaps the small of your back? It is where I have placed mine."

The two men climbed the hill that spread in front of the Basilica of the Sacred Heart, then headed left down Rue Gabrielle. The tourist shops that had lined the streets on the way up were replaced by a more residential area, with four story buildings of light stone and brick, some with shop fronts, mostly small grocery stores and bakeries. Along with a sprinkling of the ubiquitous French cafes, of course. Chernov led them to a doorway between two of those shops and up a narrow stairway bordered by cracked and peeling paint that smelled of mold and mildew. It was too dark for Baier to determine if the walls were brown or tan. Or how much of it was dirt and how much the original paint. On the top floor Chernov halted, knocked lightly, and mumbled something in Russian. The door cracked open, an inch at first, and then wider. A thin, sheepish face that seemed to be afraid of the light appeared in the crack and mumbled something in return. It was also in Russian, although he took longer to finish. Then the man stepped aside, and Chernov entered the flat. Baier followed, his eyes searching the room for any sign of danger. But the apartment was empty, except for the three men and a smattering of furniture that suggested this particular apartment was no one's living quarters. It was a Soviet safe house.

"The others will be here shortly," Chernov said.

"Others?" Baier asked.

"Marchenko and perhaps some others. I am not really sure."

"Some others? How many?"

"I do not know. I am also a bit surprised."

"If he's so bad, why does he need anyone else at all?" Baier pressed.

"That is a good question, Herr Baier. One I cannot answer. Normally he does work alone. But my colleague here," Chernov nodded in the direction of the housekeeper, "claims there may be more than one."

"And just who is this guy? Your colleague?" Baier motioned with his hand toward the individual who had let them in and then disappeared into the kitchen.

"That is the 'illegal' who operates the safe house." Chernov smiled when he looked over at Baier. "So, you see, you have already gained something new to give your colleagues. And this time you have an address."

"If I live to tell them about it."

Chernov shrugged, and the smile stayed. "We shall see."

It was another half an hour before Baier heard the knock at the door. He had declined the offer of coffee from the 'illegal' housekeeper, figuring he had enough adrenaline pounding through his system to keep him alert for another week or two. The knock was no louder than Chernov's, and the wafer of a man who had let them in reappeared from the kitchen and marched to the door. He followed the same procedure with an initial opening of no more than an inch, then a gradual widening until he retreated to allow the new visitors in. Baier noticed that the housekeeper kept a pistol in his right hand, hidden behind his back when he negotiated the new group's entry, probably a form of insurance. Baier wondered if the housekeeper had taken the same precautions when he and Chernov arrived. Probably, but Baier had not taken the time to check when he entered. He was too busy sizing up the rest of the flat.

This new bunch also included three men. So, there were now six in all—once Baier added in himself, Chernov, and the housekeeper. It was definitely getting crowded, and Baier wondered just what everyone had in mind. He reached around as though to scratch his back, but really to make sure his weapon was within quick reach. As quick as it could be in the middle of his back.

The bear of a Ukrainian, Oleg Marchenko, strolled in first. He was followed by two more, one of them the German Stasi officer Joachim Hoehn, whom Baier had last seen in Rome. The third was Ralph Pittman, and he did not appear to have come willingly. The best clue, as Baier saw it, was the Makarov semi-automatic pressed against Pittman's back by Hoehn.

"Sergei Chernov," Marchenko bellowed. "I must say I am truly surprised. I would have thought they had you buried back in Karlshorst by now. I had not gotten any word that you were here. I thought my work had been completed by someone else."

"If that is the case, then why did you come and why did you have to bring so many others with you?"

Marchenko glanced around the room. "I was hoping I would meet the man who was supposed to help spot my next target. I doubt that is you, or your friend here. Are you the reason, my target has disappeared?"

Chernov nodded. "I am afraid so. But who are these others and why are they with you?"

"These gentlemen? Well, that makes for an interesting story. Perhaps you can help explain," Marchenko said.

Baier found his English surprisingly good. Much better than in Rome, which heightened his operational respect for the assassin. If any more was even necessary.

"You've changed your coat, Mr. Marchenko," Baier said. "And you must have been taking English lessons since I saw you in Rome."

Marchenko shrugged. "And it's a good thing. This lighter coat is now much more comfortable for what has appeared to become the new possibilities of this meeting. Apparently, I was misinformed." He glanced over at the housekeeper. "As for my English, you can say that I have been to the movies a lot lately. I am a big fan of John Wayne, you know." His eyes surveyed the room, and Marchenko returned his attention to Chernov. "In any case, I am not sure how much longer we will all be here. Apparently, I was mistaken about my old assignment regarding you Sergei. It was obviously never completed, so I must assume it has now been extended." Oleg pointed at Baier. "And I see you have brought your own American friend. Why is that?"

"I have something to prove." Chernov said.

Marchenko nodded. "Good. As for these two…" He gestured towards Pittman and Hoehn. "…The German has been tailing me for the last week or so. He is the one who found this other American. He was carrying this.' Marchenko tossed the Browning on the coffee table in front of a sofa that appeared to have come from the shop just yesterday. The fall was broken by a stack of magazines piled atop the glass plate on the table. The magazines were a collection of French and American periodicals with *Life* placed prominently on the top, covering a copy of *Paris Match* underneath. Baier found it ironic, for some reason. He also hoped it was a good sign.

"I see," Chernov replied. He looked over at Baier and frowned.

Chernov and Marchenko, former colleagues but now antagonists, had finally come face to face. They stared at each other for what must have been a full minute. Chernov had finally succeeded in tracking down the man who killed his brother, but it was unclear just how he planned to take his revenge. Or if he even could. They stood not more than four feet apart, squared off as though facing each other down in a Hollywood Western. John Wayne indeed.

Marchenko broke the silence. "So, tell me, Sergei, why are you here? I do not know how you managed to get away from Karlshorst, but it would have been better for you to have disappeared. You know what must happen now."

Chernov shook his head. "But it need not come to that. I have a better proposition."

"And that would be?"

"Go away with my American friends here. They can give you a better life. They can do that for all of us, even that German over there." Chernov answered.

"And you know this how?" Marchenko asked. "Have they spoken of this with you? Is that what they have offered you?'

"Yes, they have offered it to me. And I am certain they would do the same for you, Oleg. You have much to offer."

"And how would this work? How would they protect me from someone coming after, someone just like me?" Marchenko countered.

Chernov spread his arms wide. "They have their ways, Oleg. America is a rich and powerful country. It is also a big country in which to hide, especially with their help."

Marchenko turned to Baier. "I should have expected as much from someone like your Russian friend here." He pointed at Chernov with a thick, gnarled index finger. "He is a traitor, something I would never have expected from our time together in the war."

"You were together during the war?" Baier asked. "Where? When?"

"Oh, it was back when the German invaders were still on our soil, down in Ukraine." Marchenko motioned with his head toward Hoehn, the German Stasi officer, when he spoke. "We were in the same Sepnatz unit back then. Your friend here," his head moved over towards Chernov, "was quite effective. And then he joined other units at the front as a political and counterintelligence officer. But I always felt that something was not quite right. And then he fled to the West. I have never forgiven him for that."

"Does it mean you have to kill him?" Baier pressed.

Marchenko shrugged. "Who knows? The world is a mysterious place, and these are mysterious times." He turned his attention back to Chernov. "I still must ask you, Sergei, are they rich and powerful enough? Is anyone for that matter?"

"No, they are not, Comrade Oleg." Those words came from the housekeeper, who had apparently assumed the role of chaperone. He had stepped back into the room and stood apart from the others, his gaze hard and bitter as he studied Chernov. He looked over at Marchenko. "You know I will not let that happen. Do not forget, Comrade, you have a mission to accomplish for our Soviet motherland here in Paris. And there is perhaps more you can do now. With all these others here."

The housekeeper wheeled toward Chernov and whipped his right hand inside the left half of his jacket. Baier expected another one of those damn Makarov pistols to appear from somewhere, anywhere. He slid his own hand behind his back. But he was too slow. Chernov had his own pistol—a Makarov, of course—out and aimed at the young Soviet enthusiast, the 'illegal' housekeeper.

"Please don't do anything foolish, young man," Chernov said. "It is far too soon to end that life of yours."

Chernov might as well have stayed silent.

A shot pierced the young housekeeper's chest. An incredible feat in the short time it took for Marchenko to pull his own weapon and fire it. The housekeeper and self-appointed chaperone crumbled to the floor, twitched, and lay still. There was surprisingly little blood that marked the spot. Baier was even more awestruck. The bullet, fired with astonishing quickness, must have pierced the man's heart.

The silence in the room was eerie. Baier didn't know if he had entered some sort of dream world or a parallel universe, it had all happened so fast and with such devastating consequences. He felt as though he had forgotten to breathe for a minute or two. When his heart seemed to restart, Baier' knees felt wobbly. He looked over at Pittman, who simply stared back at him, as though looking for a sign of what to do next.

The German Hoehn was quiet as well, a knowing grin the only sign that he had witnessed the shooting and even understood its meaning. If that was so, Baier told himself, he knew a lot more than either of the Americans in the room.

Chernov broke the silence. "Does this mean, Oleg, that you have decided to join the Americans?"

"Hardly. I just wanted to be rid of that nuisance. I did not trust him. He has been a meddling busybody ever since I arrived in Paris. Far too eager, and probably hoping to replace me through some kind of quick and decisive action." Marchenko laughed and swept his free hand in Chernov's direction. "Besides, he was probably Russian, and you know, Sergei, that I do not really care for Russians. I mean, given all that's happened between us over the years, and my family's own background in the independence movement."

"Then how will you explain this?" Chernov asked, as his finger pointed at the dead Soviet housekeeper on the floor.

Marchenko studied the corpse for a moment. "Well that is easy enough. I will blame you, Sergei."

"Just a damn minute," Baier broke in. He had his gun out now, and it was aimed at Marchenko. "That's enough shooting for one day. Put that thing on the floor and kick it over here."

"Or what will you do, Mr. CIA man?" Marchenko asked, more as a challenge than a request. "Do you think you can actually fire that thing at me? Are you man enough to do it?"

"If I have to." Baier tightened the grip on his Browning and slid his finger to cover the trigger.

"There are two weapons on you now, Oleg." Chernov's weapon was also out and aimed at Marchenko.

"No, I do not think so, Sergei," Marchenko said. He wheeled in Chernov's direction, his gun aimed at the Chernov's heart.

But the first shot did not come from him. Instead, a bullet exploded in Marchenko's stomach in a burst of blood and intestine. A second shot drilled a hole in the front of his neck. Marchenko dropped his pistol and grabbed for his neck, as though he could stop the bleeding that poured down his shirtfront. His face held a look of complete amazement, as though something like this was simply impossible to imagine. But he was not looking at Chernov or either of the Americans. Instead, he stared at the German Hoehn, whose grin was gone. His face held a look of determination, and his right hand a pistol that had brought an end to the career of the Soviet assassin.

"You goddamn German pig." The words seemed to bubble forth from Marchenko's mouth as he spit blood down his shirtfront. It was all Marchenko could say before falling to the floor in a heap. His body made a small splash in its own blood, then lay still.

All eyes turned to the German Stasi officer, who glanced around the room. His pistol ranged from the Americans to Chernov, then back to Pittman before finally settling on Baier.

"Just what is your game?" Baier asked. "And what do you hope to accomplish now?"

"Yes, and please no more shooting," Chernov added. "You have nothing to fear from Herr Baier, I assure you."

Hoehn shrugged and re-holstered his pistol inside his jacket. Only then did Baier recognize that he had exchanged the Makarov pistol for a Luger. "Oh, there is no need to worry now. Not for any of you at least. The work here is done, and it looks to have been a very successful day for you Americans," Hoehn said. He pointed at the bodies on the floor. "I mean, two of your enemies eliminated…"

"But why? Does this mean you are coming with us as well?"

"No, hardly. I will remain on our side for now. I believe my prospects are better there. I really do not care for the Americanized Germany you are creating in the West. I never did develop a taste for Coca-Cola." He paused, and then let his smile widen, as though amused at his own thoughts. "I can always visit Disneyland out in, where is it, California if I want to see the real America."

"So, have you bought into the other side's ideology? Or are you just nostalgic for the old Germany?" Pittman asked.

Hoehn shrugged again. "Not really. You see, any ideology died for me in the snows of Stalingrad. Later fighting, especially on the *Ostfront*, only confirmed that."

"You fought at Stalingrad? Then how is it you're still alive?" Pittman's jaw had fallen open far enough that Baier worried his lower teeth might hit the stack of magazines.

Hoehn nodded. "Yes, but I was one of the lucky ones. I was wounded in early December, before the encirclement was completed and while there were still flights to carry out the wounded."

"Yes, I'd say you were lucky," Baier added. "Very lucky. You could get lucky again today, you know."

Hoehn shook his head. "No, I do not think so. These feelings may not last, of course. Just think of me as one of the lost men of Central Europe for now. But I think I will observe what happens in Germany from the other side."

"Then why shoot the Ukrainian Marchenko?" Baier pressed. "You could have returned a hero."

Hoehn shook his head. "Not really. I have no real interest in whether that man survived. My superiors probably feel the same way. Oh, maybe they care a little. But we have other fish to fry right now, as you Americans might say."

"Then why were you here?"

"Well, we did want to see how this would play out. I will give you a warning, perhaps because I want to show you that my intentions and commitment are not all that simple. It is a dilemma many of us face nowadays as our country and Europe are rebuilt by two competing systems."

"And that would be?" Pittman asked.

The Stasi officer glanced over at him, and then back at Baier. "Right now, my superiors are in a defensive mode. That explains your treatment the other night, Herr Baier, more than anything else. Our interests now revolve more around negating your operations and activities as they are directed against us, all in the interests of protecting the Communist state in Germany. So, we are learning what we can of your methods and goals, the better to block those operations. And we no longer see ourselves as simply the poodles of the Soviets. We realized this year that we must act by ourselves, since we cannot always rely on Moscow. So, this whole episode was as much an experiment as anything else. Or perhaps more of an observation." He paused. "I guess it will be interesting to see how this new competition plays out."

"But that still doesn't explain why you killed this man," Baier said. "If you were here only as an observer than why become so directly involved?"

Hoehn studied Marchenko's corpse, then looked out the window at the dome of Sacred Heart before looking back at Baier.

"Well, that was more of a personal matter." He shook his head and held up a hand. "No, I had nothing against that man. But for most of my life, I have been following orders from one regime or another, one organization or another. I simply decided it was time for me to do something on my own initiative and for my own reasons. Those had nothing to do with this individual."

"And what would those reasons be?"

"For one thing, I decided that you two Americans deserved to walk away from this encounter and continue your work with Herr Chernov here. At least for now. There are others, but I will keep all that to myself for now." He paused and moved towards the door. "I cannot say how I might react if we meet again. But it could be interesting."

Baier and Pittman watched as the German faded away in the shadows of the stairway. The silence was broken by Sergei Chernov, who walked up to the Americans with his coat over his right arm and a fedora he must have found in the front closet in his left. "Shall we go, gentlemen?"

Baier and Pittman looked at each other. "Yes, I believe we should," Pittman answered. The French police could show up at any minute."

"Yes, we'd better get started," Baier agreed. "We've got one helluva a cable to write back to Washington."

Baier turned to Chernov, his hand outstretched. "Let's go, Sergei. I know some people who are very eager to talk to you."

CHAPTER TWENTY

September 20, 1961

"The American General Clay has been here for over a month now." Yuri Kirillnikov, the KGB chief, or *Residenz* in KGB parlance, surveyed the garden outside his third floor window in Saint Antonius Hospital, the KGB headquarters in the Karlshort section of East Berlin. His office was located in one wing of the functional arrangement of several rectangular blocks, a huge concrete assembly surrounded by a mixture of gardens and tall pine trees. "Did the Americans you encountered in Paris say anything about that? About what they expect he will be up to in the weeks ahead?"

Joachim Hoehn sat back in the cushioned chair at the top left-hand corner of Kirillnikov's desk. His legs were crossed, and he looked more relaxed that he had been at any time over the last month, or even longer. It was almost as though he was more comfortable now in the presence of Soviet colleagues, than those in the East German Ministry of State Security. And these people had been his sworn enemy for much of his life. History truly does make for strange bedfellows.

"No, they did not. We all had other things on our minds." He let out his breath with the puff of the smoke from his American cigarette. A Winston. He agreed with the American commercial, that a Winston tastes good, like a cigarette should. The Soviet officer had raised his eyebrows when Hoehn produced the package, a small indication of disapproval. Hoehn remembered then that the Russian preferred Marlboros or Players, depending on which PX he visited in the west. "What are you curious about?" Hoehn asked. "Ultimately, I mean."

"Just what this means, of course. Are the Americans preparing a more robust response than they have shown so far?"

Hoehn took another drag on his cigarette before answering. "I couldn't say, Comrade. I would expect as much. This man Clay does have a history here."

"I suppose you were too busy trying to get out of that safe house alive."

Hoehn nodded as he scrubbed out his smoke. "Absolutely. I would never have thought of the American as so violent, so dangerous. To just shoot those men in cold blood…." He sat back and shook his head.

"He never threatened you directly, though, did he?"

"No, he did not. He was too busy worrying about Marchenko, and after that our former friend Chernov."

"Whom he kidnapped?"

"Not exactly. Sergei was a willing victim, in my eyes. It was our other compatriot, the housekeeper. When he tried to intervene, this American gangster shot him as well. I should think he deserves a medal from you people, and his family a nice pension."

Kirillnikov nodded, his eyes resting on a stack of papers on his desk blotter. "I agree. I'll start the paperwork today. I doubt there will be much resistance. I take it there was no sign of any of our people there, or in the area even? I mean, my people, actually, KGB brethren."

"No, Yuri. I saw no one. I suspect they have learned to keep their distance from operations involving the Ukrainian Marchenko." He smiled. "Although that will not be a problem now."

"Yes, of course. But this will play well in our campaign to explain the necessity of the new wall here in Berlin. You know the sort of thing: the nest of spies the Americans have built over there, and how badly we need to put an end to western threats to the security of East Berlin, prevent the resurgence of German militarism in the West from endangering the stability of East Germany and Europe in general. You know the lines, I am sure."

Hoehn smiled. "Yes, I see. Good luck with that. Are you disappointed by the loss of Chernov?"

"Just a bit. Now that we know what he has been up to and the type of man he is, it would have been nice to drag him back home to learn more of what he had been doing with the American. Since there was no longer any prospect of turning him against the Americans, it would have been good to learn the full extent of any damage the two had been able to inflict. I still am not certain how much he can tell the Americans about our efforts and planning here in Berlin and Germany more broadly. He was pretty well plugged in back in Moscow, though, despite the suspicions about his past. Some of his material could be quite damaging."

"He does seem a bit less complicated than you originally thought. But would he have had that sort of access in Moscow? Really?"

Kirillnikov shrugged. "It is hard to say. Few will admit to having been his friend now, so it will be difficult to retrace his steps. It really is unfortunate that he got away the other night."

"Have you given up on trying to turn him again?"

"Yes, I suppose we must. It looks less and less likely now. But one never knows in these matters."

"So, eventually a shot in the back of the skull? Somewhere in the U.S.? That is, if he cannot be seized and brought home?"

Kirillnikov nodded. "Yes, most likely. And it is probably better that we can avoid a trial. It would have gotten ugly for us. I just hope that there is not much new that he can reveal to the Americans. They probably know most of what he has to say already." He studied Hoehn's impassive face. "But as I said, one never knows for sure. So, in that case, it would have been better to try to work with him before he fell into the Americans' hands." The Soviet sighed. "It was probably a mistake to put Marchenko on him. Sometimes we are too hasty in these sorts of affairs. That may have forced his hand. It is not always easy to walk away from your homeland, you know."

Yes, I realize that."

"I am sure that you do."

Kirillnikov paused to look out the window. A slight breeze

blew through the branches of the trees outside, a brief bit of relief on an otherwise warm and humid day. Not what he had expected here in Berlin as the Fall approached and the month of September wore on. It was now well into the second half of the month. But he would gladly take whatever extra warmth the skies provided after a life in Russia. Moscow would be thinking of snow in another month or so.

"And how is your relationship with Gracchus going?" Kirillnikov asked.

"Well enough, I believe. He still seems to harbor some distrust, but I believe I can work around that. Maybe even convince him that I am to be fully trusted. He does seem uncertain about my time on the Eastern front and in your less than hospitable prison camps."

"Imagine that. Well, you know how much it will serve both our purposes that your relationship with that man prospers. In his own way, he is a dedicated Communist, but also a bit of a German nationalist, you know."

Hoehn leaned forward. "We all are, Comrade. At least most of us."

"Ah, but you have yours under control. I suppose that your experiences during the war did a good deal to temper that."

"Yes, they did. Of course, they did."

"Is there any chance you will see the American again?"

"If you wish. That could be a tricky proposition, though."

"How so?"

Hoehn looked to the side and trolled in his pocket for another cigarette. "You already know how dangerous he can be. Those Wild West sort of Americans have a tendency to shoot first and talk later."

"A real cowboy, eh?"

"So it would seem. But more than that he appears to be a true believer."

"In what. He is a Catholic, correct?"

"Not so much in that. At least not that I saw. No, it is more in the American way of life, as they call it. And the role of his organization in protecting and even promoting that."

Even though his parents are German. And he was born in Germany, correct?"

"But so much has happened since then, Comrade. He may have an affinity, but not a loyalty."

"I'm sure you can find a way to use that, or at least work around it."

"How do I explain that to my superiors in Normannenstrasse? They know you like to keep a tight rein on work against the American target."

'We will think of a way, I am sure. We might even offer it as a joint effort, an example of our comradely approach against the western imperialists."

Hoehn stood. "Very well then. I will broach the subject with my superiors. Same time next week?"

"Yes, that should be fine. Was Gracchus aware of you coming here today?"

"Yes, I told him I had to report to you about the death of your officers and the disappearance of Chernov. Gracchus almost disrupted the entire operation, you know."

"Yes, I do know that. His was more a matter of interference than assistance. But thanks to you and our relationship, he did not succeed. What do you think his real purpose was?"

"I believe he wanted to show you up, Comrade."

"That is all?"

Hoehn nodded and took the last drag on his Winston. "Yes, I believe so. He never really understood what your plans were. He has become distrustful of Moscow."

"Is he alone?"

"I cannot say for certain."

"Well, good. We can leave it at that. Of course, we lost some good officers, but we still learned what we needed to know about Chernov and his relationship with the American. And something of what he has been up to. It would have been nice, of course, to learn more, but I believe we can still build on what we do know. Perhaps Chernov will learn to become more helpful to us, eventually. He has no other choice now. Not if he wishes to survive." Kirillnikov paused while he stood and reached his hand across to the German. "To our future cooperation."

Hoehn took the hand. "Yes, of course."

• • •

"So, how is my brother?"

Hoehn considered the figure of his wife at the sink. She rinsed the lunch dishes, then shook her hands before grabbing the dish towel to make sure they were dry.

"Hopefully, fat and happy with the Americans," Hoehn replied.

Maya Hoehn leaned with her hip against the countertop. The beige cotton slacks outlined her thin legs and compact hips as the white top was beginning to spill over the waistband. The top buttons of the blouse were undone, which seemed to accentuate the movements of her body. She tucked the shirt tail back into her pants with slow movements of her hand, smiling at her husband the entire time. Hoehn felt the stirrings of desire, as he usually did when his wife looked at him this way. He had never thought he would marry a Russian, certainly not during his time on the Eastern Front or during his days of captivity. It was ironic, he remarked on many an occasion, how he had only met her after he returned from Russia, during a trip to Paris. But it had been love at first sight. He never thought such a thing could exist, especially not after his experiences under the Third Reich and during the war. But it had. At least for him.

"Are you sure? Will I ever be able to talk to him, to see him again?"

"Maya, I promised that I would see that he was safe. I fulfilled my promise. If I hadn't acted as I did, he would probably be dead by now. Or in a Soviet prison. I am sure the Americans will treat him well. They usually do. As long as he has stories to tell that they find valuable."

"But does he have something of value anymore?"

"Yes, I believe he does. Valuable enough to overcome any resistance by certain people who trust no one from our side, regardless of their history."

He thought of the tales he had heard of the man Angleton, who refused to trust anyone from the Soviet services. The man, as best he could tell, was a fool, and he was crippling the Americans in their efforts to learn more about the Soviet Union and its intentions. Which was a good thing, as best he could tell. But he would not give his wife those sorts of specifics. It would only worry her. And needlessly, he was sure.

She moved from the sink and ran her arms around her husband's shoulder. She looked deep into Joachim's eyes and brushed her lips across his chin. Then she placed a full kiss on his lips, moving her tongue inside his mouth and around his teeth and lips as she did. "Thank you, husband. I suppose you would like your reward now."

Hoehn smiled and kissed his wife back. "Yes, that would be nice. It is always nice."

Maya pressed her hips tight against her husband. "Okay. But can you tell me how much longer we must live here in this barren country?"

"A while yet. I am still not sure of my own future here, or how Europe will look a few years from now. I realize you miss Paris and the kind of life one has in the West. And I appreciate your willingness to return with me."

"Yes, I know you find it difficult to be away from Germany for long. But is this really Germany for you?"

Hoehn rested his head against his wife's. "As much as the other one is. I'm afraid the Germany I knew is gone forever."

"And whose fault is that?"

"I know, I know. So, I will just have to try to make the best of this situation."

Maya turned from her husband and took his hand to lead him upstairs. "Just don't wait too long, my dear."

CHAPTER TWENTY-ONE

October 27, 1961

He had wanted, above all, to avoid Alexanderplatz. Even the memories of that night a month ago brought the pain back to his ribs and arms. So instead, he waited in the beat up Volkswagen he had procured from motor pool just down the street from the *Museum Insel*, the Museum Island, whose two world-famous museums housed some of Berlin's—no, Germany's—most treasured artifacts and reconstructions from antiquity. The Pergamon Altar was perhaps the most famous, but the Ishtar Gate of Babylon was spectacular as well. That way it would not raise any immediate alarms if a Westerner's car, even one with diplomatic plates, sat for a moment in Neue Friedrich Strasse, kitty-corner from the Cathedral just across the street.

Baier scanned the crowd that passed through this holy land of German classicism, looking for the distinguished face and nearly invisible body of Ludwig Volkmann. They had agreed on eleven o'clock, and Baier had arrived 15 minutes early. Not really as long as he would have liked to check for any surveillance, but then he did not want to leave himself exposed for too long. If he had brought the Mercedes he'd used on his previous visits, then fifteen minutes would have been a quarter of an hour too long. That is, if he had gotten the chance to park at all.

The crowd was sparse. That, of course, was to be expected, given the tensions in the city that had seemed to grow exponentially ever since August 13. The crisis had been going on for almost two months now, and the dispute over the East Germans assumption of control over movement between the eastern and western sectors still stood. In fact, the tension had increased alarmingly. And this despite the repeated warnings between Moscow and Washington over the threats to the post-war arrangements and the prospect of a nuclear war. Maybe that was why the Americans were now providing military escorts for U.S. diplomats trying to gain access to East Berlin. General Clay had taken that step when the East Germans claimed the right to control the border crossing for everyone, including the Western Allies, and they had tried to prevent the U.S. Minister—the highest ranking American diplomat in Berlin—from attending the opera in East Berlin five days ago. On top of that, the Soviets did not appear to be doing anything to rein in their satraps. Baier just hoped that things did not escalate further before he got Volkmann over to the West. After that, all hell could break lose for all he cared.

Baier could feel the sweat gathering in his palms as he slid his hands over the steering wheel, praying—yes, actually praying—that Volkmann would not be late. At one point he even promised to enter a monastery late in life if this pick up was successful. He would give himself no more than fifteen or twenty minutes more if the German failed to show on time.

Then the passenger door swung open, and Ludwig Volkmann practically crawled into the front seat. Baier checked his watch. 11:03. Thank God for Prussian punctuality. This had to be as good as it could get in a situation like this. Some good really could come from their obsession with precision, he told himself. His Baden-born parents would never have believed it. It was like the far corner of southwest Germany was a polar opposite of Prussia.

"Thank God," Baier exclaimed.

Volkmann blew out a breath that seemed to carry nearly all his energy. "You mean you doubted I would show? Do you not trust me because of my Communist past?"

Baier fired the engine and pulled away from the curb. "Hardly. You've proved yourself enough in the past. Enough for me, at least. And there is no question of your courage. But given how long you've been on the run and in hiding, there is no telling when and how you could get yourself free to make this hook up. I'm just grateful Wolfgang Horhmann was able to maintain contact." Baier sighed. "No, after all you've been through, I never really doubted your intention of leaving all this…" Baier's arms swept the horizon "…behind. And for good."

"Well, there is the prospect of reunification. I believe that is still your country's policy. That would allow me to return."

Baier laughed. "I hardly think that's a realistic prospect these days. Not with what has happened in Berlin in the last month and a half. It does not look like anyone now expects that to happen. Not in our lifetimes, if ever. Your side, anyway, seems to have given all that up. Or should I say, your former side?"

"Yes, please do. Sad that, nonetheless. But we shall see."

Baier handed over the set of new documents to Volkmann. "Yes, we shall see. But until then here is your new passport and identification for today. They are American, I'm afraid. I hope that doesn't offend your left-wing sympathies too much. But anything else would almost certainly create problems at Checkpoint Charlie, given how your side is making it virtually impossible for West Germans to visit."

Volkmann smiled and settled back into his seat to study the documents. "I guess that will have to do for now." He read the passport's first page then chuckled. "Could you not have come up with a better name than Dieter Hessling? Who thought up that one?"

"Well, I did."

"So, you have read Heinrich Mann's *Der Untertan*? What is the English translation?"

"I believe it is something like *The Underling*, although I think there is also a Penguin version with the title, *Man of Straw*. And, yes, I read that in my younger years. It was required reading in our house. My parents insisted."

"Hmm, I prefer the former English title. And I congratulate your parents. But using the name now, is this your idea of a joke or a play on German history? Hopefully, not a commentary on my character."

"No, certainly not on your character. But in a way, yes, I guess

I am having a bit of a laugh at the ironies of German history. But more to the point for today's mission, you'll notice that you are holding an official passport. Your story is that you are a German Jewish refugee from Berlin who fled to the States in 1933. And you've come back here to work with the U.S. Mission because of your expertise in German affairs and language skills. So, if anyone questions you, you can respond in German or whatever English you have."

Volkmann smiled. "Very well then. Dieter Hessling it is. Are you not worried that we may get an East German border guard who is a lover of German literature?"

"I think that will be the least of our problems today."

Volkmann paused to study the barren architecture along Unter den Linden as Baier swung the car to the left to catch Friedrichstrasse and the last leg of their journey to the city's western side. The shattered walls and tips of still ruined buildings peeked through the side streets as the car rolled past.

"Tell me, Herr Baier, why is it you bothered to come back over here for me? Is this sort of thing usual for you?"

"Actually, Dieter…" Baier gave him a knowing look, "…it can be. This is not my first time on an operation like this."

"But why not just leave me to my own talents for survival? I have gotten along well enough thus far. I still have friends over here, you know."

"In that case, why did you agree?" Volkmann was silent. "I think because you know full well that your days of freedom over here are numbered," Baier continued. "You may not be aware, but the place where we met that evening with Hohrmann has been compromised. It was where the Stasi took me for their interrogation and beating not too long ago. And they mentioned your name as well. In fact, I'm surprised you haven't been grabbed and hauled off to Normanenstrasse yet."

"I was aware that the authorities had become suspicious, but I must admit that even I was surprised at how far along it had come. But as I said, I still have friends here who are willing to help when necessary." Volkmann nodded and looked out the window on his side. "And these people have proven to be true friends. Their assistance has kept me one step ahead of the Stasi. Tell me, though. how did you survive your encounter?'

"There was only so much they could do to me. But they also wanted to send a message to my people in the West."

"And how did your people receive that?"

Baier looked over at his passenger. "Well enough, I think. But we will have to see. Like so much else and so many others around here these days, we are adjusting. It also might please you to know that my superiors agreed to have me come back to Berlin long enough to make sure we got you out."

"Well, that is impressive. And I do appreciate it."

"There is another matter as well, Herr Volkmann. I mean, Dieter."

"Yes? And that is?"

"How the other side got to know so much about my movements and plans. It was almost as though they knew where I was going before I got there."

Volkmann smiled and nodded. "That is because they did, Herr Baier. Perhaps not every time, but most of them, I am sure."

"And how did that come to pass? Do you have an idea?"

"I know of one way that I can tell you. There are probably others."

"And that would be?"

Volkmann looked over at the American to see how he would take the new information. "They have a source in your Mission here. This one works in the travel department. She was able to pass along your travel plans as soon as they were made."

Baier stared straight ahead. "Well, goddammit after all." He thought for a moment. "How did that person come to work for the other side? And was it an East German or a Soviet penetration? Is there a difference?"

Volkmann smiled and nodded. "Oh yes, there is. And she is an East German asset. I believe she was recruited in what you Americans call a 'honey trap.' She is a native Berliner who fell for some kind of East German Lothario." He leaned forward to get a better look at Baier's face. "Yes, there actually are such men in Germany, Herr Baier."

Baier nodded in turn. "Okay, okay. I can get that." He glanced over at his passenger. "Are there any others I should know about?"

"I am sure there are. But I only know of this one." Volkmann sat back as the car turned down *Friedrichstrasse*. "This is my gift to you for helping me today."

"Well, thank you for that then. Perhaps there will be more you can do for us in time."

"Yes, perhaps. And may I ask you another question, Herr Baier?"

"Yes, of course." Baier smiled. "I might even try to answer it."

Volkmann laughed. "Good. Your other mission with the KGB officer, has that been settled?'

Baier shrugged and smiled. He thought back to the meeting with the National Security advisor McGeorge Bundy and Foy Kohler, the State Department officer in charge of the Berlin task force. Baier had accompanied Chernov to the White House for a briefing on the operation that had brought his 'fucking Russian' to the United States and Chernov's report on the policy discussions inside the Kremlin over Berlin. He had told them what he had heard and observed from his post on the KGB's own Berlin task force. According to Chernov, Moscow did not plan to force the Americans and their British and French allies out of Berlin. They realized that the Americans enjoyed an overwhelming military superiority. Perhaps not in and around Berlin, but certainly everywhere else in the world. Nonetheless, the Kremlin was determined to support East German efforts to stop the bleed out that was robbing their satellite of any chance to stabilize its government and to assert East German control over East Berlin. "In that respect," Chernov had concluded, "you have already conceded victory to them. But you will be able to remain in West Berlin, as far as Moscow is concerned."

Baier glanced over at his passenger. "Yes, that mission has been settled. But that's not why I came back. It has nothing to with that operation."

"So, what is it? Why are you here again?"

"Because I wouldn't have been able to look myself in the mirror each morning if I had not tried to get you out. They were going to kill you. You know that, don't you?"

"I see. You are certain? They were not going to let this all pass?"

"No, I seriously doubt it. And I am as certain as one can be in this business. There is a history of that sort of thing with the people on your old side, you know."

"In that case, I have to thank you, Herr Baier."

"Thank me when we're through. Now, try to act naturally."

"I always do, Herr Baier. You must do the same."

"It gets hard sometimes in this line of work. But I think we'll be okay."

Those words escaped from Baier just as they approached the border crossing at Checkpoint Charlie. The two men fell silent, their eyes glued to the scene unfolding in front of them. Baier inhaled a lungful of air, as though he needed to store the oxygen for the challenge before them. Directly in front of them on the eastern side of the crossing stood roughly ten tanks, all painted a solid black and without markings. The soldiers lounging at the sides of the tanks wore black clothing, also without any insignias or ranks. The engines were running, as though they planned to move forward as soon as the men climbed back on board.

"What the hell…?" Baier muttered. "Who the hell…?"

Volkmann gripped Baier's arm. "What is it? What is this?"

Baier shook his head. "I have no idea. But I am not stopping."

As they drove slowly forward, Volkmann rolled down his window.

"What are you doing?" Baier nearly shouted.

"Hush," Volkmann replied. "I can hear the soldiers grumbling." He leaned toward the open window, trying to catch what he could from the scrambled conversations outside.

"Anything?"

Volkmann nodded. "Yes, I think so. They are definitely Soviet soldiers. Some Russians, but mostly Central Asians. They do not have any orders yet and are wondering themselves what they are supposed to do."

Baier gave the car a little more gas to speed their approach as he wove between the tanks that seemed to grow in size as he drove through their lines. "Let's get this over with."

To both their surprise, no one paid any attention to the puny little Volkswagen bug as it drove through the crossing. As soon as they had crossed over to the west, Baier let out the breath he felt he had been holding since they first approached the crossing. Volkmann, too, seemed to relax as he sunk back against his seat and let his hand hang out the window to catch the air sweeping past their car as it drove towards the ruins of the Anhalter Bahnhof.

Then they saw the column of American M-48 tanks rumbling right at them. Baier swerved to the right, and the two wheels on the passenger side rode up over the curb and onto the sidewalk. As the tanks lurched their way toward Checkpoint Charlie, Baier and Volkmann pivoted so they could watch the show through the rear window.

"I hope we haven't just witnessed the beginning of World War III," Baier said. As he spoke, Baier also hoped that Chernov had not misspoke on that afternoon in the White House. Time would tell. It always did.

ABOUT THE AUTHOR

Bill Rapp began his adult life as an academic historian on modern Europe but quickly decided that he needed a career that was a little less sedentary. So, he spent the next 38 years working at the Central intelligence Agency as an analyst, diplomat, and senior executive. But he never lost his love of literature, especially mysteries and spy thrillers, and started writing fiction as an escape from the pressures of a life in the world of intelligence around twenty years ago. In the Cold War Thriller series, Bill combines his background and experience as a historian and intelligence officer to bring an element of authenticity and insight that places the suspense of espionage in the political and policy context where it belongs. Bill also has a three-book private detective series set outside Chicago, where he grew up, as well as a thriller set against the backdrop of the fall of the Berlin Wall, an event he experienced during his assignment to the city.